The Book of Orm

The A J Dalton
Fantasy Collection

www.kristell-ink.com

Orm A J Dalton © 2015
Warrior of Ages A J Dalton © 2015
From the Diary of St George A J Dalton © 2015
Knight of Ages A J Dalton © 2015
The Non-dragon A J Dalton © 2015
The Dark Arts A J Dalton © 2015
Rusalka Nadine West © 2015
The Nine Rules of the Nisse Matthew White © 2015

Paperback ISBN 978-1-909845-77-0
Epub ISBN 978-1-909845-78-7
Kindle ISBN 978-1-909845-79-4

Cover art by Oliver Flude
Cover design by Ken Dawson
Typesetting by Book Polishers

Kristell Ink

An Imprint of Grimbold Books

4 Woodhall Drive
Banbury
Oxon
OX16 9TY
United Kingdom

www.kristell-ink.com

In memory of David Gemmell,
who showed us so much.

Contents

Orm

A J Dalton

ORM CRIED MUDDY tears. He cried for what he was, and for what he was not. He cried for shame.

He wiped snot across his face with one of his over-soft and small hands, and held up the fat slug. It slowly squirmed, almost questioningly. What would a troll want with a slug? Trolls didn't eat slugs. Trolls ate rocks and ore, and crunched on bones.

What sort of creature was it that wanted to eat a slug? A creature that was less than a troll, that was what. A creature that had broken its teeth on rocks it had scavenged from a waste pile. A cringing thief who had pathetically failed to digest any rock or metal type, a snivelling thing that had been unable to achieve any *bond* to see him grow hard and strong. He was a weak creature, worthy only of the scorn of his proud and hulking kind.

He put the slug in his wide slobbering mouth and quickly swallowed. It slithered down inside him. He felt it enter his empty gut. Would it die or simply ooze around in there? He was frightened he'd end up *bonding* with the foul thing. Then he'd surely become even softer and weaker. He'd become a giant slug himself. Would he end up eating leaves, mulch and dung? The humiliation did not bear thinking of. He'd prefer to smash in his head with a rock before it came to that. He'd have to watch carefully for signs of any *change* coming over him, for his skin becoming slimy and sticky.

3

They'd been right to banish him from Trollheim. He wasn't strong enough to mine even the softest and least valuable of the rock seams beneath the mountain. He'd only been an embarrassment and an annoyance to his kind. His father and his littermates had turned away from him in disgust. His littermother had refused to let him feed from her teat any longer – her milk was better given to the likes of Utholde, the largest of the litter, for he was sure to bring riches and standing for their tribe. Orm was merely the runt.

When he'd been caught stealing rocks from another's waste pile, and word had got out that he'd only succeeded in breaking his teeth on them, Trollheim had shaken with laughter and mockery so loud that it was a wonder the very mountain had not collapsed. His father had sworn to kill him there and then, as was his right. But the King, who was Shining Dovregrubben – unusually entertained by what had occurred, and ever ready to make things more difficult for one of the less favoured tribes – had insisted Orm be banished instead, in the hope that there might be more hilarious stories in the future.

Orm's father had roared his frustration and swung a boulder-sized fist, hurling Orm from their den. The young troll had landed badly and there'd been the shameful sound of bones cracking. Utholde had come then, and kicked and battered his littermate all the way up the tunnel out of Trollheim, all the way out into the cursed lands of humankind and their brutal sun-god.

The only troll who had not sneered and threatened Orm was Hjerte. Orm had played with her once when they were young. He had drawn a picture of her on a wall in coal and she had gazed at him for a while. Then she had followed and watched when Utholde had thrown him out of Trollheim. Somehow, Orm had felt all the worse for her being there. He had growled and snarled at her to leave. She had tried to follow him. He would not think of her banished like him! He had roared challenges at her until she had retreated. Then he had turned and lumbered away, seeking shelter from the flames of the sky. His skin had blistered and begun to smoke before he made it into the deep shadows beneath a stand of fir trees. When he had turned to look back at the tunnel, Hjerte had gone.

He felt unwell. The slug was not sitting well in his stomach. Maybe it was poisonous to one of his kind. Besides, he would never be able to find enough slugs to survive. He needed to find something else. His stomach gurgled.

He rose and descended for the foothills – although his eyes constantly ran now and he could barely see in the glare of the world above ground. His skin pained him – he did not have anything near the sort of thick hide he would need to resist direct sunlight. His feet were sore – for they'd never toughened properly. The pine needles and stones on the ground hurt him, and threatened to hobble him. He pondered stopping, finding something to cover his feet and waiting for the sun-god to hide his face. Yet his hunger was so great he was unable to hold onto the idea of stopping. His need to eat something – *anything* – overrode all else.

Suddenly his nostrils flared as he caught the scent of something. There was a small and fast-moving creature in the area of half-light just ahead. Before he knew it, he was bellowing and charging forwards. The startled creature skittered across the ground and shot up the trunk of a tree. It leapt onto a branch, and then to the branch of another tree. Orm hit the tree with his shoulder, but was not big enough to bring it out of the ground. He fell back and landed heavily on his rump. He yelled in outrage. But the creature with the bushy tail was now well beyond reach. Squirrel? It had smelt so good.

Drool stringing from his chin, he climbed back to his feet. Maybe if he could resist bellowing, and could learn to charge more quietly, he would get hold of such a creature. He snorted. Probably not. He had to find something slower.

Orm moved further into the lands of men. He was afraid, but the ravening need in him was greater.

~

The wind brought the smells of the lowlands to him. So powerful were they that it was almost as if he could see it all. The loam of deep forests first. Beyond, vast tracks of rich soil, full of nutrients and the potential for life. Dung degrading, making him salivate. And then, beneath it all, near addling his wits, the sweet, sweet scent of blood. Not dull troll blood either. Blood so thick with minerals that he felt stronger just for inhaling it. He could all but taste it. He picked up his pace.

Then something darker. An unpleasant note. Something that soured the taste in his mouth. Something rank and poisonous. Iron. The one element that trolls could not tolerate. Even the strong among his kind – coming too close to a seam of such ore – could sicken to the point of death. Yet the danger here in the lands of men was worse still. Much much worse. For here, there was the insanity of pure iron – lumps, spikes, flat things, rounds, narrow pieces, even boulders of it! His head felt like it was splitting.

He stumbled. He didn't want to venture any closer. But the sweetness of the blood! He was torn, caught. Like the greedy troll who is about to hurl himself into the bottomless pit for the rare metals in its walls – he will fall forever as he claws wonder into his maw. He believes he will never die, for the pit never ends, and he becomes ever stronger. He will be a troll-god in the neverworld. Unless the pit does end. In which case he's in for quite a nasty moment.

Like others of his kind, he didn't like to think too much, but it seemed quite important at this point. His stomach growled urgently. It had a point. Decision made, he forged onwards, ever closer, fighting nausea.

Dizzy and disoriented, he made it into the mountain's foothills. There were more creatures now amongst the trees, but they seemed to sense him, for the birds fell quiet or took wing, smaller things instinctively stopped rustling or slithering, and larger things quickly moved away. He did not belong or fit. All knew he was here, and that he shouldn't be. Just as he had not belonged or fit amongst his own kind. It made him sad and angry all at once. He almost didn't want to exist . . . and they didn't want him to exist either. But there was nowhere to go. Nowhere. Maybe he should step back out into the sun and let it consume him. None would miss him. Hjerte? Maybe.

Something bleated. He shouldered his way forward. Orm hesitated. A smallish horned beast eye-balled him, unblinking. Why did it not flee? It could only be more dangerous than it looked. Then it chewed ferociously, and huffed. It could only be a *goat*, a fearsome creature of legend.

Terrified that it was about to attack and gore him, Orm did the only thing possible – he attacked first. His every instinct was to fall at the beast's feet and beg for mercy, but such an abject display would mean he was worthy of only the most horrible torture and pathetic death. He wanted to run, but turning a back on an aggressor could only be a fatal insult or mistake. He whimpered as he threw himself forward.

The goat-monster raised a hoof. It was about to dash his brains out! With utter contempt too. Orm staggered and fell short, flat on his front. The goat hopped onto his back, wiping its feet and pushing him down into the dirt. Orm moaned in shame and rolled.

The goat did not like that. It made an angry noise, its hooves rapping upon the stony ground once more. Trip, trap! Trip, trap! It would haul his guts out with its horns or throw him off a bridge, as in the oldest stories of his people. The mighty billy goat gruff was about to visit its rage upon him!

Orm lashed out and covered himself as best he could. The demonic thing fell silent. Where was it? Did it circle him, contemplating how best to end him? Did it choose the piece of meat that might most please?

Orm all but lost his stinking urine. Yes, let it end. He looked up, ready. The goat lay dead, its neck at a funny angle, its tongue sticking out.

Orm blinked. There was blood. Intoxicating, even at this distance. He dragged himself over to the body and began to suck and worry at it. He near passed out for the flavour of it. He fixed one of the goat's legs between his jaws and wrenched it free, swallowing even as he did so. Blood sprayed. He lifted the corpse back above his head so that the dark ichor could run straight down into his thin belly.

He groaned, giddy with pleasure and relief. His stomach churned.

There was an angry shout. He opened his eyes, struggling to focus. He caught the smell of a man-thing. Across the clearing was a crooked white-hair dancing from foot to foot and waving a long stick threateningly. Words were gabbled that made no sense, but sounded like the darkest of magicks. Orm reeled. Was he bespelled? His head would not clear.

He held out the goat, hoping to pacify the enraged wise one, but he only seemed to cause further offence, for the elder spat and quickly turned away. Orm went to go after him, but found his legs would not support him. He slumped to his knees and tasted nausea and something worse at the back of his throat. Had there been iron in the goat-demon's blood? Then there would be no surviving.

His eyes became heavy and closed. He collapsed face-first onto the forest floor.

~

There was all-consuming darkness. He knew himself in the troll neverworld. He could not see his hands or body. Then a distant light shone more brightly than Golden Dovregrubben himself. Orm was forced to shield his eyes. He roused himself.

Excited yelps and howls came from everywhere. There was no sun-god here, it seemed, for this forest was much darker than the one before. Yet flames flickered among the trees and moved towards him from different directions.

He found their scent then. Many man-things. They bore iron, baying beasts running before them and at their feet.

The judgement of the troll-gods would be visited upon him. Orm levered himself up to meet it, as he knew he must. He was surrounded on all sides.

Animals of tooth and claw ran in from behind him. He had expected it and hurled them back with more strength than he had previously known. More came in, from two directions at once. Strangely they could not penetrate his hide, and he smashed snouts and broke limbs and ribs. Wolves that served men, they were. Six at once from all around. As one leapt from the ground, Orm caught it by the throat and dashed it straight into the next one. A heavy creature slammed into his back and tried to bear him to the ground. At the same time teeth clamped to the back of one of his ankles, to further unbalance him. He reached over his shoulder, caught something and yanked hard. Bone snapped loudly and there was an agonised howl. Orm thundered his challenge and kicked back savagely. He connected hard and felt a crunch. There was a piteous whine.

The air was thick with their excitement, blood, pain . . . and fear. He tasted it and found his own blood rising to a frenzy. 'Orm is TRRRRROLL!' he boomed, the forest echoing over and over.

The man-wolves slunk back from him, drooling and snapping, lips curled back. They circled him slowly, then to feint and twist away suddenly. Orm stamped down on an injured one that was unable to get away. He pulled its head back and bit deep into its neck, drenching himself in its crimson life. The wolves would not be drawn, though. Now they merely sought to keep him where he was. They would make him wait for the arrival of their masters.

And their masters came. Out of the surrounding shadows stepped fearsome men of iron. The three largest wore it in plates, had bucket-shaped helmets over their heads, carried long swords and matched Orm in height. There were several dozen others with them, clutching pitchforks, mallets and an assortment of tools that Orm did not recognise. And there was an iron hatred in their eyes.

The blood-rage still upon him, Orm moved quickly for the nearest man in plate and smashed in his helmet with one heft of his fist. The man promptly fell in a clattering heap. But Orm's fist had all but broken in the assault as well. It was a blazing agony that travelled all the way up his arm and that soon saw it hanging limp and useless.

The men cried their outrage and pressed in on him. The second plated man raised his sword on high and took slow menacing steps forward under the weight of his armour.

'That's it Thomas! Get him!'

'We will not suffer evil amongst us!'

'—monster back to the mountains!'

'Thor protect us.'

'And Christ our saviour!'

''Tis the devil himself. Send him to hell!'

The ring tightened. There was no escaping the man in plate. Orm jumped forwards before the blade could come down, and simply shoved him back with his good arm and bulk. The man stumbled and toppled with a yell, taking several down with him and breaking the circle.

Here was his only chance. Orm leapt, even as foaming wolves raced into the breach. They all surged in on him at once. He bellowed and rolled, crushing and maiming as he could. There were terrible shrieks, sudden squelches, oaths and curses, the sickening smell of gore and loosed bowels, and the taste of blood in the air, blood everywhere. It filled his eyes, and all was red. The torches burned red and threw up raving and flickering shadows all around. Chaos and wild confusion. If only it would somehow hide him and let him get away.

Yet it was a maelstrom that had caught him up, and it would not so easily let him go. It had merely been taunting him. Now it would cruelly punish. The third hedge knight's old blade found Orm's gut and drove home. For an instant Orm did not feel it. He wrenched his body round to better face his assailant, but cut himself deeper still in doing so. He smashed down on his tormentor's hands. Everything shattered: fragile human bone, the weapon itself, and any sense of hope Orm had kept.

The men fell about him, their hounds growling but cringing with them. Orm looked up in despair. All was lost. A foot-long piece of the sword had broken off inside him and was working its way down into his insides.

He cursed the sons of man and tottered away into the forest. The bravest of the wolves made to pursue him, but its master commanded it back. After all, the troll could not survive such a wound.

He managed a dozen uncoordinated steps, and a dozen more, the spike pushing its way into his core. It would soon pin him and he would do and know nothing again.

His quivering nostrils told him he headed back towards the mountains. It would be good to see them one last time, and to breathe the selfsame air as his sweet Hjerte. If only he could see her before the end. He would apologise for the harsh challenges he's offered her when she'd only sought to comfort him. He knew himself a fool then, stupid and unworthy. The troll-gods had been right to inflict such torture upon him, for now he understood exactly what he deserved and the important things that he'd neglected. Such a painful lesson, such a wondrous blessing.

There were tears of regret in his eyes when he could go no further. Tears of shame and joy. He half lowered himself and half fell there in the dark of the forest. Finally at peace, he closed his eyes and stopped breathing, his innards pierced through with iron.

~

Something called him, something beyond his comprehension. He awoke in the forest of the sun-god once more. What further torment or mercy was this? The grievous injury to his abdomen was all but healed, though he still felt the whitehot iron within, molten and unforgiving.

He rose as if lifting the weight of the world and trod heavily, one foot and then the other. The ground shook as he thumped forwards, the branches of nearby trees giving and their leaves fluttering. Every movement was exhausting, but while he had strength he would bring himself to the closest thing he had to a home as he could. And he seemed to have reserves of strength he'd never quite realised before. In fact, with every pace he took towards Trollheim, he felt that strength increasing.

Had he somehow *bonded* with the iron? Surely it was not possible. He had to be in some sort of delirium. A delirium in which he no longer feared and no longer flinched. A squirrel chattered angrily at him for disturbing the peace of the woods, and he waved apologetically.

'Orm sorry for chasing squirrel. Orm leave now,' he rumbled.

He offered it a grin. Alarmed, the squirrel gave a squeak and high-tailed it off into the treetops. At least the squirrel hadn't attacked him, unlike everything else in the lands of men, lands which reeked of terror and destruction. No wonder men were so short-lived compared to the older races. Men did it to themselves. And were best avoided, of that he was certain. Not for nothing then that the older races had withdrawn from the lowlands and hidden themselves in misty valleys, forgotten fjords, remote fast-nesses and the highest or darkest of caves and undermines. He would leave the places of men and never look back. Better to die in Trollheim than live amidst such madness and desecration as this. Better to die at the hands of the strongest amongst Shining Dovregrubben's tribe than never more to experience Trollheim's majestic beauty.

He crashed onwards, no interest in who heard him passing or approaching. He felt free and happy, despite what awaited him. They were feelings with which he was not entirely familiar. They were good feelings he decided. He wanted to keep them, and would fight for them as necessary, he was sure. He would gift them to Hjerte if he could, if she would allow it. Ah, sweet Hjerte.

He marched up into the foothills, decimating a path through smaller trees. It was only for the very oldest trees that he stepped aside, out of respect and so as not to antagonise their attendant, and no doubt powerful, dryads. He was a mountain troll rather than one of the forest trolls of the high reaches, but even he knew better than to go looking for trouble with forest sprites and dark elves. Only men with axes were mad enough to seek that sort of trouble. Mad and self-destructive.

Orm shrugged and climbed onwards, up and up. He breathed deeply, enjoying the labour of it. He felt the impossibly deep and slow breathing of the mountain too, and it soothed and reassured him. This was where he was meant to be. Maybe it was this that had been calling to him all along. It was this that had brought him back from the dark. This.

He saw the entrance to Trollheim high above and dug his feet in with renewed determination. A large shadow moved out to confront him! Utholde. The sun flashed off the giant troll, white metal having grown up of late around his joints.

'Utholde knew cowardly Worm would try to return!' Orm's littermate sneered. 'Utholde knew Worm would not be brave enough to endure exile. Must Worm heap greater and greater shame on all? Utholde should have killed Worm before.'

'Praps Orm's brother should have. Orm's brother might now become sorry for not doing so.'

'Utholde is no brother of Worm! Worm is nothing but dung to us. Dung-eater! Worm is untroll. Worm is disgrace to all trolls, with such weakness and whining. Worm will not be allowed to live another moment. This shame must end.'

'Orm will not apologise for his nature, *cannot* apologise for it. If we must fight, brother, then we must fight, for that is *Utholde's* nature, and Orm cannot hate Utholde for it, *will not* hate Utholde for it.'

'Enough talk! Worm babbles like a man-thing. UNTROLL!' Utholde spat, descending like a rock-slide upon his smaller littermate.

Orm was buried under by his brutal brother, battered down into the ground. And then battered again, punched and flattened. Utholde's attack was crazed, but it rapidly slowed. His fists were cracked, and knuckles were broken. He stared at them in disbelief.

'Orm's brother stinks of silver,' Orm breathed. 'Orm's brother is vain and soft.'

'Silence!' Utholde demanded, but his consternation was plain. 'What have you become, Worm?'

'Enough talk,' Orm grunted and grabbed his brother's fists in his hands. He crushed them mercilessly.

Utholde threw back his head and the mountains echoed with his horror and humiliation. Over and over.

Orm forced his way up, lifting his brother with him and then raising him fully over his head. He turned, readying to hurl his brother down the mountain.

'Pleeease!' Utholde whimpered.

Never had he thought he would have Utholde in such a position. His brother's begging sickened him . . . and saddened him somehow. Orm knew Utholde would have joyfully thrown him to his death had their places been swapped. Why then should he not do it? Because he was not Utholde, that was why.

'Will Utholde remember this if Orm lets him live?' Orm asked.

'Yes . . . b-brother!'

'But Utholde will think Orm weak if he lets Utholde live. He will think Orm ruled by feeling and unworthy of his strength.'

'No, no! Never, brother!'

'Orm cannot believe Utholde. Orm is untroll and exiled. It is Utholde's duty to forbid and frustrate Orm.'

'Brother, hear me! Utholde swears before the troll-gods that he accepts Orm as his brother and tribe. Utholde will follow Orm and his words!'

'Orm's brother knows what this means?'

'Y-yes. Utholde knows.'

He lowered Utholde and glared at him, challenging him to show any hint of defiance. Utholde kept his eyes down, his head low and his shoulders slumped. 'Then stand tall at Orm's side, brother. Be proud to stand so, for Orm is proud to have his brother there.'

Utholde pulled himself up and looked down at his littermate. 'Orm says things that are . . .strange.'

'Praps Orm *is* strange. Praps Orm has been too close to the man-things. Now, brother, take me to the one called Hjerte. We must travel fast and unseen.'

Utholde hesitated.

'Speak!'

'She is kept close by Shining Dovregrubben, for his amusement. He does not touch her, but she is forced to shame herself by eating coal.'

'Why would he do this?' Orm seethed.

Utholde shifted his weight, clearly uncomfortable. 'Word reached him of her loyalty to you. He calls it treason and treats her cruelly for it.'

'And Utholde helped bring that word to Shining Dovregrubben.'

Utholde nodded miserably. 'She would not be Utholde's. Utholde was . . . was angry.'

'What cares the King? Hjerte is no threat to him.'

Utholde shrugged. 'Utholde did not know the King would do such things to Hjerte. The King seems to . . . *enjoy* her unhappiness. He says it is a warning to others. None likes it, but none dares challenge the King when mighty Blytung is there to guard him. Utholde . . . is sorry, brother.'

'None dares, says Utholde. Well *this one* dares!' Orm ground. 'We will go to the hall of Shining Dovregrubben, and we will let all know that we bring challenge for the treatment of Hjerte. Let all see and hear us. Go ahead of Orm, brother. Cry challenge!'

'You dare?!' Shining Dovregrubben boomed down from his throne.

His golden hall was packed with the largest and eldest trolls of each of the tribes and clans. They jostled for space, eager for the spectacle.

'Orm dares!' the small troll called back, his voice falling dead and flat. He squinted despite himself, dazzled by the candlelight reflected from the pillars and mirrors of gold arrayed all around. It was hard not to look as if he quailed before the glorious Troll King.

Shining Dovregrubben smiled then. His eyes shone and mesmerised. He spoke reasonably, indulgent and understanding. 'You are young, of course, quite given to giddiness. And you are in love are you not, young Orm?' There were deep chuckles around the chamber at that, nudged elbows and knowing nods.

Then the King frowned. 'You were exiled on pain of death. It is treason to return.'

'Orm says what Shining Dovregrubben has done to Hjerte is treason against all trollkind! Orm brings challenge to the throne!'

There was utter silence in the hall. All eyes turned up towards the King upon his dais. The gleam and shimmer of his overfed bulk held them captivated. They waited upon his every word and whim. His will was all.

'You are tainted by your time in the lands of men!' the King blazed. 'You are foul with it. You bring their corruption to this place, with every word and deed. You will not be permitted to speak again. Blytung, come forward! End this miscreant forever! Bring the she-troll so that she may see.'

The huge area of shadow behind the bright throne shifted and came forwards. The roof of the chamber or the mountain itself seemed to be falling in as Blytung the mighty leaden troll advanced. Many a troll quaked at the mere sight of him. He was the greatest amongst them, and all but straddled the throne, such was his size. Held in one boulder-sized fist was a grimacing and struggling Hjerte.

'Down here, oaf!' Orm yelled, refusing to let his voice shake.

Blytung ponderously lowered his head and peered at Orm. The leaden troll snorted, much in the way that the goat-demon had when Orm had faced it.

'Blytung holds the she-troll like she is his dolly and he needs comfort. Can Blytung not face Orm more bravely than this? Coward!'

Trolls whined to hear Orm so antagonise the behemoth. Blytung's brows rose in surprise, then came down in violent displeasure. The leaden troll looked at Hjerte in his hand and then carelessly cast her down into the watching crowd. Utholde was there to break her fall and keep the others of Dovregrubben's tribe from immediately laying hold of her.

Blytung drew an enormous breath. The air in the chamber noticeably thinned. Then he spoke, his voice rocks ground to dust. 'Blytung will swallow this pathetically small troll whole!'

'Orm would not advise it. But simple Blytung follows the words of this pretty trinket of a King, does he not?'

'Yes!' Blytung agreed without hesitation.

The giant's hand swept down. Orm made no effort to avoid it, even as he was lifted towards Blytung's cavernous maw. 'In one go!' Shining Dovregrubben laughed, encouraging his guard. And Orm was unceremoniously crammed into mighty Blytung's mouth and promptly gulped down. Blytung burped loudly.

Hjerte cried out in anguish. Utholde sighed, heavy with grief. Trolls moaned, appalled to see one of their own so ended. Yet all the while Shining Dovregrubben clapped and nodded, the lesson delivered to his people and his power over them ever greater.

Blytung hiccupped, a strangely high-pitched sound for one so large.

The King giggled.

And another hiccup.

The King chuckled more loudly.

Blytung held his stomach in discomfort. He opened his mouth, but was unable to make a sound now. His knees collapsed under him and he slumped, near toppling the throne. His outsized belly glowed red. It suddenly fractured, the sound detonating and causing every ear in the chamber to ring.

The leaden troll convulsed, but was held powerless as a burning hot creature climbed out of its front. Blytung's blue blood sizzled and smoked on the creature's skin for some seconds, but then was burned away. Blytung gurgled and died.

Every troll retreated as far as their numbers would allow. The majority crushed themselves back against the walls of the chamber and hunkered low, while a few prostrated themselves completely and begged for the mercy of a quick death.

The furnace-red being turned to confront the throne.

'Stay back. I am your King. You *will* obey me! Kneel before me and I will allow you to be my new guard. See, I will gift you such gold as you have only ever dreamt of before,' Shining Dovregrubben gibbered.

The golem rose onto the first stair of the dais. 'I am the iron troll. I have no need of gold.'

'No! Take Hjerte as you wish,' Dovregrubben wheedled.

And another step upwards. 'She is not mine to take. I merely come to free her . . . and all trollkind.'

'Do not! You will bring an end to all trolls. You cannot bring iron amongst them.' A note of cunning now. 'See how I shine. Watch the light twinkle, Orm. Hear my voice and let it guide you.'

Another step. 'You will shine no more, worthless King.' So saying, Orm laid his hands on Shining Dovregrubben, and the golden troll's lustre dulled in the instant. He froze where he was, becoming brittle, and then shattered, shards hurled across the chamber.

None moved, or dared breathe.

Orm stared around the chamber, the heat in him slowly fading. As it did so, he took on a black-grey hue. He was unsteady on his feet and near swooned.

Utholde separated himself from the terrified group against the walls and moved to support his brother. He helped Orm into the seat atop the dais and then stood proudly at his right shoulder. 'Does any here challenge?' the silver troll's voice rang out. There was not a whisper. 'Then all our kind will now be ruled by the iron troll. All will acclaim him. Orm! ORM! ORM!'

The voices of trollkind were slow to rise, but soon they roared as one: 'ORM!' Over and over. The mountain range echoed and amplified it. 'ORM!' Valleys and fjords trumpeted it across the land. 'ORM!' The earth and heavens reverberated with the knowledge and announcement that there was a new king in Trollheim.

~

'Hjerte?' Orm asked when his people had at last stilled to hear him.

She came forward tentatively.

'You are free, Hjerte.'

'Free?' she frowned, the word clearly unfamiliar on her lips. She met his eye. 'I am free to choose then?'

He nodded, feeling himself quite as small and nervous as he'd ever been.

'Hjerte chooses Orm.'

His heart leapt, but still he misdoubted. 'Yet I am of iron.'

'Hjerte is of coal. Orm's touch will not hurt Hjerte.'

He grinned. 'Then you will be my queen?'

'Freely,' she blushed.

He felt quite giddy.

Utholde came to the floor before the dais then. 'Brother, with the iron troll to lead us, surely we can take the lands of men as our own. They will not be able to stand against us.'

'No,' Orm said clearly for all to hear. 'There is nothing in the lands of men for us, only war, self-destruction and self-confusion. It will see us fall out amongst ourselves as we squabble over worthless prizes and trophies. As a people, we will seek trophies no more. I command it. Gold is forbidden to all trollkind from this day forwards. None will desire it, and none will seek it out. None. It is also commanded that the story of Orm be made into drawings and song so that all trolls may remember those lessons that will keep us strong.'

'Utholde is sorry, brother, but Orm learnt much from his time in the lands of men. Why should we fear to take such lands? The man-things are small, are they not?'

'Was not Orm once the smallest of his kind, brother? So hear me. They are best left alone. They are quick, numerous and terrible, like the squirrels of the forest. The day that there is challenge between all trollkind and mankind will be the last of days. Pray to the troll-gods that day never comes. I have spoken. Now I must rest awhile.'

Taken from a series of drawings and markings found in the Okstindan Mountains (Norway), that series often referred to by academics as 'The Book of Orm'.

Warrior of Ages

A J Dalton

I

HE SAT ON his small porch high up in the mountains, watching the clouds. They towered and marched across the sky in ranks. In all his long years reading the omens of the world, he'd never seen the like. The sun had long since been hidden from view and the air been turned to cold shadow. He tasted snow on the rising wind. It was still meant to be autumn.

'The ache in my bones says there's trouble coming,' Raggar muttered.

The youth should have returned by now. Raggar looked off along the path that ran past his cabin and into the mountains. There was no sign of him.

'Come on, lad. Leave it much longer and you'll be properly caught in a storm. And it'll be a bad one too, unless I'm much mistaken. You'll get all turned around, lose your way and freeze to death. Or fall. Or break a limb, which will just draw things out longer. Or become delirious and kill yourself for whatever reason. And those are just the more pleasant possibilities.'

The Pillar Mountains offered scant shelter to any living thing. They were more than a test for any man – let alone a foolhardy youth thinking to scale one of the peaks to prove he had come of age, who was now ready to take himself a wife and have a seat at the monthly meeting of the Vale's farmers.

'I'm getting too old for this,' Raggar grumbled.

You should have thought of that before you accepted his offering, Raggar the Violent whispered.

It was hardly accepted, Raggar the Pitiless countered. *The youth left the food out on the path and ran off before we could confront him. Just plain cowardly, I call it. Ill-mannered too. We owe him nothing for such an insult. Let the storm have him!*

Weren't complaining when we ate the food though, were you? observed Raggar the Relentless.

You know the deal, came back the Violent. *The locals provide us with what we need, and we offer them our protection in return, no matter what must be faced. And they otherwise leave us alone, so that we do not get dragged into the nonsense of their other affairs. Besides, we need the exercise. Sit here much longer and we will waste away. Enough of this chatter. A warrior speaks with his actions!*

Wait, Raggar the Immovable cautioned. *We protect them from enemies: we cannot protect them from themselves. The youth has put himself in this position, to test himself. He must be allowed to succeed or fail as he can. Should he fail, whether through foolishness or some other lack, then that outcome must stand. Not even the gods themselves would dare interfere in a choice freely made by a mortal.*

Raggar raised his eyes to the heavens as he considered. 'Wouldn't they?'

With a groan, he rose from his favourite – and only – chair, his frame all but filling the porch. He took up his massive warhammer and hefted it a few times. It seemed sullen, as if unhappy at being ignored for so long. *I know how it feels,* chided the Violent.

'Enough of this chatter, isn't that what you said?' Raggar growled. There was no answer except the howling of the wind.

He rattled the chains which he wore over his shoulders, across his torso and around his waist, shaking out the kinks so he would have a full range of movement. They were difficult at first, complaining harshly, but finally fell into line and place. They had rusted again – how long had he sat contemplating this time?

He circled his arm experimentally – they were loose and limber. *See? It can't have been that long, can it?* the Immovable decided.

He swung the warhammer up to rest on his shoulder. It felt good to have it there again, like meeting an old friend. His old friend Letter, who had guarded him from and visited punishment upon enemies the length and breadth of the continent. Letter had always been faithful to him, and he in return had remained faithful to the weapon. They had sustained each other through the decades, fighting for countless kings, emperors, warlords and mercenary captains, the names of whom he'd long since forgotten. When there had seemed no wars left to fight, when humankind had finally sickened of the slaughter and realised it was bringing itself to the edge of extinction, Raggar had removed himself from the world of men to these mountains. He'd had no qualms about all the death he had dealt, for it had finally forced humankind to confront itself, and know itself. Even Letter had seemed content for a good while.

But now the world had turned. A new time of war was coming. He saw it more and more in the omens – as the world reacted to and was changed by the will, whims and wiles of gods and mortals alike. Weather wizards altered the sky to increase crop yields, at the command of greedy kings who wanted greater taxes to fund their armies and ambitions. Various demons and gods allied themselves with different kingdoms, to see their number of worshippers increase, and the various monarchs and rulers welcoming any priesthoods that controlled the people and gifted the throne with new sacred or arcane powers.

It was time. He stepped from his porch and followed the path deeper into the mountains, his stride lengthening as the storm rose behind him. Letter bounced on his shoulder, as if excited at the prospect of what was to come. Somehow it knew. It was in the very air. A building pressure or charge. Raggar's temples tightened. He ground his teeth.

At last! Raggar the Berserker hissed somewhere deep inside, as if part of the growing storm itself and knowing that its terrible fury would soon be unleashed.

Raggar fought for control, even as he broke into a run. The sky rumbled and then cracked and zagged. He was in murk one second, then a white light more brilliant than day the next. Grit and sleet stung his skin. It was near impossible to see, but he knew the path better than one of his own thoughts.

The wind keened like a wild animal and leapt at him, as if to force him back. He caught a scent then and frowned. Did his senses deceive him? Would they dare set foot in these mountains?

He did not slow, knowing that they could not be far away and had senses as keen as any predator. He powered up an incline and, coming over the top, found a half dozen cromagnon at the base of a crag. Even as he watched, one of them flung a rock the size of a human head up at the terrified youth clinging precariously to the rockface twenty feet above. With no room to manoeuvre, the youth could not avoid being hit, and cried out in agony. He barely managed to keep his grip. The cromagnon were each close to eight foot tall, heavy-boned and dressed loosely in a variety of skins, some of which looked distinctly human. For all that, they seemed unusually lean – had hunger seen them become so desperate that they had no choice but to venture beyond their usual territory?

Raggar swung his hammer, breaking the head of the nearest one, which went down without a sound. Letter carried on descending in a downward arc and Raggar pivoted with it, looping it behind him and over his head a second time. The hammer cracked down on the next cromagnon's shoulder and then the whole group knew he was upon them.

They bellowed in anger, and bared huge teeth used for rending flesh and crunching through bone. The four that stood moved in on him at once, meaning he would no longer have room for any sort of mighty swing. He punched forwards with the head of his hammer without hesitation, bringing it up under the powerful drooling jaw of the largest of them, then pushing the long metal handle out to stab another in the ribs a split second later. As two more of the cromagnon fell away, they impeded one of those still trying to reach him.

Yet the last of them caught Raggar side on and swept him up in a crushing embrace. Raggar let himself be lifted, then butted down hard with his forehead, smashing his assailant's nose. He butted again. Blood sprayed everywhere. And again. A thud and squelch, and the cromagnon was toppling backwards to the ground.

Raggar rolled free, but Letter was not to be found. He roared savagely, daring the cromagnon that still stood to challenge him. It rushed in, foam at its mouth, nostrils flaring and its eyes staring. It intended to eat him alive.

Raggar stepped, planting the sole of his foot on the outside of the cromagnon's leading knee, bringing his weight to bear. The cromagnon was forced to twist, or have its joint ruptured, allowing Raggar the instant he needed to punch it hard to the throat. Its airway crushed, it staggered and went to its knees. It clawed at its neck and fell onto its back, moving slower and slower.

A massive blow caught Raggar to the side of his head and he went spinning. In the chaos of the fight and lashing storm, he had not seen or heard the cromagnon he'd stabbed with Letter's handle rise to come at him once more.

Maybe you're losing your edge, the Pitiless mused, not that the Berserker was listening. His rage increased.

Somehow Letter was back in his hand and he was violently pounding the cromagnon's head to mush. His unblinking gaze swung round to take in the cromagnon with the shattered shoulder and side. It was trying to drag itself. Its eyes pleaded and it whimpered.

As if any cromagnon would show mercy, the Pitiless snorted. *Wait!* The hammer came down. The Pitiless sighed. *You ended that too quickly . . . too mercifully. It deserved worse.*

The Berserker remained heedless. His head turned every which way, looking for further enemies, any enemy. His eyes looked up, and saw the mortal there beyond his reach. He shouted with an incoherent savagery. The youth trembled and hid his face.

Surely it wasn't over. It was never over.

It is over. Listen, whispered Raggar the Watchful.

There was only the cataclysm.

But the storm is already abating. It seems to be blowing itself out.

No.

Yes. It passes as quickly as it came.

Where were the fierce tears of heaven? Where was nature being torn apart?

Perhaps the storm was not entirely natural. Think. Nothing about any of this seems right. The strangely eager storm that forced you to go looking for the youth, the cromagnon who should never have come so close to the Vale – it was all designed to achieve what?

Now he had pause. He had spent long enough reading omens to understand some force had sought – and succeeded in – manipulating him. It was all to remove him from his place watching over the Vale! To entrap him. Perhaps he *was* losing his edge.

He spun on his heel and set off at a loping run.

What of the youth?

He must still complete the test he has set for himself. We cannot complete it for him.

Raggar's hand went to his throbbing brow. There was a sticky wound at his temple and his eye was swelling shut.

It can only improve your looks, the Pitiless advised him.

Our concern should be whether it will hamper our ability to kill, the Violent admonished.

It is not over. It is never over, the Relentless murmured.

Quickly, the Watchful urged.

We should not exhaust ourselves, the Immovable warned. *Who knows how soon the next confrontation will come?*

The sooner, the better. The Violent grinned, also speaking for the Berserker.

He came back to the porch. The clouds over the Vale had cleared enough to reveal a thick pall of smoke above one of the farmsteads. He swore there and then that whoever had conspired to take him from his vigil would pay more dearly than they had ever imagined.

Raggar hurried down the pass that would take him into the Vale. A figure awaited him at the pinchpoint in the path, the place where he could hold back an entire army should he ever have need.

He slowed warily, to give himself time to get the measure of what he faced. Whoever it was, they had not sought to conceal themselves. They were either arrogant or stupid, which was pretty much the same thing as far as he was concerned.

The man's clothes were incongruously fine, as if he were dressed for some royal court. He was unusually tall, his features were absurdly delicate, and there was something quick and knowing about his eyes. In fact, this was not a man at all, unless Raggar missed his guess. He hefted his hammer threateningly.

The being smiled indulgently. 'Well met, good Raggar. Allow me–'

'Who the hell are you?'

'–to introduce myself. I am Sharim. Perhaps you have heard of me?'

'Nope. But then I'm not really up on the latest gossip and rumour. What do you want?'

The smile did not falter. Sharim's eyes caught him and the two of them were suddenly within touching distance. 'I am a god,' Sharim said gently, his breath intoxicating and his gaze enthralling. 'You have lived and fought for the longest time, old friend. Is it not time you rested?'

We do not want to rest! Raggar the Relentless swore.

We have not fought and have not suffered this world and its people so long then to give up our life so easily, the Violent averred.

'Warrior,' the god said kindly. 'Let the aches and pains of your body trouble you no more. Have done with it.'

It is our *body*, the Immovable insisted. *We like its aches and pains. They let us know we are alive.*

Raggar looked Sharim directly in the eye. Should he spit in that eye, blacken it or have it out? He raised Letter between them and grinned evilly. 'If you want this body, come try take it off me, godling. I have made a promise to the people of the Vale.'

Sharim blinked and swayed back slightly. He reasserted himself. 'You can keep a better watch over them once you join the pantheon. Did I not say? There is a place for you amongst us.'

'I have a place here.'

'Are you so vain, mortal, that you would dare turn down our offer? You can be a demigod, man!'

Enough of these words! Smite him! the Violent begged.

Raggar wrestled for control. 'Why would a godling waste his time on a mere man? What is it you want? Why do you stand in my way? Why do you prevent me descending to the Vale? I do not have time for this!'

Sharim showed only sympathy. He sighed. 'I had hoped to spare you this, for all that you have already endured on behalf of an ungrateful humanity. You are already too late, good Raggar. You saw the smoke. And it will take you at least an hour to reach the unfortunate farm below. Too late in so many ways, my friend. Do not be too heartbroken, but you are from a bygone era. A relic, if you like. The world has changed since you were last a part of it. The Vale is nothing like you remember. The Vale that now exists bares no relation to the one which you swore to protect. None at all. Join us and you will see.'

'So you say, Sharim. The world must have changed indeed if it would have one such as you as a god. What are you the god of? Lies? Twisted tongues? Betraying words?'

The god allowed himself a sneer of contempt now. 'The god of knowledge, carping mortal! And, yes, that includes *self*-knowledge. Nothing is hidden from me, Raggar the Ever Vengeful. Raggar the Destroyer. Raggar the Riotous! For all that they used you, mortalkind were only relieved when you chose to involve yourself no longer in their affairs. They wanted – and want – no further part of you! It is only conceit, false pride and perverse jealousy that now sees you attempt to return. You know what I say is true. Deep down, somewhere in there, you – Raggar – know that it's true.'

Raggar the Watchful was silent, as was the Pitiless.

Raggar gritted his teeth. 'I have sworn to protect the people of the Vale, and that I will do no matter what must be faced.'

'You will contest the will of the gods?' Sharim asked in utter disbelief. 'Do you really think the pantheon will permit such blasphemy? You are mad. It is the only thing that can explain it.'

'I have given my word!'

'To a bunch of farmers. All of whom are now dead.'

'What do you mean?!'

'How long do you think you've spent up there in self-absorbed contemplation? Are you really so dull as not to have noticed the passing of the seasons, ages and generations? The original farmers to whom you made promise have passed on. Their offspring remain, but most have not even heard the stories of you. Do not mistake your current stubbornness for any sort of virtue. Know thyself.'

And know thy enemies, the Watchful counselled. *We have read the omens long enough to know that this one does not tell us the whole truth. Gods rarely do, I suspect. They are best avoided.*

Smite him! Or so help me—

Raggar struck in the instant. Sharim hardly had time to show his surprise, but his foreknowledge had been fastest of all. He completely disappeared before the blow could land.

That may not have been wise, the Watchful considered. Yet the others sided against him, so the lone voice subsided.

'We'll worry about it should we ever meet him again,' Raggar nodded. He stepped cautiously through the pinchpoint and, satisfied he was not about to be ambushed, quickly set about the descent, in the direction of the thickening column of smoke.

~

The farmstead was little more than smouldering timbers and heat-cracked stones by the time he arrived. Nothing of the thatched roof remained of course. In fact nothing of anything really remained. He crouched and examined five blackened and twisted corpses. The farmer, his wife, a younger man and two younger women.

He glared up at the iron-grey sky. 'Where were your rain and storms when they could have saved this place from the flames, eh? Well? Answer me!' There was a distant and surly rumble. He would have spat in disgust then, but out of respect for the dead resisted.

He walked the surrounding area, looking for signs of what had gone on. To the south, the ground had been churned to mud. It looked like twenty or so mounted men had ridden up, murdered the family, torched the place and ridden back the way they had come. The nearby barn filled with hay had been left entirely untouched.

Armed southerners intent upon giving a message to the people of the Vale. An argument over the cost of grain and crops? An avaricious warlord demanding rulership of the place? Bandits offering protection? *A band of mercenaries looking to scare the people on behalf of religious, political or trade-related paymasters? Any of those*, the Watchful pondered.

The details do not matter, the Pitiless yawned. *It's the same old winning combination of selfish ambition and destructive envy, that's all.*

The details do *matter*, the Immovable maintained.

Something shifted within him and an older voice came to the fore. *The results always matter more than the reasons. Who lives, who dies and in what numbers. The promises we make mean nothing until we deliver on them.* It was the Ever Vengeful who spoke.

We go then, the Relentless prompted. *We find the twenty and see them ended. Even though they are on horseback, they will stop to rest. We will run through the night and catch up to them. Or if they ride on, we will hound them until their horses drop. Should they change horses, still we will pursue them; until there is no horse left standing on the continent.*

We like this plan, the Violent nodded.

Wait! the Watchful begged.

Do not dare suggest we bury these four before leaving, the Pitiless pre-empted. *If necessary we can inter them once we have visited ourselves upon those responsible for their deaths. Delay too much and we risk losing the trail.*

Just listen.

Something made him hesitate. He tilted his head. There was something. He stopped his breathing and forced his grinding chains to silence.

He heard the hiss and pop of the farmstead's fired remains. Whenever the wind taunted them, they would flare or glow an angry red at what had been done to them, but they were broken and would slowly die back down. How much longer before their very last spark was gone? Hours? Less?

He stepped inside the space that had once known joy and laughter, perhaps even singing and dancing. Work and dreams and achievements, be they simple or otherwise. And those precious things that would have been passed on through future generations, from four people, to eight, to sixteen, to thirty-two, and so on, until they were shared by an entire and better world. They would have been passed on . . . were it not for the vain and murderous men who had come here.

There was a part of the dwelling that had a stone-flagged rather than earthern floor. It had to have been the kitchen. He spied narrow stairs – to a cellar or pantry – under a fallen beam that was only partially burnt through. Pushing the debris aside, he squeezed himself down into the gap. Surprisingly, the air was that bit cooler here.

And there, on the bottom shelf, beneath a rack of hanging meats, was the bundle that instinct and the omens had told him was there. A small infant that grizzled weakly and struggled to see. Its skin was cold to the touch, and so he gently picked it up and held it in the crook of one large arm. He warmed it with his breath for a few moments and then went back above ground to crouch where it was warm.

That's all we need, the Pitiless grumbled.

An orphan, the Immovable shrugged.

Those that came here can never justify the crime they have committed against this innocent, the Relentless amended.

It must be avenged, as must the five who were most terribly taken from it, Raggar the Ever Vengeful demanded.

Raggar took the blanket in which the infant had been wrapped and knotted it into a sling. He placed the infant inside again and then tied it snugly against his back.

He took Letter into his hands and took long but careful steps at the side of the churned path left by the killers. He steadily increased his pace until he adjudged he was travelling faster than those who were riding, and then settled into a predatory pursuit.

~

It was full dusk as he came to the wide plain to the south of the Vale. It was here that the killers had chosen to set their camp.

They are arrogant in their numbers, the Watchful smiled. *Their fires are too large – they will have no night vision because of it. They have posted no guards and they have arrayed themselves with no sense of defence. And they have picketed their horses on the north side of their camp – blinding them in precisely the direction from which they are pursued.*

They do not deserve to survive, the Pitiless observed, the Ever Vengeful silently agreeing.

Perhaps they are more subtle than we give them credit for. If they serve Sharim in any way, they will know *the Vale is not entirely undefended. Indeed, the fact that they left the Vale as quickly as they struck at it suggests they anticipated the possibility of retaliation. Their camp is too inviting for our taste – undoubtedly a trap. They are expecting us*, the Immovable asserted.

It would be a shame to disappoint them, given that they have gone to such effort, the Violent observed. *Letter thirsts for their blood.*

The infant stirred against his back and began to rouse. He brought the babe forwards into the cradle of his arms. It looked up at him with bleary eyes, and then large eyes, eyes the colour of smoke rising from a funeral pyre.

We have made a promise, the Relentless reminded. *No matter what must be faced. The child should not have to make this mute appeal to us. Do not wait for it to cry out its anguish, for then we will only be serving the Vale's enemies.*

Normally Raggar would have waited until the wolf hour – the time between the setting of the moon and the rising of the sun, when men are least able to resist the call of sleep and death – before venturing into such an armed camp. But he knew the longer he waited the greater his chance of losing any possible element of surprise – indeed, he counted himself fortunate that the horses had not already sensed his presence. A sudden shift in the wind and he might still be undone.

Yet there was a greater truth. He could not deny the child. He struggled even to meet its gaze properly. He had already failed it once in not being there to save its parents. He had been too slow to react, even though he had seen the omens in the approaching storm, even though deep down he had *known* he needed to act. Maybe he had not really wanted to believe a new age of war was starting. Maybe he had tried to convince himself that all would be well and that the undisturbed peace of his cabin might go on forever. He had allowed himself to become distracted.

For nothing lasted forever, not even the mountains themselves. The warring winds and time would eventually grind then down and turn them to dust.

Selfish fool, the Pitiless spat, *with your self-deluding fantasies of forever. Would you imagine yourself immortal? Wretch. You are as vain and proud as any mortal, if not worse than them. You are no better than those killers below, no more deserving of life, and you know it. You only hesitate for fear of losing that which should not be yours. Am I wrong? Then why haven't you already placed the child down and leapt amongst the dross below?*

The Beserker pulled at him, then battered at his will. He knew he would not be able to hold . . . not forever. He nestled the child into an area of longer grass, even as the Berserker transformed his face into a rictus grin.

He took his giant warhammer and rose up. His vision became sharper, all his senses keener. He smelt the horses, the woodsmoke and unwashed men. He tasted the residue of their excitement and bloody desire. He heard the heavy breathing of the few who drowsed, and felt the waiting of the others. He understood these men entirely – indeed, had once been much like them.

Raggar went silently forward. He moved with calm assurance through the enemy's exhausted mounts. They parted for him with hardly a querying snort. Then onto open ground, gliding forwards as fast as possible before the Berserker's incoherent warcry could turn the night to screaming chaos.

Letter cracked the skull of the nearest man, who sat murmuring to a comrade – one – and then destroyed the shocked face of the other. Two. A man sitting nearby began to turn at the strange sounds that had ended the low conversation. His eyes widened . . . and the warhammer crashed up under his chin, lifting him right out of his seat and flinging him half a dozen feet. Three.

A lone shout went up and time seemed to slow. Raggar whirled, booting a tough who made to rise to the side of his head and then bringing Letter slamming down and through the chest of a recumbent fighting man. Four.

The camp sprang to life. 'Now! He's here. Up!' came a harsh and guttural command from beyond the central fire. Blankets were cast aside and a dozen armoured soldiers rolled to their feet, weapons ready. They had indeed been expecting him – and those he had just killed had been a few extra sellswords taken on precisely to act as a sacrifice and bait for him.

There are bowmen among the soldiers, the Watchful fretted. *The distance to them is too great. We will not get to them in time.*

Excellent. We do not want this over too quickly, the Violent rejoiced.

They'd better pray they don't miss. We will give them no second choice, the Immovable promised.

The Berserker did not listen. The Berserker did not care. The other voices were as stray meaningless memories or complaining ghosts of the past.

He charged forwards and leapt the wide fire, hurling his hammer as he did so. The enormous weapon spun lazily, and was clearly going to fall short of the line of men arrayed against him. Two bowmen – who had initially started at the wild apparition appearing out of the flames – now saw their chance. They stepped up and trained their bows. Letter hit the ground and bounced low, awful momentum sending it to crack the shin of the first bowman, who toppled into his comrade with a cry. The aim of the second was lost and his arrow went well wide of Raggar.

'Guard the bowmen!' the commander barked. 'Move!'

Yet Raggar was already upon them. The flat of his palm sent the head of the second snapping back – five – and he stamped on the already twisted leg of the first. Six. He had Letter in hand before the first sword came swinging in. He batted it aside, his warhammer with the longer reach, and jabbed with Letter's anvil end. It seemed barely to touch the man, but it was enough to stave in his skull. Seven.

Two men came at him at once, one high and one low, both feinting and testing him. They had clearly trained together. Raggar set himself.

Do not wait too long. There is a third bowman!

Shut up. We're trying to concentrate.

An arrow was loosed. The air whistled. The two swordsmen began to repeat the same feinting pattern, hoping he would be drawn onto them this time. Raggar flinched left. The man to the right slashed forward and down, even as Raggar reversed Letter's direction and arched his back as far as he could. His hammer mangled the attacking swordsman's wrists, and the arrow passed harmlessly over Raggar's bent torso.

'Sweet Sharim have mercy!' the crippled swordsman begged.

The blade of the first swordsman was turned by Raggar's chains.

That was too close. If the idiot had stabbed instead of cut, he would have skewered us good and proper. He'll die for that.

Raggar smacked the end of Letter's handle into the southerner's eye, breaking socket and nose in one. He headbutted the man for good measure. Eight. He jumped right and, as if to console him, hugged the soldier holding out his ruined hands. The bowman's next arrow slammed into the fellow's back. Nine. Raggar threw the fast-dying man into a trio that were seeking to close on him, six others behind them.

'You're too close, you fools!' the faceless commander shouted angrily. 'Get back!'

The men staggered as they tried to retreat under the weight of their comrade. Raggar sprang after them.

'Look out! Don't flee him, you dolts! Stand your ground. Spread out.'

Ribs turned to wreckage despite armour. A jaw near torn off a broken face. A leg shattered so badly that it looked to be going in two directions at once. Tears of agony and grief. Snot dripping from teeth. Screaming, so much screaming. Prayers to gods, mothers, sweethearts and children.

A ceaseless roaring now. Was it him? The pounding of his blood and heart? The enemy? Simply the Berserker? The outrage of the pantheon?

There were horses suddenly bucking, bumping and trampling all around. In their terror they gnashed and bit at each other and their masters alike. Letter smashed down between the eyes of one battlesteed coming straight for him. The beast went straight down with hardly a sound.

Sorry, whispered the Watchful.

How many left, Watchful?

Er . . . eleven dead, one incapacitated? I think that's right.

You think?! Pay attention, damn it!

But the horse—

Forget the horse. If we die because of your flaming sentimentality, then we will torment your shade for the rest of eternity, mark our words.

There! the Watchful rushed. *See the legs behind that horse? The bowman. Get him!*

Better, the Pitiless conceded.

The bowman dodged left and right in the tumult, trying to get a bead on the Old Man of the Mountains. A horse galloped past, and he was suddenly face to face with Letter. It was the last he knew.

'Oafs! He's there! Must I do everything myself?' the commander hollered.

Raggar now saw the brute of a man who had overseen the slaughter of the innocent family of the Vale. The commander was a head shorter, but no less intimidating for it, as he was all broad muscle and blunt features. His eyes shone a baleful red and there were runic scars upon his cheeks. This was the servant of some power that was beyond human.

'You men!' the commander snarled. 'Form up on Dead Head and go at him as one! Hold together and you will triumph. For Progress!'

Dead Head stepped out of the near dark and into the glow of the fire's light. He was not overly muscled, but he was bizarrely tall, his long levers able to wield a two-handed sword that stood as tall as any man. His eyes were hooded and dull, as if in a trance. He was flanked on each side by a regular soldier.

Watchful, is this all that's left?

The horses must have trodden a couple of others under.

How disappointing. Still, Dead Head looks challenge enough. He has the longer reach.

The Berserker was laughing like a loon. He capered, then threw himself back into the fire.

'Where'd he go?' one of the soldiers asked querulously.

'To your right!' the blood-eyed commander called. 'No. That's your left!'

The soldier to Dead Head's left side had his shoulder demolished by Letter coming out of the dark. Dead Head swept his prodigious blade in a flat wide arc, slicing the soldier completely in two through the waist. The top half of the torso slipped sideways and the soldier watched in horror as his guts and spleen spilled down his legs.

There was a whisper behind them and Dead Head continued to turn with the mighty sword. The other soldier had anticipated it and raised his weapon to deflect the blow. It wasn't enough. Dead Head's heavy scythe cut through the defence and lodged fatally deep in the man's chest. Dead Head raised his sword – and the soldier with it. He frowned and shook the blade, trying to dislodge the encumbering body. Letter caved in the back of the giant's skill, and saved him further effort.

Nineteen, give or take.

Raggar turned quickly, seeking the commander. There was the fading sound of hoofbeats in the night.

Go! urged the Relentless. *We will run him to ground soon enough.*

The child! the Watchful interrupted. *We do not know how long it will take to overhaul that unholy captain. Meanwhile, the child will die of exposure or be consumed by the wild animals hereabouts. The life of the child* must *be our priority.*

Damn sentimentality, the Pitiless sighed.

Raggar trod quietly up to the last horse in sight and caught its tether. It was skittish, but finally gentled. He secured it to an ownerless sword that he stabbed into the earth.

Then he walked the camp, checking for signs of life. Several men were in their dying throes and he showed them an abrupt mercy. One was simply unconscious, and young by the looks of him. Raggar rested Letter's anvil on the youth's chest and kicked him awake.

Wake him up so he can see his own death coming, the Pitiless approved. *They did no better by the family, I'm sure.*

The young soldier's eyes fluttered open, then rolled in terror. He gulped over and over.

'The rest are dead,' Raggar informed him matter-of-factly. 'Care to join them?'

'N-n-no. I-I-I–'

A whining coward, the Violent opined. *He is not worth our time. Have done. We promised the child to see them all punished.* The Pitiless, the Ever Vengeful and the Relentless could only agree.

'I . . . I'm sorry. I have only been a Retainer for a week. My job was just to watch the horses.'

'You did not speak out when they murdered those farmers,' Raggar grated. He knew perfectly well how such things went.

Tears. 'S-sorry. I was scared!'

Words! the Violent spat. *What has become of soldiers these days?*

'Why kill them?' Raggar asked flatly.

'I don't-I don't–'

'Use your brain, boy. What are you a Retainer of? What is it they want of the Vale? Think or die. There are other things to which I must attend.'

'I am a Retainer of both the Empire and the cause of Civilization,' the youth chanted, clearly not for the first time in his short life.

'What is this *Civilization*? A religion?'

A nod. 'The priests say it will see the lot of all people improved. Civilization will see us individually improved.'

'It didn't improve the lot of those farmers, did it? Answer me.'

'N-no, sir . . . milord!'

'Where does your troop hail from?' It was no doubt the place to which the unholy captain had fled.

'A-Altimor. The capital of the region.'

'And what does the Empire want of the Vale?'

'I-I'm not sure, but the cause of Civilization must be brought to all.'

Especially those that are rich in resource, the Immovable observed. *An Empire with priests and soldiers is always in want of meat and grain.*

Raggar lifted the anvil. 'Go, before I change my mind. Tell your masters I said they should never trouble the Vale again. Should they ignore my direction, I will take this Civilization of theirs, ram it down their throats and choke them with it. Do you understand me?'

'Yes, milord,' the youth squeaked, jumping up.

We promised vengeance on all those involved! the Ever Vengeful fumed.

'Run!' Raggar roared after the disappearing soldier.

What is it you do? the Pitiless, Relentless and Violent protested as one.

We give the enemy the chance to bethink themselves, to doubt, and to know fear, perhaps to surrender or to be plagued with misgiving when battle is joined once more, the Immovable promised.

We give them greater time to prepare and scheme.

Heavily, Raggar went back to where he'd left the infant, fell to one knee and gently raised it back up. It smiled to see him and tried to catch one of the long wisps of his grey beard. 'We killed all but a youth and their captain.

The child's face changed. It cried in distress.

'Do not be afraid, child. I will not rest till he is put down. I swear it before every god and demon. Though it cost me my life I will see it done. Even should I die, I will find a way. Any who seeks to deny me will receive the same treatment as I will visit upon the unholy captain. I give my life and all that I am in payment. I will pay the price of your parents' deaths, for I should never have allowed such an atrocity to occur within the Vale protected by my promise.'

The night had stilled, as if listening to the oath and bearing witness. The oath could not be unsaid by him or anything in existence.

~

The old couple started at the heavy blow on their door. They had been enjoying a moment of peace before the fire, after a long day of pickling vegetables and laying down stores for the coming winter.

'Maggie, wake Calan,' Jedd murmured as he rose and crossed the room. 'Who's there?'

'Raggar of the Pillar Mountains. I have a young child who needs warmth and feeding. I claim hearth rights.'

Jedd shooed his wife to go fetch their son. 'Er . . . just a minute.'

Another blow and the door jumped in its frame. Again, and it burst its latch. Raggar stooped and came inside. 'Sorry but I must insist. This is still the farm I left in my son's care, is it not?'

The old farmer stood with his mouth hanging open, while his wife stared in disbelief. 'Ye gods, it really is him.' Then he seemed to remember himself and lowered himself awkwardly to his knees, gesturing for his wife to do likewise. 'Forgive us that we did not admit you sooner! We did not think . . . well . . . forgive us. We have always kept the old ways.'

'What are you doing, man?' Raggar frowned. 'This is no way to greet a neighbour. Get up. Where is my son?'

'S-son? I do not understand. Y-you . . . well . . . you . . .'

The farmer pointed a shaking finger at a crudely carved figure placed above the hearth as some sort of protection. It depicted a powerful warrior in chains, with long hair and beard, a warhammer strapped to his back and a babe held in the crook of the one arm. It existed in an identical pose to the one that Raggar himself currently held.

What is this? the Watchful said in utter bewilderment. *It is beyond our understanding. How can this be?*

We do not like it. It smacks of prophecy, foreknowledge and this meddler Sharim, the Immovable responded distantly.

'Where is my son? Daran?' Raggar blinked.

'D-Daran?'

'Yes! Daran! Are you entirely wit—' He took a calming breath. 'He owns this farm, does he not?'

'My father was Daran,' the farmer answered quietly. 'That is the only Daran that has been in these parts . . . holy one. How should I best address you?'

'Where is he?' Raggar asked numbly.

'He died a good twenty or so years back.'

Noo! the Relentless howled, for he loved as fiercely as he pursued every other emotion.

Can this be Sharim's doing? Can he make time pass so? the Watchful wondered. *Or is all this some trick to wrongfoot us?*

The infant was wailing now. Raggar sightlessly held it out, and the famer took it from him, with reassurances that they would soon have some milk warmed and have it settled. Raggar barely heard.

'Who is this?' asked a new voice, a brawny youth having appeared from one of the back rooms. From his hair and clothing it was clear he had just been sleeping.

'This is Raggar of the Pillar Mountains,' the farmer's wife replied softly as she took the unresisting old warrior by the hand and led him to a chair by the fire. The furniture creaked ominously under him, but it held. 'He is here to . . . he has brought us this infant.' She suddenly looked frightened. 'Raggar, where is the infant from?'

'A farm south of here. Razed to the ground by mercenaries and Retainers of the Empire,' he said woodenly.

'What?' the youth cried in alarm.

'Did you not see the smoke? I killed the majority. The captain escaped though . . . to Altimor.'

The youth was already taking up some lethal looking tool and heading for the door.

'Cal! Wait!' the farmwife begged.

The farmer's head dropped. 'There'll be no stopping him, Magreth. You know that. This is something he must do.'

'Take the horse I rode here on,' Raggar said without looking up.

Cal was gone. Magreth ran out into the night after her son.

The farmer shook his head and, still rocking the quietening babe in his arm, went to put some milk on the hearth. 'She'll be back soon enough. Cal was betrothed to one of the girls south of here. We get up and finish early hereabouts. Could be why we didn't see the smoke. Is there . . . is there any hope . . . that . . .?'

'No,' Raggar said, looking into the flames. 'Only the infant survived.'

They fell to silence then, with only the occasional fizz and crackle from the fire and hungry protest from the infant. After a while, the farmer dipped some cloth in the milk and gave it to the child to suck on. He redipped the material every half minute or so.

Raggar finally roused himself. He looked across at the farmer. 'Tell me about this Empire. And its cause. This *Civilization*.'

The farmer pulled a face. 'I know little enough. It was born in the south and has been growing steadily my entire life, this Koraline Empire, and now it is here on our doorstep.'

Koraline? Koraline? Do we know that name? the Relentless demanded of the others.

Something . . . the Watchful mused. *Some old memory. But we cannot catch it.*

'How is it I have not heard of it? I have travelled the length and breadth of this continent and not encountered it. And yet it has taken near the entire continent. By what power has it done so?'

The farmer shrugged tiredly, looking down at the child. 'At first, through astute alliances, I think. Then it began to seize parcels of land under something it called *wider law*. Few dared dispute this law, when it was backed up by the Emperor's Retainers, men and women in possession of terrible weapons and fearsome magicks. And apparently many genuinely wished to join the Empire once they had heard the Emperor's priests of Civilization, handpicked individuals of powerful persuasion and zeal. Great Raggar, they say it is an empire of both body and mind. Surely such a thing cannot easily be resisted.'

'And this Emperor?'

'Koralus the Eternal.'

Koralus. Hmm. Yet it was so long ago, so long ago. Daran had passed on in the intervening years. Sweet Daran. He wished . . . wished he'd been able to say goodbye . . . to say important words.

We have never been good with words, the Violent confessed. *Our deeds—*

Are not yet done! the Relentless avowed fiercely. *If Sharim has changed the passage of time around us, then we will find him and force him to change it back. Not all is yet done.*

We have personal issue with this god. Yet who knows what else he has wrought upon the world? How else has he manipulated the natural order and worked to upset the balance of things? Surely he oversteps. Why does the pantheon not offer him censure? the Ever Vengeful brooded.

We will take it upon us then, the Pitiless said simply.

'Good farmer, you will take the child in.' It was more of a statement than a question. 'I head south to Altimor.'

A vague nod. 'But who will protect the Vale? What will we do?'

'I head south to protect the Vale. From what you say, this Empire is intent upon its own expansion. I must go and persuade them otherwise, else they send their Retainers and priests to the Vale in ever greater numbers.'

Besides, it's about time the people of the Vale started thinking about standing on their own two feet. We cannot protect them forever. There is no forever. We know that now better than ever. Daran, forgive me.

Raggar lifted himself out of the chair.

The child began to grizzle. 'You can't be leaving right now. See, the babe wants you to stay.'

'I have promised the child the head of the unholy captain who brought the Civilization of the Empire here. I will not rest until I have delivered that head.'

'Will you not at least stay the night or until Cal has returned?'

Magreth re-entered at that moment, hands wringing. 'I could not stop him.' She took the child from her husband's arms, to comfort herself as much as the other.

'I must go,' Raggar repeated. 'I will not give our enemies a moment longer than I must to marshall against us. The sooner I intervene, the more harm that may be prevented.'

Unless the Vale would be better off ceding itself to the Empire. Maybe that will see all harm avoided immediately, the Watchful pointed out. *Who are we to decide on behalf of the Vale that the Koraline Empire must be resisted? Perhaps we are leading them into a war that cannot be won. Perhaps we are condemning them all to death where they might otherwise have been well and happy.*

Shh. Does an innocent give itself to a wolf just to pacify it? No. The Retainers of this Empire are unhesitating and unprovoked murderers. They cannot be allowed to go unchecked, or ultimately all will suffer. A dark age will overtake this continent and bring an end to all. Besides, we have sworn ourselves to seeing the captain and those who directed him brought to account. We swore to the people of the Vale, no matter what had to be faced. So enough, Watchful, enough. Abide.

Magreth nodded. 'Ride well, holy Raggar, and know our prayers go with you. Avenge us on the killers of my son's love.'

II

We are being followed, the Watchful warned.

Raggar sighed and scrubbed at his gritty eyes. He'd taken a rarely trodden path out of the Vale and hoped to have eluded the boy entirely.

A chip off the old block, eh? the Relentless smiled.

Raggar deliberately took a path dropping down into a wooded hollow and pulled Letter free of the chains across his broad back. 'Boy's a fool,' he groused, setting himself to wait for the sound of hoof-fall.

As the minutes passed, he became increasingly impatient. He was wasting valuable time with this nonsense. 'Come on.'

'Is this an ambush, mighty Raggar?' a youthful but uninflected voice asked behind him. The farmer's son had ridden around the outside of the wood and approached from the opposite direction.

Raggar turned and glared. 'So you've hunted before.' He spat on the ground. 'Doesn't mean anything. Doesn't mean you're coming with me. Go home, boy.'

'Who says I will let you come with me, old man? I can leave you far behind with this horse.' His face hardened. 'And I have a greater claim to this cause than you do. This is mine, and mine alone.'

I like him, the Relentless chortled.

Shut up, idiot, the Immovable snarled. *This is no laughing matter. We will* not *add this boy's death to our conscience as well. Our debt to the people of the Vale is already great enough.*

His life is his own. The Pitiless shrugged. If he wants to throw it away, what do we care?

'Have you ever killed a man, boy?' Raggar asked evenly.

The youth hesitated. 'I have killed.'

'Animals on the farm, maybe. But *a man?*'

'I have lacked the opportunity and cause until now, but I am of your blood.'

Good answer, the Violent allowed.

Raggar slid Letter across his back once more. 'Very well, take your best shot.' He threw his arms wide. 'One shot to put me down. Show me that you can at least fight like a man.'

The youth did not hesitate. He came forward, having tied the horse before entering the hollow, and set his feet.

Punching up from the ground at least, the Violent observed.

Cal rolled his head and loosened his arms, then bunched his work-hardened muscles and delivered a thunderous blow to Raggar's gut.

Raggar bent slightly and rocked back on his heels, to channel the strength of the punch into the ground. He straightened up and looked down severely at the youth. Did this stripling remind him of a younger version of himself? Did he remind him of Daran? No. 'You were given a free shot. Did you kick me in the groin or smash in my knee to bring me down? Did you slam my jaw back into the top of spine to unstring me? Did you hammer into my solar plexus to stop the breath in my lungs or cave in my chest? No, you did none of those things. You fight with some childish sense of honour. It will see you dead in a heartbeat. Were you to face any sort of brawler, mercenary or veteran, you would be nothing more than sport. Go back to your farm where you will at least be of some use. Your folk will not be able to run the place without you. Do not let your grief make you selfish. Do not lose yourself to this.'

The young man remained clear eyed and determined. 'The harvest is in. My folks are hardy enough to see out the winter. I could not live with myself were I not to see Brin avenged. I will *not* hide from this!' There was true feeling in his words now. 'And you will teach me. You will not talk me out of this.'

'Enough of words, then,' Raggar snorted. 'Ready yourself. I will take my shot now. You may not be able to deliver a blow to fell a man, but let us see if you have the courage to face one. Or will you flinch and cringe like a coward?'

To his credit, the farmboy stood straight and steady. Raggar delivered a massive blow to his midriff. Cal went backwards and slammed into a tree. Somehow, he kept his feet, though he was bent double. He groaned and spewed the contents of his stomach onto the ground. He crouched down, struggling to breathe.

Raggar turned and walked away.

Why did we only hit him in the gut after telling him off for doing the same? the Violent wanted to know.

'We didn't want to hurt him too badly,' Raggar murmured.

We are becoming soft.

He is still on his feet, the Watchful pointed out. *Perhaps we should have been less kind.*

We were teaching him a hard lesson and dissuading him from his current stupidity, not helping him to join his Brin in the ever after, the Immovable internally shouted, ending the matter.

He strode out of the hollow, not looking back.

~

Mushrooms, berries, nuts and garlic leaves. Is that it? We should have taken the horse from the boy and eaten that. Our need is the greater.

We will have meat once in Arlford.

He had marched all day and was now approaching where the plains to the south of the Vale met the river Arl. The Arl was wide and fast-flowing, and dangerous in many places, but there was a crossing place at Arlford. Nearly all goods being traded between the northern and southern reaches of the region had to pass through Arlford. There had always been a market there, where goods of every kind could be found. It was also a place where men of every type could be found – mercenaries to protect caravans from bandits; hawkers and hauliers; sellers of weapons; labourers; flesh-traders from more distant parts; a motley of minstrels and jugglers; conjurors and charmers;

itinerants and philosophers; priests and mendicants; whoremongers and doxies; physickers and the purveyors of potions, tonics and elixirs; arrangers and well-guarded lenders; and then a good number of simple butchers, blacksmiths and ostlers. All life was to be found at this meeting place of humanity.

When described to someone who had never been there, Arlford often sounded colourful and exciting. But viewed up close, it was pretty much all one colour in various shades; and that colour was brown. The main streets on either side of the river were always churned up, even in the hottest summers. With horses and herds so regularly brought into town, the streets were a constant slurry of dung. It covered boots, buildings and faces alike. Brown even got into the water, judging by its brackish taste and the particular flavour of the local ale. It hung in the air and was breathed deep into lungs.

That was how Raggar remembered it at any rate and, judging by the fug he could see over the town even at this distance, it had changed little since his last visit. If anything, it seemed to have grown bigger and become even browner. The copses of trees and open spaces all around seemed to have taken on its hues too.

We really should have taken his horse, the Watchful groaned. *It would have stopped him following us.*

What?!

Raggar turned and looked back along the trail. Sure enough, descending towards him, as the ground gently dipped all the way down to the river, was the tousle-haired farmboy, jaw set.

'Sharim's maggoty pizzle!' Raggar cursed. 'He's as stubborn as . . . as . . .'

As we are?

Shut up!

'You've made your decision then,' Raggar said as Cal drew up. 'You know my views on it, lad, but it's ultimately your life to do with as you please. Let's just hope you live long enough to learn from this folly. If you are to travel with me, then there are some rules. Tell me now. Do you agree to these rules?'

'Do I get to hear the rules first?'

'No.'

Cal chewed on that for a moment. 'I agree then. Now what are they?'

Raggar held up a hand. 'First, you do what I tell you. Second, you do what I tell you without question, argument and quibble. Third, you do all the cooking. Fourth, you do not expect me to save your sorry carcass, especially if it gets in the way of me completing the task to which I have sworn myself. And fifth, you keep up at all times, because I will not be slowing down for you and your various injuries and needs.'

Cal nodded, and said nothing.

'Good.' Raggar turned on his heel. 'Come on then. Try not to get in trouble in Arlford. Do you know how not to get in trouble?'

'Not speak to anyone?'

'It's a start, but you need to make sure no one fancies talking to you either. There are predators in Arlford who will see you for what you are – a green, back-o'-the-woods innocent who's an easy mark. You need to make yourself look mean and dangerous. Now, given how fresh-faced you are, that's gonna be difficult. So your choice is either to wait outside Arlford till I'm done, or you play the loon, one that's gods-touched or something. Or you head back to the Vale. Which is it?'

'I will play the loon. I will talk to the horse and pretend that I can hear its reply.'

'Yes. And mess up your hair more. And wipe dribble down your chin. If anyone approaches you, shout and make to grab at them. Ask them to kneel in the mud and pray with you. I know! Chant the name Sharim a lot. Tell them it is blasphemy if they do not pray with you. Tell them Sharim speaks to you. If they refuse, shout loudly that they are a sinner. That'll scare 'em far more than any blade or bloody threat. Got that?'

'Got it, great-grandfather.'

Raggar stopped, pivoted and met the youth's eye. After a moment, he nodded. 'You are sure you want to do this, lad? You are raising arms against an empire. Do you have any idea what that means? You are but one man. I will not always be here. You will be alone. And it will not end. For each soldier that falls before you, there will be two to take its place, till you are sickened by all that you have done. You will stand atop a pile of the dead, a pile that will grow and grow. You will be drenched in gore so none you have ever known will recognise you. And you will not even recognise yourself, or your own bloody thoughts and mind. It will make you into the very monster that you believed you fought against. Do you see that you will come to hate and fear yourself? And for what? What will you have achieved? You will have given your own life to it, sacrificed it upon that hill of corpses that you have made. But for what? A wrong that you barely remember after all the years of killing. A dim and fading memory. An idea of what was once right and wrong, before it all turned to chaos, before they were all dead, when it still mattered. For once they are all gone, right and wrong will be as the wind. So tell me, lad, why you would want any part of that for yourself, your parents or the Vale. Tell me, boy, why you have not turned that horse of yours and ridden home to those that love you, miss you and worry for you. Tell me why you are not at your parents' side in their final days as storms build all around. Tell me why you are not with them when they only wish to have you there for comfort and so that they might tell you of things important to their hearts.' And now his voice rose well above the competing air. 'Tell me, damn you!'

Yet the youth was not shaken.

There is something not right about this one, the Watchful averred.

In a hollow voice Cal replied: 'I know what you say is true. I know it. I already feel it . . . for my life ended when Brin died. I found her burned body, you know? I held it to me – just as I had always held her – and she broke in my arms. I kissed her next, and her lips crumbled beneath mine. I taste it still, and will forever.' His eyes were like snow. 'I cannot be at my parents' side now, for they are full of love and care, and I will bring them only misery, heartache and finally death. I would be a blight to them. I would be no son. Please, do not ask me to return to the Vale again, for I cannot.'

Raggar swallowed. He scratched beneath his chains, considered the sky and then cleared his throat. 'A good enough reason, s'pose. Not sure an engraver could get all that on your tombstone, but maybe you can commission some idiot minstrel to come up with a song to make your parents proud. Well, time's a-wasting, so let's get on.'

'Just what is it we're looking for in Arlford, great-grandfather? This unholy captain of whom you speak?'

'Aye!' Raggar called as he set off. 'Could be he's come here for a change of mount and a decent bed for the night. He might be hiring himself some new men and thinking himself safe. Looks like his sort of place, and it's the only proper town hereabouts, as far as I remember. Or he might be getting himself a riverboat south to Altimor, though that's a winding route and probably too slow. We'll see. Now stop asking questions.'

~

They queued at the gates to get in, lined up with locals who had largely come to sell baskets of eggs, barrows of late fruit, game and wooden goods. Some were clearly labourers coming to hire out their strength, youth and knowledge of a craft – they could easily be identified by the tools they carried and their artisan apparel. There was also the occasional mercenary who discreetly paid the guards to be allowed entry.

At the front now, however, was one who was different, judging both by his long unadorned robes, and his conspicuous refusal to bribe the guards. ' . . . that is none of your business,' he could be heard saying.

The smaller of the two guards bristled. 'We don't want your sort round 'ere, Tender or no. If you can't pay proper like honest folk, then stand aside for those that can.'

'Honest? What does this town know of honest? Since when was a Tender of Garlan turned away by the people of this farming region? Would you forsake his bounty and blessing? Do you really want to see how your market fares without him?'

'You threatening me?' the pugnacious guard demanded loudly, for all to hear. 'Don't take kindly to that, does we, Horth?' The larger guard shook his head with a stupid grin and brandished his stave.

The folk in the line pretended not to hear or notice what was going on. Raggar made an impatient noise. 'This is going to take all day. The killer will be long gone at this rate.' He eased a couple of people aside and, Calan close behind on his horse, came forwards to tower over the guards.

The short man – who was all stubble and blotchy features, smelt of stale ale and was wearing the remains of a greasy chicken dinner down his tunic – glared up angrily at the intrusion. 'What the hell do you want?'

'I am looking for a captain of the Empire. He has runes cut into his cheeks. Did he come through here?'

Open suspicion and aggression. 'Who wants to know?'

Raggar shook his chains, pulled Letter free and growled. 'Me.'

The short guard's eyes widened, as if only now properly seeing the warrior before him. He took a step back, his bottom lip trembling. 'I-it's *him*. The demon! By all that's holy!' He took more steps back, bumping into Horth and pulling him out of the way. A shrewd-faced but otherwise nondescript fellow who had been resting on a seat just inside the gates got up and disappeared into the town.

The folk behind Raggar and Calan set to whispering and edged backwards on mass. One swore some oath or vow, peeled off and trundled his barrow away in the opposite direction. The path before them now clear, Raggar shrugged and led Calan into Arlford, the Tender slipping into the town in their wake.

'The main inn's at the end of this thoroughfare, where it meets the riverside,' the big warrior said back to Calan. 'Or at least it used to be.'

The street was full of peddlers, stall-holders, the curious and crowd-pleasers. More well established merchants had wares on display from open-fronted storehouses to either side of the street, where there were wooden walking boards to protect the more discerning buyer from the mud, spit and filth in the middle of the course.

A mother glanced towards them, apparently didn't like what she saw, and ushered her children away. There was a sudden clatter as a shop pulled its shutters down. Several casual traders abandoned their pitches and hurried off down side alleys. A few made a show of looking up at the darkening sky, then rapidly began to pack their goods and livelihoods away.

Hard-eyed knifemen stepped away, watching them warily. Smudge-faced but nimble youngsters – presumably cut-purses – thought better of coming to play near the new arrivals and chased each other off.

'Everyone seems to be finishing early,' Calan noted. 'Maybe it's some holy day.'

Raggar shook his head. 'Maybe we smell bad and that's why they're all fleeing. Lad, you don't need to be a seer to know there's trouble in the offing. Keep your wits about you. Forget the whole talking-to-your-horse thing. Stay close. You do have weapons about you, yes?'

'A short axe, a half-blade and a bag of stones.'

'*Bag of stones?* What are you saying? For wooing one of the loose women of this place?'

Calan flushed. 'No! The throwing kind.'

'Sharim's weeping arse, boy! We're not hunting rabbits and squirrels. Just do what I tell you. Forget staying close. Keep out of the way altogether!'

Don't want him too close to that maniac the Berserker, after all, the Watchful offered. *We'd end up minus one great-grandson otherwise.*

'As you say, great-grandfather.'

'Look, just go find a stable along the riverside and see about finding some feed for the horse. I'll come find you once I've finished asking around at the inn. Head off to the left there. No arguments or questions, remember.'

Calan gave him a level stare. 'No arguments or questions. A favour rather. Do not kill this captain should you find him. His life is mine.'

Can we really make that promise? the Relentless and Ever Vengeful challenged.

Maybe it would be better if we spared the boy, the Watchful pondered.

The captain will get what he deserves either way. The boy asks little enough of us, the Pitiless allowed. *Whether it is by our hand or the boy's, we will have seen the infant to whom we have sworn ourselves avenged.*

'Very well, lad,' Raggar replied solemnly. 'You have my word. Now begone for a while.'

The Good Faith inn was much as he remembered. Outside, the same wooden sign, though clearly repainted, swung from the metal bar high above the entrance. For those not well versed in their letters, there was a depiction of a labourer bringing in the harvest under a smiling sun. To the side of the worker's field there were well-fed cattle and their Tender.

There was very little of good faith about the interior of the inn, however. Every patron, be they blade-for-hire, trader or farm worker, had some piercing or bludgeoning implement on display or close at hand. Voices were kept low and private. The two dozen or so occupants watched for trouble, while avoiding any direct eye contact that might be adjudged too challenging.

The background chatter hushed as Raggar stepped into the low and heavy-beamed main room. At a nod from the innkeep, a minstrel sitting by the wide fireplace played a gentle and soothing melody.

'Welcome!' the broad proprietor boomed, waving Raggar over to the board from which flagons of frothy ale were served.

Raggar crossed to the man. Chairs scraped as three mercenaries stood. They went to the door, their drinks left unfinished.

'You look thirsty!' the innkeep said jovially. A fresh flagon thumped down in front of Raggar. 'On the house.' He had a full orange beard, thinning hair on top and the thick forearms of one used to hard work. His face was open, if a little forced.

Raggar chose not to reach for the beer. 'I am looking for a particular Retainer of the Empire, runes cut into his cheeks.'

The innkeep's smile slipped slightly. 'We don't want any trouble here. This is an honest place. Truly.'

Raggar frowned. 'Do I know you? You seem familiar.'

His smile weakened further. 'This inn has been in the family for hundreds of years.'

'And all in your family have had the same copper hair?'

'Ye gods! It *is* you, isn't it? The d-demon!' the innkeep near choked, looking around nervously to be sure they were not overheard. 'My grandfather said you'd promised to return should this town ever offer bad faith again. Please, demon. I run an honest business. Do not destroy me. I beg you.'

What's he going on about? the Watchful asked. *I don't remember the details of the last time we were here.*

We clearly left a lasting impression, the Violent chortled.

I suspect we were drunk, the Pitiless added. *And someone or some group or other tried to take advantage of us. We probably knocked a few heads together and the story got exaggerated over the years or some such nonsense. Nothing important.*

'The Retainer,' Raggar reminded the innkeep.

'Yes, of course. Er . . . he was here in the early hours of this morning. He took a room to clean himself up while my boy went to get him a fresh mount from along a-ways. He took supplies to fill a pair of saddlebags and then he was gone. He seemed in a . . .' Understanding dawned. ' . . . hurry. You are on his trail, demon, yes?' Hope now. 'It is not my inn you have come for? I have provided you information in *good* faith. Yes. I have not offered you bad faith!'

All but giddy with relief, he is. The Violent was sour.

Shouldn't count his chickens then, should he? the Watchful rallied. *Get ready.*

Raggar spun and hefted Letter in one giant hand. Behind him the innkeep squeaked in alarm. The inn's customers looked up as one and saw Raggar intent on the door. All heads turned just as the main door flew open and a half dozen of the town-watch came rushing in. A tall and imperious figure swept in after them. His eyes were a harrowing white and he wore a vague and sadistic smile. He was hairless and had a large boney cranium. His robes were priestly and far cleaner than they had any right to be in a working town like Arlford.

The priest's men-at-arms fanned out, short stabbing sword in their hands, and pushed customers roughly aside – the majority of whom gratefully made for the exit.

'So, this is the demon that threatened the good people and guards of our town,' the priest sniffed. 'A primitive creature. My, but it stinks of carrion and corruption.'

Just our type of person, the Violent happily opined. *This should be fun.*

Be wary, the Watchful cautioned. *See him drifting forwards. We should strike immediately, before his men can get past the tables and properly flank us.*

A few of the inns patrons – farmer types – had retreated to the far wall, apparently torn about whether they should be leaving. They looked unhappily at the priest and wonderingly at Raggar himself. What was it they wanted of him? Why did people always want something of him?

'You claim the town as your own, do you, pretty priest?' Raggar growled. 'By what right? I was about to enjoy a quiet drink, but instead I get this. You are rude, priest. Ill-mannered.'

'Ah, the forked and weaseling tongue of a demon,' came the quick and smooth reply. 'We *know* you, demon. We *know* how you revile and defy the gods and their priests. We *know* how you have lived unnaturally long by feeding on violence and the lives of others, how you have feasted on their fear, outrage and dreams. We *know* how you hate the Civilization, progress and freedom of the people. You would keep them ignorant, cowed and terrified. We *know* you! And you are *nothing!* You will be *exorcised!*'

Careful. He has continued to drift forwards. Leap with Letter extended now. There is a chance we can end this before it starts.

We have to be sure, and we dare not let his words be the last the farming folk hear before they flee. They will think of us as nothing more than this rampaging and murderous monster otherwise. They will turn towards the priest's faith, no matter the outcome here, and then all will eventually turn on us. We will be doing the Empire's work for it.

We care not if they are so simple-minded and weak-willed as to be swayed by the priest's words, the Pitiless rejoined. *The men-at-arms close in. Strike.*

'I am just a man,' Raggar said clearly. 'A man who will *not* be bullied by thugs and the ever-growing demands of an empire's priesthood. I will *not* apologise for living, do you hear? I will *not* ask permission of any to walk this land freely and drink ale produced of its grain. And I will *not* be insulted by the likes of you and let it pass!'

Raggar leapt, Letter rising and moving into a devastating arc.

The priest did not flinch. He extended his sandaled foot and touched the flagstone ahead of him with a toe. 'Lodestone.'

Letter was yanked out of its trajectory as it passed over the flag – and the weapon's anvil came crashing down. There was a loud crack and detonation.

The priest took hurried steps back as Raggar made to grab for him. Then Raggar's chains were dragging him back and down. Immensely heavy all of a sudden. The more he strained against them, the greater the force resisting him. One of his knees buckled.

Up! the Relentless shouted.

I don't understand what's happening, the Watchful wailed.

Bugger understanding it. Move! the Pitiless demanded.

'Kill him,' the priest commanded his attendants coldly.

One moved in with his blade and lunged. Raggar made to bat it aside, but it was already hitting the floor, having been unnaturally pulled down. He grabbed his attacker's forearm and pulled further forwards, taking him off balance.

Poke his eyes with the other hand. Just so. His head pulls up, baring his neck. Then we tear out his throat with our teeth. Messy, but effective. And the other guards are appalled and hesitating, which gives us vital moments to slip our chains—

'Forget your blades. Batter him with the wooden furniture,' came the priest's calm instruction. The remaining guards came on once more.

There were feints and then a heavy oak stool came down with a crack on Raggar. Pain flared the length of the forearm he had raised defensively. Had wood or bone given way? He was still tangled in his chains and kept down.

He reached for and snagged a nearby stool for himself, as he caught a blow to the back of his head. The room tilted. With a roar, he slammed the seat back over his head and felt it connect solidly. Then he threw it straight into the face of the next nearest, who was too close to duck in time and had his nose split open.

Raggar was clubbed across the flat of his back as he tried to wrestle free of his chains. He cursed foully. 'Whoever did that will pray they'd died a hundred other deaths before I'm through with them!'

A thwack to the back of his head and he could hardly see anymore. The Berserker seized control in the agony and confusion. He thrashed, a vein bursting in his forehead as he near tore himself apart. Muscles and limbs contorted. Links creaked then separated and whiplashed, metal mangling the ankle of a thug off to the side. The guardsman fell screaming.

Raggar's ancient armour suddenly sloughed and cascaded off him and he was up, taking yet another blow from the guard to the rear, but this time only glancing. Raggar leapt at him, grabbing the man's crotch and collar in the same moment. He upended the man and brought him down headfirst onto the flagstones. And again. And again. Then he hurled the all but headless body at the priest, who had to take a long step sideways to avoid being hit.

The Berserker jumped up onto a table and now hurled himself at the sneering cenobite. He had lurid visions of what he would do to this creature.

Yet the priest was all calculation and not about to be fazed by an oncoming enemy. Another flagstone touched: 'Liquefaction. Mortification.' And another careful retreat.

The Berserker could not avoid the flagstone and his feet sank deep. The stone suddenly became solid again and he was trapped.

'Oaf,' the priest pronounced. 'You, man, see him dispatched. I have rendered the rabid troglodyte defenceless for you.'

There is another guardsman! the Watchful was shrieking. *And those that were merely injured are regaining their feet.*

Match the guard, match the move, become the move. The Violent was chanting, the Relentless, Pitiless and Ever Vengeful beginning to echo it. Raggar matched the rhythm of his breath to it, watching the guard stalk forwards. He swayed his arms in time with the guard's, mimicking the cadence, increasing his sway as the man rushed in with sword held close. Raggar twisted his torso with the man's, clasping him and encouraging the sword-wrist round and past them.

He head-butted the bridge of his attacker's nose hard, caving it in. He head-butted again and the man lost all coordination. Raggar took the sword and pushed the flailing man away. Then he hammered down with the end of the sword. Chips of stone flew.

We'll never get free in time, the Watchful said. *See the shrewd priest pulling his sinuous blade. He has reach and will surely find us out.*

Not if we hurl this sword and bury it between his eyes, he won't, came the obdurate Immovable. *Won't look so shrewd then, will he?*

He maybe has conniving and twisting magicks to pull our blade from the air. And he may be able to throw his with the unstoppable force of a hurricane.

Quit fretting, Watchful. Honestly, you're getting worse with age. It's not like we have any more to lose now than we did in the past. If we die, we die, albeit we'd prefer it to be at the hands of one more . . . well, one less . . . verminous and detestable.

One who does not throw away the lives of underlings so casually.

Every king, warlord and god has been casual with the lives of others. That is why we cannot respect them, Watchful accepted. *Look out.*

Another incantation. 'Intersterces.'

The priest's blade rippled through the air, sheering it like silk, as loud as a whisper in a temple. The room seemed to fray apart, colours bleeding and warping. Images starred as if seen through a faceted crystal. Even time seemed to fragment.

Multiple magical daggers came at Raggar from high, low and aslant. It was impossible to avoid them all. They sliced, nicked and skewered. Blood swelled, spilled and ribboned down him.

He did what he could to fend, pivot and be in all places at once – and may have succeeded if his lower legs were not held immobile. Daggers were flicked away, to clash with others and then wink out. Others he clapped between his hands and flung back at the priest – who vanished them before they could come close. Yet more got through and found Raggar's flesh.

Tiring quickly.

His limbs shook, his strength draining away with his blood. He threw the short sword that he still held. It looped more lazily than he had intended, and its heavy hilt caught the priest on the cheek, interrupting the conjuration. An ugly gash and thin trail of blood marked the religious acolyte.

'How dare you! I will see you expire in a slow torture, demon.'

'Not without the permission of Garlan,' interrupted a voice from the door.

The priest's head whipped round and he hissed in anger. 'Tender! This town is no longer yours. Your altars are no more and the people no longer care for your ignorant and backward ways. You cannot stand against me. I will see you finished along with this demon, this abomination with whom you choose to side. Your sacrilege cannot be allowed to go unpunished.'

Raggar recognised the Tender from the gate into the town. In stark contrast to the priest, everything about the Tender – robes, features and manner – were simple and unadorned.

Cal stepped from behind the Tender, appraised the room and hurled a stone. It smacked a rising guard in the temple, instantly felling him.

'Th-thought I told you to stay outside,' Raggar slurred.

'Apologies, holy Raggar. I am but a simple youth who has become over excited with the sights and sounds of this place. I find I cannot contain my enthusiasm.'

'Holy!' squawked the priest. 'You are the demon's blaspheming familiar. Your tongue will be pinned to your palate. Intersterces.'

Nothing happened. The Tender shook his head. 'This inn and its land were consecrated in the name of Garlan long ago. You cannot raise magicks against me or any I choose to protect here.'

'Heathen! Dispersal. Eradication. Infernication. Intersterces. Malinc–'

'Lad, shut him up,' Raggar loosely waved.

A stone struck the priest between the eyes, staggering him. Raggar caught the end of the man's flaring robes and pulled him into proper reach.

'No,' the servant of the Empire spat, his face a savage rictus of hate. Raggar slapped the dirk out of the man's grip, grabbed him about the head and swiftly snapped his neck. There was a moment of silence, the priest went limp, and hit the floor with a thud.

His legs coming free at last, Raggar found he could not stay upright. He swooned atop his victim.

Little stones. Who would have thought? asked the Violent, but there were none to answer him and he spoke no more.

~

'Amazing,' Cal was saying distantly.

'Garlan's blessing still has potency here. Had he suffered such injuries off consecrated ground, I may not have been able to save him. He would probably have bled out.'

'Some of the wounds have disappeared completely. Others are nothing but faint scars.'

'Are there no Tenders where you come from, young man? I am Gardel, by the way.'

'And I am Cal. *Thank you* for what you have done.'

'It is nothing. I am indebted to the two of you if anything. I would have had a mite more trouble in this town were it not for the two of you. I might not even have been allowed to enter. To think that this place has so easily forgotten its debt to Garlan the Grower. There was a time when there would be simple shrines to him in every field and on every street corner. But now . . . now, all the people talk of is *progress*, *the power of the mind* and *the rise of mankind*. It is almost as if they would replace the traditional gods with themselves, and the physical world with their dreams. It is a type of madness, I think, and can lead nowhere good.'

'I do not pretend to understand it, Tender Gardel.' Cal kept his voice low. 'It is because of the Church of Civilization, yes? Why then has Garlan allowed this Church to spread into lands and amongst his own congregation?'

There was a sorrowing sigh. 'Garlan and his Tenders are generous by nature. All share in the harvest, so that all may survive and give thanks for his bounty. Even a prosperous farmer needs well fed labourers. If the lowest field-workers in a community are not cared for, then crops will rot ungathered and all will fail. As per this generous spirit, we have always tolerated the worship of other local and parochial deities. Their strengths have always added to our own. Yet it was this selfsame open-handedness that then allowed the Church of Civilization to spread amongst us. We did not really understand the nature of the threat until now. We have allowed a wolf into the fold, I fear.'

'What then will you do, Tender?'

Raggar roused himself. 'The wolf must be hunted down and skinned.'

The Tender's grass-green eyes widened in surprise. Apparently he had not expected Raggar to come round quite so soon. 'The High Tender has asked me to travel to Altimor, to come to an understanding with the Overlord,' Gardel said softly.

Stiffly Raggar rose from the pool of drying blood in which he had been lying, and looked around for his chains and Letter. 'Waste of time. The wolf will grin and nod but, as soon as your back is turned, snatch another of your lambs.'

Gardel frowned slightly, accentuating further the lines of his careworn face. He looked older and more tired than his thick brown hair said he should. 'Perhaps, but even the wolf has its place in nature. Without it, rabbits become so numerous that they destroy the famer's crops. Without it, deer become too abundant and destroy the shrubs and weaker trees of the forest, slowly killing the forest and destroying the places where birds and other winged birds might live. The birds then descend upon the farmer's fields and hedgerows just to survive. Without the wolf, the mountain aurochs proliferate, begin to spread into the lowlands and trample or devour the farmer's seedlings.'

Calan nodded thoughtfully, but Raggar showed no sign of agreement as he noisily began to don his armour. The old warrior finished, slid Letter across his back and met the Tender's patient gaze. 'Would you deny the hunter his livelihood, Tender?'

Gardel did not hide his uncertainty. He hesitated, then lowered his head. 'No, good warrior, I would not.'

Raggar made a satisfied noise. 'Very well. As thanks for your seeing to the scratches and grazes that I suffered, we will see you safely to Altimor. We too head that way.'

Gardel smiled. 'You should be fully recovered by the morning, good Raggar, and I would be grateful of the company.'

'We will be leaving immediately. Also, there are some rules–'

Calan rolled his eyes.

'–First, you do as I tell you. Second, you do what I tell you without question, argument or quibble . . .'

~

They left the inn by the back door, just as evening was turning to night. Raggar had spoken quietly to the innkeep, the latter agreeing to hold the weapons of the fallen townwatch and priest as payment for any damage done to the inn. Much enriched, the man was then quite content to keep the unconscious and dead secure until at least the next morning.

The ancient warrior led the youth and Tender across the bridge spanning the river Arl, went to a wide barge and negotiated a place on deck for the three of them and the horse, to depart the next morning. The sharp-faced barge owner asked which inn they were staying in, spat in his palm and shook on the deal. Raggar then took his companions into the quiet streets in the southern part of town.

'Great-grandfather, I thought we were leaving town immediately,' Cal offered.

'We are. Now keep quiet and be sure than none follows or hears us. Get in the deeper shadows. The gates are not far ahead and I do not want the night-watchman to see us. Wait here.'

Raggar carried a firkin of ale he had taken from the Good Faith inn. He raised it on high now as he tottered into the middle of the street, looked up at the moon, toasted and drank deeply. He started to sing a bawdy tavern song, his pitch and phrasing all over the place. He stumbled round a corner in the direction of the gate.

'Tender, do you understand what is going on? We have left the horse at a stables at the riverside. Will we be going back for it, do you think?'

'I suspect not, Cal. The stabling of the horse and the places we have arranged on the boat for ourselves are just a ruse . . . to mislead those who might think to pass on information about us or think to pursue us. Come tomorrow morning, we will be long gone. Raggar understands his enemies and the weaknesses of humankind all too well. He is far more than the simple and direct brawler that he appears.'

Cal nodded.

'May I ask you some questions about him?' the Tender followed up.

'I know little enough.'

'You called him great-grandfather. Do you simply mock him with that name or is he really such a relative? Yet how can that be? Was your mother particularly young when she had you?'

'I do not fully understand it myself, Tender. I overheard some words my father shared with him, that is all. Raggar spoke of Daran, who was my grandfather, so . . . well, I don't know.'

'And you called him *holy* Raggar. Why is that? Do people so revere age where you come from?'

'Again, I overheard my father use that name,' Cal admitted. 'I shouldn't have been eaves-dropping.'

Silence fell between them.

It was then Raggar returned. 'Come on, then. We can't stand here gossiping all night.'

He led them back round the corner and onto the gate, which was unbarred and ajar. They passed an unconscious night-watchman, who stank of ale and was arranged with his arms around a firkin.

'He will be none the wiser when he awakes, and will put his sore head down to too much drink,' Raggar assured them. 'If we are in luck, he will awake before any find him, and he will swear that he remained vigilant and at his post all night.'

'Should I check that you have not done him any serious harm?' the Tender offered.

'No. It will only waste time. Besides, I didn't hit him that hard. Let's go. Tender, you swore to do as I told you, remember? Would you so quickly go back on your solemn vow?'

'The oath I made to serve Garlan will always come first. All life is sacred to him, even if–'

Raggar gestured to Cal and went on through the gate. The youth did not hesitate to follow. Muttering to himself about the stubbornness but usefulness of mules, Gardel performed a quick blessing and hurried after them.

III

Raggar had allowed them a few hours' rest late in the night, and even a small fire, but he had awoken them at dawn and set them on the road once more. Young and fit though he was, Cal struggled to keep up.

'Good Raggar!' Gardel called ahead. 'I am well used to travelling on foot from region to region, and even have certain magicks to hold back weariness and injury, but if you do not ease up then you will arrive at your destination without a single companion. And you swore to see me to Altimor, remember? Would you so quickly go back on your own vow?'

Damn the pair of them, the Relentless chafed. *They are slowing us down.*

Leave them behind, the Pitiless encouraged. *We warned the youth we would never go back for him, after all.*

But the Tender has it right that we promised to see him through, the Watchful came back half-heartedly. *We usually keep our word where we can.*

And we are not invulnerable, the Ever Vengeful cautioned. *Carry on like this and we will lame ourselves, perhaps never reaching Altimor at all.*

'Sharim's pox, Tender!' Raggar declared as he came round. 'Would you have me carry you like a child or some sack of turnips?'

'No, good Raggar,' Gardel replied evenly. 'Just ease up some. Much faster and we will overtake time itself.'

Raggar was caught by that. He looked off into the distance and rubbed his chin in thought. 'Overtake time? Is that how it happens? Is that possible?'

'Great-grandfather, look.'

'Is that how he seemed to disappear, and how everything was suddenly moved on? Can he do it in reverse, or does it only go forward?'

'Great-grandfather!'

Raggar blinked. 'What is it, boy? I'm not deaf, you know. I'm stood right here.'

'There. Do you see? Up along the road. Is it a cart?'

Raggar peered through the dim light of early dawn. About half a mile along the way, where sparse copses and uneven ground met the dark horizon, was something set off to the side. 'Could be.' He sniffed. 'Certainly a scent of horses. They're not hidden, so probably some trader camped for the night. Let's see.'

Wouldn't be bandits this close to town, the Watchful agreed. *And none can know we're coming, so can't be an ambush.*

Drawing closer, they perceived that a heavily laden cart had lost a wheel and veered into boggy ground. There were two horses in the cart's traces, standing patiently enough. The sizeable cartwheel that had slipped its axle dangled from a taut rope that disappeared over the far side of the cart's load. Loud gasps and oaths could be heard from back there.

'Hello!' Raggar called.

'Gah!' The rope slipped. The wheel thunked down and toppled onto the road. There was a vehement curse.

They waited. A rotund and sweating merchant came round one end of the cart. He wore a padded coat and trousers which, while not of the finest material, were clean and patched in only one or two places. The weighing scales of the merchants' guild were conspicuously stitched into the right breast of the fellow's jacket.

'Well met!' the round-nosed and bejowled character beamed. 'Fine gentlemen, would you be able to render me assistance? The guild would be most grateful, not to mention myself. And I am Samul Sitwell, at your service!'

'It would be our pleasure,' spoke up the follower of Garlan. 'I am Tender Gardel, and these . . . are my companions!' He waved Raggar and Cal towards the cart. 'We are travelling south, much like yourself it seems. Do you head for Altimor?'

Raggar silently set his shoulders beneath the bed of the cart and nodded to Cal to lever the wheel up. The brawny youth crouched and got his fingers beneath the metal rim of the wheel.

'Why, I do as it happens. Perhaps we can keep each other company on the way–'

Cal straightened his legs and the wheel came up. In turn Raggar slowly straightened, lifting the entire vehicle.

'–as I would happily offer a lift to a Tender who might bless my enterprise, and two fighting men of such obvious strength and ingenuity. A fair bargain, yes?'

Cal slotted the wheel back onto its axle, and Raggar used Letter to tap a thick windblown branch into the axle's pinhole.

It might allow us to travel faster, the Ever Vengeful considered.

It seems too good to be true that we should meet him precisely when we need him like this, the Pitiless pointed out.

Almost like he was waiting for us, the Watchful agreed. *But how could he have been?*

'A strange time of day to be travelling, Master Sitwell,' Raggar said.

The merchant pulled a face. 'I know. Believe me, I would much prefer to be abed with my good lady wife at such an hour, but the goods I was waiting on did not arrive into Arlford until late last night. And I have to get them to Altimor within two days if I am to catch the market and fulfil the orders I already have. Some of my clients are too important to disappoint or inconvenience, don't you know?'

'If you are in a hurry, then you will be taking the route through Wormdale, yes? The road may not be so easy, but it will save you half a day.'

The merchant's easy smile faltered. 'I am more interested in saving my skin, however, goodman. None takes that route. The pass through Wormdale is known to be haunted. It is said a witch rules that territory. It is an unnatural crack in the earth more than any true river valley. They say there are caves that lead down to the very bones of the earth or the very Pit itself, for steam rises out of them, and who knows what has crawled up to the surface to await unwary travellers?'

Sounds nothing like the Wormdale we know, the Violent mused. *Wasn't it all flowers and pointless prettiness when we last went through it? There was certainly no gossip bandied about of any witch.*

'Fear a witch and you give her power over you,' Raggar answered, helping the cart back onto the road. 'Is that not so, Tender?'

Gardel tilted his head. 'There is some truth in that. Those whose faith in Garlan is strong will know themselves protected and will not need to fear. And yet, there are certain powerful creatures upon this earth whose territory it would be wise to respect and therefore avoid.'

Cal was frowning as he climbed into a seat amongst the cart's load. 'If none takes that route, how is it so much is known of this Wormdale?'

The boy has the right of it. It sounds like local superstition and fireside tales. It is a route which may well put us ahead of the captain, so we must take it. If he gets to Altimor before us, then he will find protection amongst his cronies and will be hard to winkle out. It will take all the longer and be all the more effort to see him annihilated.

'Whatever you decide, Master Sitwell, the lad and I will be taking the route through Wormdale. We will leave you at the fork in the road as necessary. Let's go! Tender, as we go, you will also need to decide which way you will travel. I know I promised to see you to Altimor, but a prior promise I made to the lad's people must be honoured before all others. I am sorry.'

'I understand, good warrior. I will think on it and pray for guidance, but I suspect it is my duty to ascertain whether Garlan's bounty within this Wormdale has been corrupted or despoiled. If it has, then it is my duty as his Tender to restore it.'

Samul Sitwell clucked to the horses and flicked the reins. The cart swayed forwards. It slowly picked up speed and was soon moving faster than even Raggar could travel.

~

They travelled into the afternoon, Gardel and Cal dozing as they could. Raggar eyed the clouds – thin and ragged off to the left, where the road turned to follow the circuitous path around Wormdale, and thick and bruised straight ahead. A ragged pennon or the livid contusion of the injured. There wasn't much to choose between the omens.

'Master Sitwell, tell me of Sharim.'

The merchant ran a hand through his oiled, black hair. 'Good warrior, I am not one to speak ill of any god, of course. My customers are varied enough that there is always someone I might offend.' He grinned good-naturedly. 'What would you ask of me, however? I will answer you as I may.'

'He is the god of the Koraline Empire, yes?'

'We-e-ell, I wouldn't say that precisely.'

'What would you say then?'

'Er . . . well, what would I say? Sharim the Seer, Sharim the Sage or Sharim the Social Benefactor – no matter the avatar you may prefer – is the principal deity of the Church of Civilization. There are lesser deities as well, for the Church is not intolerant, and the Empire encompasses peoples of different cultures and traditions. I struggle to name the lesser deities, mind you. Be that as it may, Emperor Koralus does not rule the Church, so the Empire and the Church are not quite the same.'

'I see. Who rules the Church then?'

'Er . . . the priesthood?'

'And who heads this priesthood?'

'I am not entirely sure who the current High Priest is in Cha'Ithan. Needless to say, news is slow to get up here from the Enlightened City.'

'I am from a farflung place myself, so do not know much of this. I had not heard of Sharim before. He is some new god, yes? Where did he come from? Or is he one of the old gods renamed?'

The merchant's brow furrowed. 'Sharim has always existed as far as I know. He is immortal and eternal.'

'*Knowledge* and *advancement* are holy to him?' Raggar pressed. 'Mere *ideas*? Things invented in the minds of men?'

Stories and lies. Fantasy and delusion. Deceit and distraction. He must be one of the old gods posing as something more noble . . . and attractive. Or a demon? Yes, a demon perhaps.

Samul Sitwell now looked distinctly uncomfortable. 'These things are somewhat beyond my learning, goodman. Yet *advancement* and self-betterment are advocated by the Church, that is true. Surely it is for the good of all if we work to raise ourselves above the baseness of animals. Should we not look up to the gods for example, rather than to the beasts in the field? Should we not emulate the sacred divine? The Church has brought learning to many who had not previously known its advantage. Now I can avail myself of numerate and literate workers to complete simple invoicing and stock taking tasks, where previously I had to do it all myself. It has freed me up for other things, and allowed me to expand my business. Can you not see the Empire and Church have benefited all?'

Gardel – whose eyes had come half open while Sitwell spoke – snorted, but otherwise held his peace.

'All I see is that it has allowed you to place yourself over other men,' Raggar responded. 'Your wealth and power have increased thanks to this advancement, no doubt, but I do not see it has benefited all.'

'I provide jobs, and pay my workers well!' Sitwell countered heatedly.

'It is for them to say whether you pay them well,' Raggar shrugged.

'My reputation–'

'Is clearly your primary concern. So! We are at the fork, I believe. This is where we part ways. Lad, you awake? Tender, have you made your decision?'

'Indeed I have. I will accompany the two of you. I placed my faith in you back in Arlford, and have seen or heard nothing to make me rethink that decision. Besides, the manner of that first meeting was surely auspicious and a sign from Garlan. I will go with you if you will still have me.'

'We would be pleased, Tender,' Cal answered, and Raggar nodded.

As they made to climb down from the cart, Sitwell exclaimed, 'Friends! Pause a moment, I beg you. Have I misspoken? If so, then I apologise. Be sure I meant no ill by it. I am ever ready to learn. If I have been in error then you need but say so and I will attempt to make amends. I would ask you not to judge me harshly, for I would very much like to keep in your company. Arriving in Altimor all the sooner would be of great advantage to me, and your fearlessness has convinced me that I would take little risk in passing through Wormdale with you. Forgive me if I was full of my own importance before–' Here, his voice broke in what sounded like genuine regret. '–it is a manner we merchants adopt in order to instil confidence in any potential customers. It can become an unfortunate habit, I am now well aware. It promotes arrogance and puts off those with better self-awareness than myself.' He met the eyes of each of them in appeal. 'I will be more honestly myself from now on, if you will allow me to go with you. And my cart might still speed your own journey, yes?'

A pretty enough speech? the Watchful wondered.

Cal looked dubious, the Tender quite moved. Both looked to Raggar for a lead.

'Very well. We will vote on it. What say you, Tender? Will Master Sitwell accompany us?'

Gardel hesitated but a moment. Then: 'Garlan is a god who knows how to forgive. Therefore, I vote yes.'

'Lad?'

Cal glanced between Raggar and the Tender, clearly undecided. At last his jaw firmed, although his voice was not quite so decisive. 'I also vote yes.'

We can outvote them, surely! came a veritable chorus.

It was not fair on the boy to have him vote second. If he had voted no, he would have been at odds with the Tender. And if we had then voted yes with the Tender, the boy would have lost all credibility amongst the group. Not fair, declared the Watchful.

Fair? sneered the Pitiless. *Fair is no place or tribe of people. It is meaningless. It is the complaint of those too cowardly to fight for themselves.*

It was a test of the boy, the Immovable concurred.

Not one he could have won though.

There is no other sort of test, is there? If there is a clear option by which to win, then it's just the most obvious and sensible thing to do. Not a test at all.

'Well that's the decision made, then,' Raggar said without expression. 'Drive on, good Master Sitwell, so that we may be well into Wormdale before evening falls.'

Cal could not hide his ill ease, until Gardel gave him a reassuring nod and invited him to sit close.

'There's just one more thing, Master Sitwell,' Raggar said lightly.

'Of course, good warrior. Anything.'

'There are some rules. First–'

Cal and Gardel rolled their eyes as one.

'–you do as I tell you. Second, you do what I tell you without question, argument or quibble . . .'

The way down into Wormdale was somewhat precarious, as the path twisted first one way and then the other, but the horses remained sure-footed and were entirely obedient to Sitwell, even when they came perilously close to a drop. Besides, the road surface was relatively compact, and the roots of the gnarled trees growing all around seemed to hold the edges that might have otherwise crumbled away.

There were no signs of life, the skeletal wood through which they travelled stark and silent. The light inevitably faded and all turned to gloom. Down and down they went.

Nearly all of them jumped when Gardel chose to speak up. 'Well so far so good! Although it does feel we're descending into a tomb, eh?'

'Did you have to say that?' Sitwell whined.

'Perhaps some light then?' the Tender offered, and raised a gentle nimbus around them. The shadows closest to them jumped back as one and hid behind the nearest trees.

Raggar grunted. 'A useful trick. How's it done?'

'Why, it is merely the natural energy from within, good Raggar. It is easy once you have learned the knack, and if you let Garlan guide you. The young – who are so full of life – almost do it without thinking or realising. As we get older, and more mistrustful, we guard ourselves more closely and forget the *how* of it.'

'Not much hope for me then. But will it not tire you? I do not want you weakened if we are waylaid by some witch or other.'

'It requires little enough energy to maintain like this, good Raggar. It is about as tiring as a brisk walk. Yet if I were to burn bright suddenly, to illuminate this entire wood, for example, I would fail quite rapidly.'

'Perhaps I could learn?' Cal suggested tentatively.

A J Dalton

'Why, it would be a pleasure to teach you, good Cal. Now, do you sense the life within you? Do you see it, feel it or taste it? Each person experiences it quite differently. Some hear it as a rushing sound. I have even heard of those who *smell* it, as if it were a smokiness, a spring freshness or sweetness.'

'Er . . . not really . . . well, I guess?'

One of the horses wickered. 'Quite right, horse,' Raggar chuckled.

Gardel ignored him. 'Close your eyes and try. You know it is possible, because you have already seen that this energy can be redirected if it can but be harnessed. That's it. Feel the limits of your body and mind, then look inwards. Is the darkness deeper? Or do you see colours, shades and patterns? Tell me.'

'I . . . I–'

The other horse farted. Raggar hiccupped, hand over mouth, and Sitwell fought hard to contain himself. Gardel tutted, then shushed them.

'I . . . I . . . no, nothing.'

Gardel's shoulders slumped and he sighed. 'It is often like this with fighters. Perhaps unsurprisingly, they prioritise or fixate upon the material or physical world. They are so used to putting it before all else, they struggle to put it aside, even when faced with a non-corporeal threat. The exceptions are paladins.'

'What are they?' Cal asked, all wide-eyed.

'Magical knights,' Raggar growled. 'Trouble even at the best of times.'

'You have faced such?' Gardel asked with genuine interest.

'One or two, which is more than enough. It's best to take them down fast and hard, while they're still making their flowery speeches and challenges. Hit them while they're still between *thee* and *thine*, and you might just escape intact. Even then, you'll still have their entire order hot on your heels for a few decades, as they chunter on about some debt of honour needing to be repaid. The best advice is to avoid them altogether. Priests aren't much better. Present company excepted. No offence, Tender.'

Gardel breathed deeply and smoothed his features. 'None taken, good Raggar, none taken. Perhaps we will wait, Cal, until we find more conducive surroundings for our next lesson. In the meantime, I would recommend you practise identifying the currents, flows and eddies of the natural energies within you.'

'Thank you, Tender. I will do so.'

~

They passed down into the valley, where the going was easier, albeit that the trees crowded more and frequently clawed at them. There was a deep and decaying litter on the ground, dead leaves, branches and what might have been moss-covered bones. It was a putrid mulch that made it difficult to breathe. Fungi the colour of old blood seemed to be the only thing that thrived.

All sound in that closeness was deadened. They came to the river but its dark waters slid past in a whispering silence. Ghosts spoke to them just beyond their hearing.

Things unseen stirred, shifted and slithered beneath the mould. One of the horses whinnied in alarm.

'At least some things live here,' Gardel said softly.

'Who says the things we disturb are the living?' Sitwell asked in a high and breathless pitch.

Raggar held Letter ready before him. 'I have never met a thing that could not be dispatched by strength of mind or arm. Do not let this place unman you, Master Sitwell. You will panic the horses.'

'Yes, yes of course.'

'I take it none of you fancies stopping here for the night?' the old warrior continued. 'Thought not. Then we travel through the night until we are beyond this place. Can you light the way that long, Tender?'

'I shall endeavour to do so,' Gardel nodded, although weariness could already be heard in his voice.

'Lad, you are quiet back there. Not asleep, are you?'

'No, great-grandfather,' the youth murmured. 'I am remembering the old farm at the edge of Beltar's Grove, to the west of the Vale. They say that it is haunted, that something bad happened there a long time ago. I went there as a dare once, when the sun was high in the sky. The place had a feeling much like this one. There was a pall over it, and the good weather could do nothing to lift it.'

'Aye, I know the place, lad. Even knew Beltar. His farm always did well, although he had lost his eldest to sickness. Then we found out he'd been making bloody sacrifices in that Grove of his. A number of youngsters had gone missing from local farms too.'

Sitwell shivered, as Garlan choked, 'A demon worshipper?'

Raggar spat over the side of the cart. 'Aye. He'd started by sacrificing small animals, and so on, but the demon demanded more and more.'

'Why did Beltar start in the first place, great-grandfather?'

Raggar sighed. 'I told you Beltar had lost his son. At such a time, a demon will come sneaking up with all sorts of offers and promises – to allow the grieving parent to talk to the departed one last time, to hold back the sickness from other loved ones, to wreak revenge on the jealous neighbours who might have caused the sickness through a curse, and so on. The demon will ask for some small token or payment at first, to seal the bargain. Once the victim is dependent, however, the demon will then demand worship and blood, perhaps promising to bring the departed fully back to life. All too soon, the victim loses all control and sense of self. They become entirely possessed by the demon, and the demon is then able to spread their influence to others. Of course, all that they touch is despoiled and corrupted, for the demon can only survive by continually draining the essence of others. That is what befell the old farm, and why still nothing grows there properly.'

'Even Garlan struggles to heal ground so steeped in blood,' Gardel said sadly.

'And you are all saying Wormdale is similarly blighted by demons? This is a hellmouth?' Sitwell wailed, slapping the reins so that the horses stepped higher and faster.

It would be a foolish demon indeed that thought to tackle this group. But we would welcome it, the Violent decided. *It has been too long since we tangled with one and battered it into oblivion.*

We fear they have prospered in our absence. Let us hope there are dozens, else the battle will be too one-sided, and something of a disappointment.

'Fear not, merchant. Demons are wily. They will never come at us directly. Always they act through others. We must watch each other, lest one of us is lured into betraying the others.'

'What?' Sitwell protested. 'I know we have not been companions long, but I hope I have shown you enough that I may be relied upon. My word is my bond as a trader. Were I not true to my word, I could not be trader at all. My word and reputation are everything, and reason why you can trust me.'

'See? You have now forgotten your fear quite suddenly, Master Sitwell. Let the demons but challenge you on your reputation and you will thwart them easily. You need not baulk. Keep your head and do not exhaust the horses.'

Sitwell blinked. 'Yes. I see.' He smiled awkwardly, easing back on the horses.

It was us that got them all spooked in the first place, the Watchful pointed out. *Best we stop with all the stories and speculation for a bit, else their imaginations run away with them.*

Raggar fell to watching the dark after that, and the others did likewise. They travelled in silence for hours, and Raggar found his eyes more than a little sore. He closed them deliberately for a long moment or two.

'Shh!' Gardel was saying. 'Don't you hear them? So many!'

Raggar's eyes snapped back open. He listened hard. Yes, something faint. Did he feel the air stirring too? A hiss of a voice . . . voices? A crowd? An entire host coming towards them? The slightest tremor of the ground, as if a thousand feet were marching.

'Should we turn back?' Sitwell worried.

Raggar didn't answer for several heartbeats. Then he relaxed. 'It is the sound of cascading water, that is all. Watch the ground carefully in case it falls away.'

As it was, they came to a giant sinkhole down which the entire river roared, and the road went well wide of it. The air was full of spray, and both horses and passengers were quickly soaked through. For all that, the oppressive atmosphere which had so burdened them now seemed dispelled.

'It's incredible!' Cal laughed and hollered, barely audible.

Gardel nodded with boyish enthusiasm. 'The work of the gods is awe-inspiring, no? Who can doubt their power? Human empires, so-called Civilization and demons are as nothing before them.'

And the ground beyond the yawning sinkhole rose once more, up towards a ridge where the sky showed the deep blue that promised dawn was close. Sensing that they would soon be free of the strange and unnerving Wormdale, the horses leaned into their traces with renewed vigor.

'Go on, my beauties!' Sitwell encouraged them with a whoop.

Up they went, if anything faster than when they had cautiously descended into the brooding valley. Cal and Gardel had to cling hard to their places amongst the load, to avoid being thrown off, while Raggar had to brace himself in the seat next to Sitwell.

Back and forth the wagon wove, until finally they crested the ridge and entered a more shallow defile between two promontories silhouetted against the lightening sky. Yet cowled figures – one to each side – also stood silhouetted, and there was another in the road directly ahead of them.

Sitwell applied the break and drew the wagon up. 'Who are they? What do they want?'

'Maybe they're just out for a morning stroll,' Raggar replied, rolling his head and loosening arms and shoulders. 'I hope so, for their sake.'

'Local shepherds?' Gardel suggested, no real conviction in his tone.

'Be ready,' Raggar advised, then slowly levered himself up. 'Stand aside, goodman. We would love to linger and exchange gossip with you, but we have other places to be. Stand aside, I say!'

'Turn back!' came the ghastly command of the central figure, his words felt as much as heard – a crawling in the gut, something wriggling in your ear, something caught in your hair.

Sitwell moaned, swaying slightly.

'I think not,' Raggar called back. 'All are free to travel this land, whether you like it or not. And who are you to say otherwise?'

'All things have their limits and ends, Raggar the Mad. You should know that better than most, for you have ended more lives than any other. See all the lives you have taken. See!'

The words twisted and squirmed around them, sliding one moment, sensing and burrowing the next. Raggar tried to shake his head clear, as he heard Cal being sick. He could see the air worm about them, could feel it slithering as something more substantial, something more monstrous. Yes, there were shapes half seen there, closing in on them.

'Eugh! They're everywhere,' Gardel breathed. 'Look there!'

Out of the corner of his eye, Raggar glimpsed them. Glistening and hungry apparitions, their maws stretched wide. Most were wrecked things, as if slain on a battlefield and risen again. Chests were caved in, faces obliterated, limbs mutilated and jaws hanging, but all had the same starving and yearning look in their eye. They reached out desperately, pleading, angry.

We recognise some, the Relentless said. *Our enemies walk again it seems, just as we ourselves walk the world of men once more. No matter. Have at them!*

Mere ghosts, the Pitiless shrugged. *We have put them down before. No doubt we can put them down again.*

Be not distracted, the Watchful interjected. *It is the necromancers who are the real threat.*

With a roar Raggar leapt down from the wagon, brandishing Letter even as he landed. He swung wide and hard. Yet his trusty weapon passed through the wraiths and did little more than cause them to pause before they came forwards once more.

The three necromancers were chanting in concert now, their magicks raising more and more spirits to send towards Raggar, and a few towards his companions. The sweet and damp smell of the grave filled the defile. The restless dead became ever more real.

Raggar swung with furious energy, knocking the nearest off their stride, but still unable to connect properly and throw them back. Hands raked at him.

Ignore them! Leap through them while you can! the Watchful screamed.

The Berserker bellowed even louder and fought to be free.

Raggar charged forwards. Filthy nails and fingers were broken and torn free as they sought for purchase on his chains. They crowded towards him, biting the air. He powered on, pushing them down and treading them under, but the weight against him steadily increased and he could not help but slow.

Onwards, you decrepit lazar! the Pitiless demanded.

Raggar became frenzied and then the Berserker tore free, laying about him with the rage and frustration of centuries and wars beyond counting and memory. He became a maelstrom of savagery and brutality. He lost all sense of self as he gave himself to it.

The necromancers continued chanting, Raggar caught in the press and no longer making progress towards them.

~

Cal mustered himself, pulled sling and shot from the pouch at his waist and carefully stood. He set his legs wide in order to keep his balance upon the wagon's uneven load. He whirled the sling and released with a snap.

The stone flew straight and true. It struck the cowl of the central necromancer. The creature staggered backwards with a cry, a grey and withered hand reaching from its robes and going to its head. It looked as if it would fall, but caught itself and managed to remain upright.

The necromancer high up on the right of the defile reacted at once, lifting his strangling incantation above the others. A phantasm separated itself from the rest of the undead and drifted towards the wagon. The horses shied.

A young girl raised her hands in mute appeal to Cal. Her eyes held a tragic emptiness, tears of dried blood staining her hollow cheeks. Her rent shift barely covered her spare frame.

'Brin!' Cal mourned, voice breaking. He went to climb down to her.

'No!' Gardel shouted. 'Cal, do not. It is not her.' The Tender tried to restrain him, but Cal shook him off. 'She is gone. The monster but steals her visage. Do not be deceived!'

'Gardel, is that you?' sighed the image of a wan matron.

'M-mother?' the Tender whispered in horror. 'How are you here? I am so sorry.'

'I forgive you, Gardel. I understand. Come to me. I am so cold.'

Cal reached the ground and went to his sweetheart. 'Brin, what have they done to you?'

'It does not matter. We can be together now,' the lost soul mouthed.

He took her in his arms. 'My beloved.'

'Kiss me, Calan. Share your breath with me. It will make me stronger. We can be as one.'

He lowered his lips to hers, tasting mould, maggots and destruction. He saw putrefaction and knew despair.

Gardel struggled to hold back tears. How could she be here? She could not be. Yet she had forgiven him. She *knew*. Only she would know, only she *could* know. He'd never told another what had gone on in her final days.

It was an agony to see her now, to see her so . . . non-judgemental. It only made it worse somehow. If she'd been enraged and livid, he'd have been able to explain, to beg, to defend himself. This though was beyond him: this pity she showed him.

He realised in that moment that *he* was the one who could not forgive the desperate young man who had smothered his own mother because she was in such terrible pain. He had wanted her to go out calmly and at peace, with some sort of dignity. He had not wanted this once proud woman humiliated and lessened by her incontinence and constant screaming.

He could not forgive himself, could not live with the knowledge of what he'd done. Could not live with it.

He was on his knees before her, head bowed in misery and defeat. He hugged her legs and was racked by hard dry sobs.

She lowered her skeletal hands to his head, down to his temples. Her thumbs splayed out and searched to put out his eyes.

~

Sitwell gibbered to himself in terror. The horses jostled each other in panic now, nipping and gnashing, kicking out. The wagon tilted precariously and he was lucky to stay aboard. All would be sent to rack and ruin in moments.

He wanted to call for help. He wanted to yell sage advice, to break the enchantment of the devils besetting them. He wanted to cajole Gardel back to himself and promise Calan that his grief would pass in time. He wanted to soothe the horses with an even tone.

He wanted all these things, but more than anything he wanted to leap free of all this, turn and flee, all the way back to Altimor, to where it was safe. He was a simple trader. None of this was for him. Yet his legs would not obey him. All he could do was stare, mouth hanging open, as ghouls came for him, and his horses bucked and threatened to tear wagon and traces apart.

He was nothing in all this. Nothing. Bluster and air that meant nothing. Tall tales and half-truths. He was no fighting man who knew what he believed in or had a cause for which he'd die . . . or fight to live.

Why had he ever come here? Greed, he knew. The promise of advantage over competitors, with his goods brought to market all the faster. An insatiable emptiness at his core, the desire for what he did not yet have. He was no more than any of these undead, with their constant craving for blood, warmth and life.

Why did he not join these animated corpses, or simply flee? Why? Because he'd promised the old warrior and bound himself by it. That was why his legs would not let him move back towards Wormdale. He had begged the youth and Tender to let him accompany them – in the process promising to be more than he had been before – and that now held him.

Hating himself for it, he felt for the small and cocked crossbow secreted beneath his seat and trained the weapon on Cal. He fired, then reached for the cable that would quick-release his horses from their traces.

The bolt from the crossbow punched through the one temple of the corpse trying to steal Cal's breath, and came out the back of its skull. The cadaver toppled out of Cal's grasp, hit the ground and turned to dust.

'Noo!' the heartbroken youth pleaded.

Nostrils flaring, and foaming at the mouth, the panic-stricken horses plunged forwards and in amongst the grizzly dead. They barrelled through them, trampled them down and became even wilder. Hooves stove in heads, broke through ribcages and even bodily threw the enemy up into the air. More and more of the dead were crushed and stamped down into the mud.

~

His mother was bumped from behind. She clutched at his face as she tried to avoid falling over his back and shoulders, and then over his back. She hit the ground with a loud crack. Still on his knees, Gardel turned to find the disarticulated body of his mother crumbling to nothing. 'Mother!' he keened.

'Raggar needs our help!' Sitwell was calling. '*I* need your help. Tender! Calan! Arghh.'

Gardel blinked hard, disorientated, coming back to himself. They were fighting necromancers. What was he doing on his knees? He came up, looking to help his friends, yet what did he know about fighting the dead? All his magic was for healing and blessing the living. Still, did not that magic ultimately protect the living and hold back death?

He blessed the nearest shambling creature – a large man with a prominent skull and underbiting jaw – and it burst into flame, burning red and then green. The creature twisted and pirouetted, spreading the fire to others, and yet more.

'Sorry,' Gardel breathed, as the inferno of the funeral pyre began to engulf them all. 'Oops.' He realised that he and his friends were at risk of being caught in it.

He saw Sitwell grappling with two emaciated women and a child, and not faring well. One had hands around his throat, the child bit into his leg, and the other was tearing his tunic open.

Gardel cast a blessing towards the group. Sitwell's assailants were instantly aflame, coruscating energies consuming their already shrivelled flesh. Their cries were hideous to hear, full of anguish, yearning and loss.

'Hot! It burns,' the merchant yelped.

Gardel cast a healing spell in his direction.

'Face me, false Tender,' a new voice dripped from the air.

Gardel beheld a dark figure striding through the dead directly for him, eyes incarnadine and with a long scythe in hand. Here was a Tender of the Dead, more than an equal for Gardel, for death eventually came to all. Gardel began to pray hard as the dark priest cast vile curses at him and raised the scythe for what would be a fatal strike.

~

All was chaos. His heart was battered. But Calan knew a terrible anger in his grief, and that sustained him now. Even through the pall of smoke hanging over the defile, he saw clearly. He whirled his sling and snapped out another stone towards the central necromancer.

A blink, and the stone was impacting beneath the sorcerer's cowl. The creature collapsed. The spirits it had commanded seemed to lose focus, then melted away.

'That's for Brin, you misborn wretch.'

Instantly he looked for the necromancer high up on the right of the defile. The mage was illuminated by the burning dead and the morning rising behind him. Cal began to whirl his sling.

But the necromancer had seen what was happening and had already redirected some of his minions at Cal, as had the mage to the left. There was no way Cal would have time to take out both mages before the dead reached him.

He loosed the stone and, not waiting to see if it found its mark, turned to flee, despising himself for a coward. He fitted another stone to his sling and chanced the briefest looked back. There were so many right on his heels he dared not even stop to release the next missile.

'My friend,' Sitwell begged, as Cal reached the corpulent and slow-of-foot merchant, 'do not abandon me!'

'Get up on the wagon!' Cal cried, making a prodigious leap upwards. 'Take my hand. Quickly!'

Sitwell jumped as best he could, getting most of his stomach up over the edge. 'Pull!' He kicked outwards, keeping the dead from him for vital seconds. 'Pleease, Cal!'

'I'm trying!'

He heaved. Sitwell booted and humped, and then they both tumbled onto the top of the cart. Cal just saved himself from going over the other side, righted himself and clambered back up. He pulled his long knife.

The dead leered and ravened all around them. The necromancers up to the left and right still stood.

Then the dead came for them.

~

Raggar did not know if he still lived. Or whether he had died and become like the dead around him. All he knew was that he still fought and would always do so.

Letter was so slick with gore and viscera that he struggled to hold it. It struggled in his grip as if it had a will of its own – a determination to deliver greater and greater destruction. It was as if it almost resented Raggar for slowing it down.

Yet they needed each other – they wielded each other.

Hands sought to push themselves into Raggar's mouth, to choke him or tear him wide. He gnashed, swallowed, spat, head-butted and grabbed at those who were too slow to come at him.

He took Letter in two hands when they crowded him, and delivered flurries of short punching strikes with anvil and handle. Then, when there was room to move better, swung the mighty hammer in two-handed circles, high and low, dashing, crushing and smearing.

His arms and shoulders had gone far beyond aching, far beyond pained. They were a molten agony so severe he expected them to slough off his skeleton entirely.

He slipped then in the carnage and then the dead flung themselves on top of him, seeking to bury him under. Letter was trapped beneath him. He punched and chopped at ankles, heads and mouths. He was on his knees still, but his limbs trembled under the charnel weight.

A face came at his, black teeth bared. He headbutted hard, unhinging the corpse's jaw. It took its head backwards, ready to strike with just the teeth of its top jaw, but in that moment it showed its throat, which Raggar bit out.

They scrabbled at his back, trying to dig through him, fighting each other to get close, tearing each other to pieces more than they did him, for his chains preventing them inflicting any fatal wound. Their numbers worked against them, for only a few could get at him at once, and those that did were crushed or dismembered by the others.

Inch by inch, he dragged Letter forwards. The anvil-head emerged and he pushed it onwards, bludgeoning, and again, and harder. A tunnel-like gap began to clear ahead of him.

Through sheer force of will, he started to get out from under them.

There was a wild snorting and hooves flashed here and there, further helping to free him. Sitwell's horses? And now there were flames of unnatural hue, spreading quickly. Gardel? They would soon become a conflagration. He had to get free.

And he spied the middle of the three necromancer's ahead. He gritted his teeth and strained his every sinew to keep moving.

Suddenly there was a smack and the necromancer's head snapped backwards. The necromancer was unstrung in that moment, and fell where he stood.

Another of the boy's stones! the Watchful crowed.

The weight bearing down on him seemed to ease and he surged out and up, greeting the dawn with a massive shout and snarl. The two remaining necromancers took an involuntary step backwards, and he knew then that they feared him more than death itself, that he was more than death. Worse than death. He would devastate and devour them. And he relished that prospect.

'Come down here, little death-wizards!' he demanded.

Frantically the necromancers tried to re-establish their chanting, out of harmony and cadence. Raggar sprang forwards and onto the slope that would take him up to the necromancer on the right.

Magicks swirled about him, lashing and tightening, then dissipating. The air thickened, a half dozen shadowy forms coalescing. Midnight beats with tattered wings and blazing eyes came into being.

Demons of the lower planes? Those who prey upon the souls of the cursed and the damned? How can they be here?

'Whatever.' Raggar spat, his bloody phlegm sizzling as it hit the nearest demon.

'Join us, brother!' the largest beckoned. 'We will be your comrades-in-arms.'

'Sorry. Bit busy at the moment. Maybe later.'

Raggar moved Letter through the air with a speed and agility that caught the first of the demons flat-footed. He hammered it straight between the eyes, and then swept his weapon round with unstoppable force towards the second.

As a group the demons *shifted*, as if stepping out of one realm into another, and then back again, but now in a slightly different place. He missed the second of the demons, and it made sure to move back out of his reach.

'You are tired,' the largest drooled. 'We will test and taunt you a while longer, till your companions have all fallen and you no longer have the strength to lift that enchanted weapon of yours. Our kind is patient. We have waited centuries to have your soul, tyrannical Raggar, so we can wait a few moments more. Soon it will be in our clutches and we will feast upon it. Oh, how sweet it will taste! Soaked in the blood of so many innocents. So many!'

Arcane implements materialised in the demons' talons: a hooked polearm, a two-pronged sickle, a burning net, a twisted cat-o-nine-tails and a many-branched sword.

Letter? Enchanted? Since when? the Violent wondered.

Forget it. We must move before Cal and the others are over-whelmed. No, do not look back. Move, before we fall flat on our face with fatigue!

Raggar bent his aching knees and leapt, but the slope was against him and Letter came short of his tormentors again. He ran for the necromancer and the demons *shifted* to intercept him. He blundered into the net, and Letter was dragged towards the ground. He barely kept hold of the hammer, and now the net seared across his face and neck.

Ow! That smarts! the Ever Vengeful shouted. *We'll see them pay for that.*

Yet the polearm stabbed at him and he was flayed by the cat-o-nine-tails. He wrestled to get free, but the net melted into his flesh and would not be dislodged. The more he resisted it, the deeper it cut. Blood ran freely down him.

And we surely do not have much to spare, the Pitiless hazarded faintly.

Raggar reached for the Berserker, but for once could not find him.

We will not fail, the Immovable insisted.

The Watchful saw the flickering and bloated tongues of the demons anticipating their triumph, and truly understood *doom* for the first time.

'No!' Raggar grated, bracing, then forcing his ancient muscles till he felt them tear with effort. Letter rose an inch, peeling net and skin off him. And another. If he was to be undone, then it would be by himself and no other. He would not bow to such unholy parasites.

'Quickly!' the largest commanded. 'Before he wins free. Cast him down!'

The demons *shifted* and raised their unearthly weapons in unison.

'Gahh!' Raggar screamed, incoherent with defiance.

New shadows moved among them, almost faster than could be seen. The impression of claw and fang, a sinuous coil, a goring horn and dripping muzzle. The demons were bitten in two or swallowed whole, except the largest, who chose to vanish entirely.

The net constraining Raggar became gossamer thin, then a mere cobweb blown away in the breeze. He looked back along the defile and saw a wild-haired woman covered in writhing animal tattoos sending out ossidian, bullish and lupine shades to harass the dead, appal some dark figure that was bedevilling Gardel, and dismay the necromancers.

'You dare, witch!' the death mages projected. 'Our master will hear of this. He will–akk!'

Raggar pulled his hammer free of the mess he had made of the nearby necromancer. He waved across the hollow to the last one standing. The necromancer turned to get away. Raggar kissed Letter, swung his arm like a pendulum and sent the hammer arcing through the air. It flew silently for a long second . . . and then crunched into the back of the necromancer's head, bringing him down once and forever.

IV

'You are not like any other I have met,' the witch-woman said across the small fire they had built.

Raggar shrugged, scratching at the tight new skin on his cheek. Gardel had worked some minor healing magic on him, before joining Cal and Sitwell in a deep slumber. Sleep, after all, was probably the best cure and restorative, for shock, a battered spirit or spent body.

A shame we stopped being able to sleep long ago. We have seen too much.

'I am as you see me, woman. Nothing more.'

'Elha. I am Elha of Wormdale.'

He nodded. 'And I am Raggar . . . of the Vale.'

She was quiet for a moment. 'Perhaps I have heard of you. And perhaps I see you differently to others. With a third eye perhaps.'

Careful, the Watchful murmured. *All we know is she is dangerous.*

Raggar met the witch-woman's purple gaze. Beneath the animal totems marking her skin, she was young, little older than Cal. Strange as she looked, she could not be considered comely, but neither was she repellent. Simply different.

She helped us, the Violent said dully.

Ha! Her purposes may have coincided with ours by simple chance. Or she may have sided with us to create the sort of trust that might then lead us into a greater evil, the Pitiless retorted.

It might have been her who told the necromancers we were coming this way, the Watchful agreed. *How else would the necromancers have known to be waiting in the defile for us? Unless it was one of the others.*

Surely not Cal, the Violent growled protectively.

We do not know for sure it is Cal that sleeps there. Who knows what shape-shifter may wear his form? One of them is a traitor. That much is certain. The necromancers knew we were coming this way.

My money is on Sitwell. Finding him there outside Altimor was all a little bit too convenient. No normal trader travels so early that it is still dark.

'And what does your third eye show you, witch?'

Elha peered forwards through the smoke, her tattoos seeming to stir. 'Long years of hardship and pain. So long–'

'That is true of all who live, witch.'

'–A power in you that . . . I do not understand. It will not yield. You . . .' She sat back. ' . . . are unbending and will not be ruled. And yet there is something still not right, still unfinished. It drives you. I would not wish to be in your way or your enemy.'

'Then do not be so.' He glared at her.

She hooded her eyes. 'Why do you travel through Wormdale? Few would dare.'

'I am Raggar. I go where I will. Wormdale is the fastest route to Altimor. I have matters to settle there.'

'You are at odds with the Overlord and the Church. The necromancers would not have come so close to this domain unless the powers in Altimor were truly exercised. Perhaps I will join you on your journey.'

'Why?'

'Perhaps I tire of having to defend this valley alone. Perhaps you came through Wormdale because it called to you, because it wanted me to join you. The valley did not rise against your party or prevent you passing through, after all.'

'I would not have let it stop me in any event. It could have stopped me no more than the necromancers could.'

She tilted her head. 'Perhaps.'

She gives me the creeps. Tell her no, the Watchful counselled.

We fear no one. The Pitiless shrugged.

We fear for the others, though. For Cal, who is too young to know better. We have brought him into this danger.

Which is precisely why we should not have brought him. He compromises our judgement and potentially weakens us. We can still leave them all and continue alone.

That sling of his has been of use, do not forget. Perhaps we do need help. We are not as spry as we once were. Do our knees not ache, and our bones creak? Have we not been grateful for Gardel's healing, and Sitwell's wagon? Perhaps the witch will be of use also.

'One necromancer said his master would be told of your interference, Elha. Whom did he mean? This Overlord?'

The witch-woman pulled a face. 'The Overlord is merely an administrator for the Empire. The true threat is Holy Instructor Sepis, leader of the Church in Altimor. His knowledge and learning are such that he can command both the living and the dead. The necromancers will have come here at his instruction.'

'You are not telling him everything, *witch*,' Gardel accused, coming to his feet. 'You are not telling him you have made offerings to the Keeper of the Dead, just as the necromancers had made. You are not telling him that you have bound the spirits of animals to you through blood sacrifice. You are a parasite and have drained Wormdale of its life. You have consorted with demons of the lower planes, giving them the creatures of the forest to win dark magicks for yourself. You are not telling good Raggar that it was the Keeper the necromancers were really promising to tell of your actions.'

Elha leapt up and back. 'What would you know of it, priest?' she hissed, shadows spiralling and dancing around her. 'What would you know of the sacrifices I have made just to stay alive? What would you know of the sacrifices Wormdale has had to make so that I might protect it from the endless demands and rapine appetites of Sepis? He is determined to have it all. He will plunder this place, dig out its caves and delve for its every secret. He will *know* it and rule it, in so doing divesting it of its own definition and very essence. It will become an extension of his will, and his will, mind and power will grow thereby. It will be his *progress* and the *progress* of his Church. It will be his Civilization, but the wildness and independence of Wormdale will be tamed and ended. It will be no more.'

'All I know,' the Tender replied with uncharacteristic harshness, 'is that, as a witch, you take the lives of the innocent and use them for your own gain. Your magicks are blood-magicks, murderous and evil. You will have imps, demons and succubi as your familiars, play-things and servants.'

'I have murdered no one! Who are you to judge me, you smug and sanctimonious priest? I have sacrificed deer and rabbits, and then consumed them. Every farmer in your care does the same. Hypocrite! I came here precisely to leave behind such false and lying men as you.'

'Why is everyone shouting?' Cal asked blearily, sitting up. Snores continued to rumble from Sitwell.

'Me, a liar? Ha! Cunning and fork-tongued she-devil! It is you who have been so partial with the truth to good Raggar. We want nothing of you!'

The Tender seems to be working himself up into high dudgeon indeed, the Violent chuckled. *He needs to be careful, for we do not think the witch will tolerate much more from him, and her bite is certain to be as bad as her bark.*

Perhaps we misjudged her before, the Watchful considered. *After all, have we not ourselves taken innocent lives for our own ends? Yet Gardel does not judge us for that. What then does he really have against the witch? What is behind it?*

'Elha will be joining us on our journey to Altimor,' Raggar announced.

'What?' Gardel spluttered. 'You cannot allow it. Did we not vote on whether Sitwell could join us?'

'You swore to do as I told you, Tender. I have made my decision and you will abide by it, without question, argument or quibble.'

'I cannot ride with her.'

'Then you will walk.'

'Do not worry, Raggar of the Vale,' Elha interrupted. 'My animal-guides will show me hidden paths and trails so that I might keep pace with you. You will not see me, but I will always be nearby. I am no more eager to travel next to the priest as he is me.'

'Very well,' Raggar allowed. 'Now, there are some rules to which you will need to agree before travelling with us. First, you do as I tell you. Second, you do what I tell you without question, argument or quibble . . .'

Cal rolled his eyes, while Gardel glowered, and Sitwell continued to rumble.

~

They were a subdued group that left Wormdale, Raggar sitting up front with Sitwell, and Cal and Gardel back amongst the wagon's load once more. The Tender did not seem much given to conversation. And Sitwell had heavy bags under his eyes as if he hadn't slept a wink, although – before kicking him awake – Raggar had considerately left him undisturbed for the period it had taken Gardel to call the horses back and calm them.

It was full morning by the time they finally left the defile and rose up into the foothills surrounding the valley. The winter sky was a bright and milky white, so that the merchant shielded his eyes with one hand while he held the reins with the other. He squinted ahead, his face creased as if in pain, yet it was he who first spoke.

'You can see now why not many merchants choose to brave Wormdale, good warrior.'

'I suppose I can at that, Master Sitwell.'

Gardel snorted loudly. Raggar ignored him.

'I do not know these foothills so well,' the merchant continued. 'Are we likely to meet much trouble in them before rejoining the road south? We will then all but be at Altimor, I take it.'

'Looking at this place, I cannot imagine much trouble. The hills are pretty barren, no? There is little obvious shelter and I doubt there is much game to speak of. There will be the odd wooded gully perhaps, but hardly enough to support any band thinking to hide or live here. Of course, there might always be a threat from that which does not live, but we simply deal with it as we did before. That would only leave wyverns, dragons and elementals to fear, creatures that would come here precisely because it is so quiet and out-of-the-way. Any stories of winged beasts seen in the skies of late, merchant?'

Sitwell swallowed. 'N-none that I recall.'

Raggar nodded. 'Well enough. Even if we met one, it would be likely to go for the horses first. That would be our chance.'

'To slip away?'

Raggar blinked. 'Er . . . not what I had in mind, but as good a plan as any, I suppose. Leaving only elementals . . . oh, and golems.'

Sitwell made a high-pitched noise.

'Come, come, good Raggar, do not tease him so. There are no such vermin lurking hereabouts,' sang a perfectly modulated voice.

They looked up, and there upon a low knoll was an immaculately dressed individual standing in a regal pose. His coat was of cloth-o-gold, and dazzled. His britches were embroidered with silver thread and pattern, and mazed the eye. His waistcoat was a blood-red velvet and his neckerchief was restrained, so that it might better show off the clear lines of the owner's chin and cheek. His features were infinitely refined and his dark eyes impossibly knowing.

Raggar hawked and spat. 'Well, there's always you, isn't there? Surely a dandified godling is the worst of the lot.'

Sitwell whimpered and tears ran from his eyes. He flung himself from the wagon's seat and down to the ground, near injuring himself in his haste. He prostrated himself and grovelled. 'Holiest, Sharim, bless us!'

The god ignored the merchant, eyes locked with Raggar's. 'You have learnt no better manners since we last met, I see. And you quite cruelly lead these others into rebellion, sin and blasphemy. Is there no end to your vanity and crime, Raggar the Riotous?' Sharim's voice was thick with emotion – passion, sympathy and mourning. 'It is one thing to ruin your own soul by your actions, but quite another to damn these others. I come to appeal to you on behalf of these my subjects.' Conciliatory, pleading and generous. 'Is there any vestige of human mercy left within you, old as you are? Have you forgot what it is to know youthful ambition, to glory in one's faith and to experience the joy and freedom of new ideas? Tell us of these things, Raggar, he who was once Raggar the Defender of Faith. Do you not remember that man, or would you tell us he never existed and that you know nothing of what he was? Do you know nothing of faith, be it in one's self, one's fellow man or in the gods themselves? Really nothing?' Inviting and enticing, but never judging. The dearest friend and boon companion. 'Yet you hesitate. You others, then, help him. Good Tender, Garlan the Grower is my brother, but so much more than that. Do you not know me, and will you not therefore be guided by me?'

Gardel's mouth hung open. His hands were raised and clasped before him. Tears of revelation coursed down his cheeks. He nodded, otherwise transfixed by the shining divinity before him.

'And you, brave youth? You have known nothing of the pantheon, trapped as you were in the Vale, a place of ignorance that has brought you such pain. Would you not want that pain taken away and your heart healed? Would you not want to be whole once more? Would you not want to be that man you were always destined to be? A man capable of such love, tenderness and nurture. Tell me that you still understand that love. Come, tell me. Speak up.'

Raggar raised Letter and moved to spring from the wagon, but the god was quicker.

'Violence?' the god chastised. 'Always your answer. Always the example you set them. Always. Prove me wrong, warrior. Prove me wrong.'

We bloody well will at that, the Violent swore. *Come on, we hardly need his invitation.*

No! the Immovable intervened. *He seeks to snare us. This is a different game.*

We must be relentless but find vengeance in another way, the Watchful agreed.

'Was it well mannered of you to send your necromancers against us, then?' Raggar asked. 'Or will you deny you knew anything of them? Are you not Sharim the Sage? Sharim the Knowledgeable? If you did not know of them, then you are a *fraud*.' He sounded stronger now. 'Who are you really? Enough of this masquerade. Reveal yourself!'

'What deception do you attempt now, Raggar the Mad? Enough of your denials, delusions and stubborn determination. Do you not see all now engage in contrition, self-reflection and humility? Join them, or forever be separate from the rest of mortalkind. Join them, or forever know the pity, sorrow and contempt of all others. Will you not join them? Do you not see your friends beg it of you? Will you deny them also? Can you truly tell them no?'

'Necromancers fighting on behalf of Altimor's Overlord and some Holy Instructor Sepis, the latter ordering all in your name, isn't it? Death-magicks won through you. How is that exactly? How is that possible? What god is it who truly commands the dead? Are you the Keeper himself in some other guise? Are you that god who has always envied the world of the living? Are you he? Answer me, for I do no fear you and I *will not* fear you! I have faced you on battlefields times beyond counting and never been defeated. And I will not fail now, for to do so would be to lose not just these companions but perhaps the entire world of the living. You seek absolute sway, do you not? You seek to extend your dark empire across the world. Well I tell you *no*, sly and simpering Sharim. *No!* Do you hear?' Raggar's rage roared and echoed through the foothills.

The god drew himself up, towering over them. His brows were unforgiving storms and his gaze was as lightning. Murder was in his every movement and his shadow was the grave. Here finally was Death. He intoned with emptiness and oblivion: 'Do not pretend to know us, mortal. Do not pretend to know the ways of the gods.'

Sitwell pressed his face into the mud, squirming in horror and swallowing muck.

Gardel groaned and clawed at his face, for here was the one force Garlan could not hold back. Cal was hunched and bent, becoming the shaking and infirm elder from which youth instinctively recoiled.

'Arrogant mortals!' The god's words laid them low. 'Now you see your place. Bow before the pantheon or know their eternal displeasure. Your minds will be turned to mush, your souls will be stretched and shredded. One word or step more, Raggar the Sacrilegious, and the breath, hearts and thoughts of your companions will be stopped in them forever. *You* will be responsible. *That* you are permitted to know, and nothing more.'

They knew the risk they took in joining us, the Pitiless offered.
Did they? Did they truly? the Watchful asked.

Coward! the Relentless sneered, the Violent echoing him.

Do not judge. This is the trap of existence, nothing more, came the Immovable.

It is the god who is the enemy here, remember that, the Ever Vengeful rejoined.

The Berserker snarled and the others came to his call, united. Raggar threw himself off the wagon and into the face of Death. Letter swung with an awful determination and the insistence of destruction, yet found no mark. The weapon was powerless.

Raggar refused to tire or submit. With savage energy he sought to lay ahold of the god and strangle him. For the briefest of moments it seemed he would find a grip or sink his bared teeth into the deity's throat. His strength was prodigious. Yet it was in that fatal moment that the god slipped him and threw him down. Sharim stamped hard into Raggar's lower back, grinding with all his weight to crush the old warrior's spine.

'At last, warrior, you are mine. Will you beg for mercy? For now is the final moment of repentance. Now is the time you remember all those hopes you had but never achieved. Now you remember all those guilt-ridden mistakes. Now you wish you could live your life over again and do it differently. Now is the chance to see Daran and apologise for never being there to comfort him. To see his mother, about whom you have not had the courage to think. To see your own parents, whose faces have haunted you for so long. To see all those you have betrayed to the pestilence and torments of the lower planes.'

The images filled his head. He could not keep them out. They called to him, entreated him to forgive them if he thought they had wronged him, threatened him with retribution for what he had done and promised him that death was only the beginning. Daran was there, and *she* was there. So beloved. So vivid. So near. All he had to do was let go of this life, reach out to them and join with them. They would be indivisible and never parted again, by tragedy, greater forces or the world itself. There would be no need to fight anymore. No more railing and striving. He could rest at last. The peace and finality of ending.

It was all there. Within his reach and will.

Yet his other selves held him and prevented him. The Immovable stubbornly enduring, the Violent remorseless, the Relentless unbowed, the Ever Vengeful staring avidly, the Pitiless unyielding, the Berserker insane with fury and the Watchful always wary. He could not defeat or move against them.

'Neeever!' he wheezed, as ribs cracked, lungs filled with blood, and bile trickled from his lips.

'You *will* break, damn you! I am a *god* and you are nothing!'

The deadly maelstrom of Sharim's desire near drowned out all else. 'Raggar is right,' the Tender mewled. 'He has shown us what you are. This is wrong!'

Then on spectral wings and with the wail of a banshee, some horror descended upon the god. Talons scratched at his eyes, claws tore at his shoulders and fangs sank deep.

'Gah!' the titan boomed, pulling Elha off him and hurling her into the ground. 'Ungrateful bag of bones!' Her body bounced once and then fell unmoving.

'Great-grandfather!' Cal begged, casting a stone that struck the god deep in the chest.

'Garlan aid me!' the Tender beseeched. 'Ward and protect the life in him. Aid and nurture his spirit!'

Sharim slipped and impossibly missed his footing, allowing Raggar a moment of freedom. 'No! You dare not defy me.'

Yet even Sitwell was no longer offering obeisance – he had come to his knees, shaking his head in denial. Raggar struggled to mimic him.

Cal let fly with his sling again, looking to take out one of Sharim's all-seeing eyes.

'Pathetic mortals!' And in that moment Sharim vanished.

Ringing silence. All still.

Raggar coughed and shuddered.

'A chick that fails to fly but flares its wings enough to survive the fall, to grow eventually into the greatest bird in the sky! A lone wolf that comes close to perishing in winter, but follows paw prints until it discovers a pack in which it might survive! An elk that is humbled by the largest of its kind, but in so doing learns what it must to triumph in the next confrontation!'

Gardel exhorted. 'An ailing phoenix that sacrifices itself to flame so that it might be born anew!' He cast his blessing over Raggar and Elha.

Raggar found himself rising easily now, hardly feeling his age. It was all he could do not to shout out, so invigorated did he feel. Although the witch-woman did not stir, her skin glowed and there was a healthy blush to her cheeks. Raggar gently lifted her and took her over to the wagon. He placed her carefully and nodded to Cal to watch over her.

'I thank you, Tender,' Raggar said.

Gardel shook his head. 'It was not me, but my god that saved you. I have never known such strength of healing before. And I have never felt holy Garlan's presence so strongly. It makes me think he moves in equal degree to this Sharim, or whatever he is, so that some sort of balance may be preserved. All life hangs in that balance, methinks. Perhaps it is you, good warrior, who saves us all.'

Raggar shrugged. 'I pray that I do save us rather than condemn us, but it strikes me this balance is far too precarious a thing. It is too easily manipulated by the gods, though it be blasphemy to say it.'

'We must preserve this balance or lose it all,' Gardel avowed. 'I cannot believe it is truly blasphemy to say so.'

Sitwell was intent as he joined them. 'It is surely no blasphemy to defend one's right to life, or the right of others. I am mortified that Sharim would so use the dead. Yet now I see he seeks to mortify all life. I did not know it before, but he truly is the Keeper. Forgive me, friends, that I did not do more in the stand against him.'

Raggar clapped the merchant on the shoulder, half staggering him. 'You did enough, good Master Sitwell. Many would never have dared even to lift their heads up. And you stood shoulder to shoulder with us when we fought the dead.'

Gardel nodded his agreement.

Yet Sitwell looked down at the ground. 'I fear I stood with you not from courage but because I had little other choice. I would have ridden away, I think, if the horses had not begun to break free.'

'I will not hear that,' Raggar insisted. 'You could have scampered away on foot, but you did not.'

'Cal and I would have been lost were it not for you, Master Sitwell.'

Sitwell's chest rose and fell a few times, then he lifted his chin a measure. He peered up at them. 'Can we really prevail?' he asked softly. 'Against an entire empire? Against a god? Against the Keeper himself, who will ultimately see us punished, one way or another? All mortals come to an end and are finally ruled by him. Surely we should submit to the divine will of the pantheon. Who are we to tell them no? I am but a lowly merchant, with little enough to show for his life.'

'Good merchant,' Gardel said kindly. 'The pantheon does not live our lives for us. It cannot be blamed for crimes we choose to commit, or praised for more noble deeds we choose to undertake. Our choices are our own to make, and we make them as we can, based on good faith, conscience or whatever sense we can make of the world. I chose to obey the High Tender and travel to Altimor to appeal to the Overlord. Now I have seen the true design of the Koraline Empire, I know that my appeal is all the more important. I will not allow anything to turn me from my chosen path. You have chosen to come this far with us, good merchant, but you must now choose for yourself if you will continue. We cannot make the decision for you . . . and nor can any god.'

'You must also choose, lad,' Raggar called to Cal, who had listened carefully throughout.

'Nothing has changed,' Cal replied unhesitatingly.

Raggar nodded faintly and turned his attention to Sitwell.

The merchant became miserable. 'I-I . . . must I choose now?'

'No,' Raggar replied. 'But be aware, in not making the choice, you are in fact making a decision. Think on it further as we go, but do not take too long, for I am sure the Keeper will not be waiting upon your pleasure.'

And one of them is still a traitor, don't forget.

Rain lashed them, a deluge trying to blind them and take the road out from under them. The sky flashed a livid red one second and was as dark as the void the next. Day was turned to night. Raggar could not even tell if they were in the normal world anymore. Every moment he expected one of the wagon's wheels to get bogged down, lightning to strike them or the air to be pulled out of their lungs so that the torrent would drown them where they sat.

Don't need to read any moments to know someone's mad at us.

'Master Sitwell, should we turn off for one of the sheltered gullies?' Raggar had to shout even though the merchant was right next to him.

'We dare not, good warrior! The going is difficult enough on this main route – things would be nigh on impossible if we left it. See, that way there is little more than a river.'

Gardel negotiated his way forward. 'The storm cannot last forever. All Tenders must know the way of the weather. Once the clouds lose their rain, they lose their energy and substance, just as when a man bleeds. We will come through this, have faith.'

On more than one occasion Raggar, Gardel and Cal had to climb down to heave the wagon forwards, but after an hour or so the storm noticeably began to slacken. Then it simply ceased.

It was like breathing again, like having one's sight restored. Utterly soaked and spattered as they were, they all grinned like fools.

At all but the same moment, they came out of the foothills and the way opened up before them. Altimor sat at the top of a slight rise on the other side of a wide and blasted plain.

'Elha is stirring!' Cal called excitedly.

'Praise be!' Gardel exclaimed, leaning in to examine her. 'I think she will be well.'

'The sooner the better,' Raggar replied. 'I suspect we will have need of her magicks all too soon. Master Sitwell, perhaps your eyes are keener than mine. Are those really soldiers lining up there outside the gates.'

The merchant gulped. 'Aye, I think so. A great many of them. Perhaps it is some training exercise. Or there is some trouble at the mines beyond the city.'

'Mines? I do not recall there being any mines hereabouts.'

'The workings have increased much in recent years. And considerably so since even my last visit, by the looks of it.'

'What is it they search for? Gold?'

Sitwell hesitated. 'I . . . er . . . am not entirely sure. I do not think it is gold. It is overseen by the Church, and gold has never seemed their particular interest.'

'What then? There must be rumours.'

'People will always speculate, but I have never put much stock by what they say.'

He avoids the subject. 'Spit it out, Master Sitwell.'

The merchant shifted uncomfortably. 'For what it's worth, there is crazy talk of an older settlement beneath the current city. Stories of large and ancient foundations. Perhaps as old as what they call *The Time Before*, when pagan gods walked among mortalkind and made war with fell weapons and terrible magicks.' Out of habit or instinct, the man quickly looked all around to be sure they were not overheard. 'Strange altars, demon engines and other lost lore. Objects of blasphemous design and purpose.'

Ahh! See where the pursuit of knowledge has brought this Church of Civilization. They seek to learn what was once rightly forbidden. They aim to possess a power that will eclipse all others, a power that near destroyed all mortalkind in The Time Before. *Damn them, for otherwise they will damn us all.* 'I understand now how this Koraline Empire managed to grow so quickly, merchant, and how none seem able to resist it. The leaders of this Empire must have unearthed weapons and powers that should have remained forgotten. They near raise themselves up as gods. All will eventually be in their thrall. They will be a new pantheon. There will likely be a war against the old pantheon . . . and mortalkind will have little chance of survival.'

Sitwell hid his face in his hands. 'It is true,' he sobbed. 'I know it. I could not bring myself to think upon it before. Forgive me, good warrior!'

Raggar sighed. 'How can I judge you, Master Sitwell, when it appals me as much as it does you? Have you made your decision?'

A silent nod. A drawn face. But a jaw set firm. 'I am with you.'

'As am I,' Elha said weakly.

'Do all understand what we face?'

All Raggar's companions nodded. Gardel spoke up for them: 'And we understand what will come to pass should we fail. We will do as you tell us without argument, question or quibble.'

'Even though it looks like an army of near a thousand is being turned out against us?' Raggar asked.

'Is it? Er . . .'

'Are you sure?'

'Maybe they've confused us for someone else?'

'Maybe . . . maybe . . . oh, damn.'

'I know,' Raggar agreed. 'That's only two hundred for each of us. Disappointing. Hardly seems fair, does it?'

'I will do my best,' Gardel ventured. 'But Garlan tends to nurture and preserve life rather than take it.'

'My spirits will dispatch a goodly number,' Elha assured them. 'Unless their priests are able to turn back the nature of my magicks . . . which is not impossible.'

'I will start collecting more stones,' Cal promised, with no hint of concern.

Sitwell raised his crossbow. 'And I will give such an accounting of myself that my guild will commission a song lauding my valour. My wife will have something by which to remember me.'

'Ahem!' Gardel dared. 'Could we not retreat and find a better way into the city? Perhaps through the mines previously mentioned?'

'I doubt we can outrun these soldiers,' Raggar replied. 'They have mounted troops, from what I can tell. And something tells me the cursed priests of this Church will know what we are about and will have everything closely guarded. As priests that always seek knowledge, they are likely to have scrying pools and spells, no, not to mention old-fashioned lookouts, spies and informants? No, we go in through the main gate.'

'I am a man of faith, good Raggar, but even I am hard pushed to believe we will get that far,' Gardel said.

We are leading them to their deaths, the Watchful could not help saying.

Everyone dies at some point or another. Now is as good a time as any, no? And better than many perhaps, the Pitiless considered.

At least they will know glorious battle at the end, and will no doubt have the satisfaction of taking a number of the enemy with them, the Violent added.

But where is the sense in all of us dying? the Immovable came back. *Several could escape while the others kept the enemy occupied. Those that escape might still find a way into the city and a way to win through. We cannot afford to fail. Think of the consequences. And what do these four know of facing battle-hardened soldiers, let alone so many?*

'Master Sitwell, do you have any white cloth or pale rag amongst your load?' Raggar asked. 'For we will be surrendering.'

'Thank the gods!' the merchant breathed.

'What is it you do, Raggar of the Vale?' Elha demanded angrily. 'I will not be taken without a fight!'

Raggar met the young woman's gaze. 'Trust me, this is the best way. It will see us taken into the city without a hair on our heads being hurt.'

~

They were shackled, chained and marched inside the walls, precisely as Raggar had predicted. The bulk of the army that had faced them had been ordered back to barracks or to their regular duties, leaving a hundred or so and their commander to escort them through the city towards the Overlord's ostentatious palace.

Citizens jumped out of the way of the soldiers, as if fearing to be struck, or worse. Most kept to the shadows or hurried away.

A few that were conspicuously wealthy or wore robes of rank deigned to stop, whisper to each other and point. 'Look at that primitive barbarian there. And that animal-painted she-devil,' one said loudly. 'I warrant there is as much chance of them worshipping one of the beasts of the field as there is of coupling with it.' There were titters and sniggers. Then a rotten apple was thrown. It hit Raggar and bounced into the filth of a nearby gutter. An urchin appeared out of nowhere and grabbed the spoiled fruit. Other scrawny children materialised and scratched and fought for it.

The soldiers remained stony-faced and kept marching, uninterested in the scuffle. The burghers and elite of Altimor wrinkled their noses and looked away.

A bent-backed and toothless old man elbowed his way in amongst the youngsters and delivered hard knocks and blows. He ripped the apple free even as it turned to mush in hand, and got some of the mess in between his withered lips and gums. He'd strayed into the path of a large leather-armoured trooper.

The soldier did not break step, and clubbed the elder aside with the heavy butt of a spear. With a thin cry, the old man went down, his brow split wide. His head hit a cobble with an ugly crack. His eyes rolled back in his head. Then next soldier coming on stepped cruelly on arthritic fingers. The next kicked the failing body aside.

'Please, no!' Gardel begged, but he was pushed roughly down the street.

There would be no saving him after such an injury in any event, the Pitiless decided.

Yet Raggar was appalled by the casual murder. Despite all he had seen, for all the horrors he'd known on battlefields, and even though he'd been responsible for many a grim deed himself, never had he seen a life treated as if it were so worthless. The soldier had not hesitated for the briefest instant, nor had there been the slightest flicker of remorse in his gaze. The old man – who had known love, hope, misfortune and probably most mortal trials in between – had been as meaningless to the soldier as a splash of mud on his already begrimed boot.

There was no protest from any of the citizens either. No second glance. None seemed to care that it might be their own parent treated so one day, their neighbour . . . or even themselves. What had happened to these people that they would be this way? How could they have so utterly lost their compassion? Were they not properly human? Were they demons wearing mortal skin? What terrible magic was it that could so possess them?

'Did you see that? Someone do something!' Cal was arguing.

'This is the Empire and its Church,' Elha responded, her eyes constantly moving.

'Master Sitwell, is this the progress that the priesthood espouses and exhorts all to embrace?' Raggar demanded. 'Well? Must we learn to treat each other like this? Must the young and old fight and die like this? What hell would this Empire make of the world? Is this what you trade and barter in, merchant? Is it? Answer me!'

Sitwell hung his head in misery. 'The fields that once surrounded the city have been replaced with mines and new barracks. Food is always in short supply and commands a higher price as a result. I need to secure a high price because a tenth of my load is always requisitioned by the authorities here, and the guild then takes a tenth of my profit in return for a licence to trade. I have no choice, for I too must survive.'

'No wonder the Empire is so desperate to have the Vale,' Cal commented.

'Or Wormdale,' Elha added.

'Silence, traitors!' a minor officer commanded. 'Those who do not usefully contribute to the Empire are deserving of nothing. Those who do not contribute are enemies of the Empire. They are undeserving of mercy. The sooner we are rid of them the better, for then the Empire will no longer be drained, held back or undermined by their selfishness and blasphemous non-cooperation.'

'Give yourself to the Empire entirely or die,' Raggar bit back. 'The result is the same either way, fool. Mark my words, I will see this Empire brought down on the heads of its leaders. Raggar of the Vale swears it.'

'Ignorant savage!' the officer snarled. He brought back his hand to strike Raggar across the mouth.

Raggar jumped inside the officer's reach and headbutted him between the eyes. The armoured man went down flailing. Raggar stepped on the fingers of the soldier's reaching hand and ground them against the cobbles. The ancient warrior walked on without a backward look. His eyes were fixed on the palace of the Overlord. Never had he known a fury like he did now. He was determined to see the pantheon itself answer for the existence of an Empire intent upon the end of all mortalkind.

~

And they were marched into the vast audience chamber of the palace, although it was more of a banner and trophy room. The pennons and flags of fallen kingdoms and enclaves festooned the walls, as did the skins of those individuals who had proven particularly troublesome to the Empire. There was even the stuffed body of some scaled and fearsomely-posed marshman mounted upon the wall.

Soldiers stood at attention around all four walls. Raggar counted fifty or so and took in their ornate but rune-inscribed golden breastplates, and their ceremonial but efficient-looking stabbing spears. The men seemed better conditioned and more alert than those who had brought him here. Clearly these were the Overlord's elite guard.

They were dragged and pushed across the floor of thick rugs and furs until they were a dozen paces short of the marble-encased steps of the high dais. In the throne at the very top was a small man wearing black velvet and clutching a sceptre set with a pulsing green stone. He swayed and twitched in time to its rhythms, his eyes dark and glittering one moment but dull and empty the next. His face would be pale and slack, only then to become flushed and full of angry expression. It was as if two people filled the same space.

Set five steps below the Overlord were two smaller thrones. The one to the left was occupied by a tall, hairless priest not entirely dissimilar to the one Raggar had faced in Arlford. This one, though, had eyes an even starker white, and his skull had bony ridges and protrusions. His mouth opened in anticipation of what was to come, saliva stringing between overlarge and pointed canine teeth.

Yet in the throne to the right was the one Raggar had come to find. The unholy captain with runic scars upon his cheeks and baleful red eyes. Otherwise, he was all blunt features and broad muscle, as if the god who had made him had packed together an excess of clay but had not then had time to pare back and refine his creation. He was almost a human golem, and looked to have all the unnatural strength and endurance that came with that.

The captain glared at Raggar, who met the gaze with a smile that mixed ridicule with lethal promise.

The fires of the captain's eyes flared stronger. 'He should be killed this instant.'

'Mmm? Silence,' the Overlord purred and barked. 'The weapon!'

The officer who had led the escort ordered Letter deposited on the bottom stair of the dais, bowed and then led his men out of the chamber, the doors sealed behind him.

'So this is what all the kafuffle has been about? This broken down old man? Surely this is some jest,' the Overlord said with as much boredom as interest.

Raggar found his attention dragged up to the ruler holding the sickly glowing gemstone. As bent as he was on the captain's destruction, he dared not overlook a potentially greater threat. 'And you seem even less to me, boy,' the warrior sneered. 'Where is your nurse, eh? Is it this malformed priest here? What? Has his milk curdled in his teat and you have been indulged your tantrums as a consequence? What perversion is this?'

Sitwell cleared his throat hurriedly and shuffled forwards a half dozen steps. He bowed deeply. 'Mighty Overlord, forgive him. Raggar is not from these parts and does not understand our ways. He has been affronted by his arrest and speaks out of turn. There has been much . . . what might we say . . . misunderstanding? Why, your men naturally believed I was a member of this unusual party, when in fact I was just a passing trader giving a ride to guests newly arrived in our land. I am a member of the merchants' guild and all my credentials are in order, you see. I believe good Raggar has come to you asking for redress and understanding concerning unfortunate events beyond our boundaries. As have the young man, the priest of Garlan and the good woman here.'

Cal curled his lip.

'Double-dealing lickspittle!' Elha hissed.

Gardel shook his head.

'You have done well to show our guests such hospitality, merchant,' the Overlord yawned and bit. 'If the good warrior will but apologise for his behaviour, then I will listen to his request. Warrior, you represent the Vale, do you not, which seeks alliance with the Empire?'

'I am here to see both this murderer and the Empire undone,' Raggar shrugged. 'You may step down voluntarily or I will remove you. It makes no difference to me.'

Sitwell winced and shuffled forwards again, to distance himself from the others. Cal nodded with satisfaction at his great-grandfather's words. Elha showed her teeth and began to mutter to herself, shadows moving across her tattooed skin. Gardel looked upwards in silent prayer.

'Now, warrior, it is treason to issue threats against the being of the Empire. It is also . . . *non-progressive*. I have shown you patience and courtesy thus far. You will treat us similarly unless there is nothing at all *civilized* about you. And if there were to be nothing at all civilized about you, then . . . well . . . Am I not correct, High Instructor?'

The throned priest inclined his head, running a quick tongue over his spare lips. 'You speak as the Empire, Overlord, and the Empire is correct in seeking to bring progress to all, be they within our borders or beyond, for it benefits all to progress, improve and grow in wisdom,' sibilated the cenobite. 'A simple apology from the barbarian, truly meant or not, would evidence simple courtesy, social understanding and ability to progress. Acceptance of the need to progress.'

Who shall we kill first? smirked the Violent.

We enjoy the anticipation of it, the Ever Vengeful crooned. *But let us now begin.*

Hold, warned the Watchful. *Do not forget our companions.*

Sitwell has damned himself. Gardel is spineless, his ilk allowing the Empire a foothold in the first place. And Elha and the lad are spoiling for the fight, the Pitiless insisted.

There are fifty spears ready to snap into place. We will be cut to pieces. We need Letter.

'Was it progress that saw the Empire slaughter innocent farmers in the Vale?' Raggar asked mildly. 'Come, give me some weaseling, wily and weak answer. If I know anything of this Empire, it has a way of justifying any atrocity that serves it. Come, let's have your whining answer, tyrant.'

'It cannot be justified!' Cal yelled, red faced. He pointed a shaking finger at the scarred captain. 'Nothing can ever justify what you did to my Brin. I will *kill* you, coward!'

'Occasionally,' the Overlord drawled and snapped. 'Those who are apparently innocent stand in the way of progress. Their wilful ignorance causes many more to suffer in untold ways. Is the Empire answerable to such bumpkins and backward folk, those who would see the Empire brought low and undone, so that they might then selfishly exploit it or seize its treasures? Ancient warrior, you are a man of conscience, I know that. Indeed, I have followed your exploits back through the centuries and kingdoms. You are an enduring legend, self-sustaining superstition . . . and veritable demigod! Always you have defended the weak, or simply wrought havoc to teach warmongers the true consequence of their perverted appetites. You have rightly been worshipped for it. Yet the world is not as simple and innocent as it once was. *None* are truly innocent anymore. It is time you saw that bigger picture and complexity of it. I appeal to that true conscience of yours now. Help us. Guide us. Become lord of not just the Vale, but also its surrounding environs and provinces. Become a lord of the Empire. We humbly beg and entreat it of you. Will you not do it? It will give you that greater cause, opportunity and meaning that you have striven for for so long. It will allow your ways to be enshrined across the continent forever more. You will be *immortal*. You will have won at last! Think of it. No more fighting.'

Finally, all will accede to us? the Pitiless wondered.

No more fighting. True permanence! the Immovable said with an absolute desire.

We will win? the Relentless and Ever Vengeful asked in faint confusion.

No! the Violent railed against them, even threatening them. *It does not ring true to us. How can such a promise ever come to be? Throw this off.* The mindless rage of the Berserker caused the Violent's voice to resonate throughout his being. *We have never been the smartest amongst us, but do not abandon us. We will be lessened. Rise up! They fight us with words, ideas and noise. They entangle us and hold us helpless. Fight it! See the lyches leering at us. See them! See the truth of them. Watchful, aid us.*

Raggar saw himself in the Overlord's black devouring gaze. He saw the mind-vampire that was the Church of Civilization. And he saw the hellish gaze of the unholy captain, whose fires had burned the farmers of the Vale and permanently scarred the thoughts of all those that had known them. For it was not just those farmers who had been ruined, but also the caring Cal and surely all who would later hear the news. See what it had done to the youth. See how he was scarred and how his gaze burned. See how he was on the path to becoming just like that unholy captain he so detested. And that was how the Empire would finally triumph.

It had to end. 'Master Sitwell,' Raggar croaked. 'Have you truly made your decision then? I would have it of you now, good merchant, for the sake of us all.'

Every eye in the room went to the portly and apologetic figure of Samul Sitwell. Sitwell cringed, his eyes going to the floor. His breathing quickened and sweat glistened at his brow, despite the coolness of the chamber. The Overlord frowned slightly. What was this? Why would the warrior pay any mind to the fat and weak fool who was like so many others of the Empire's subjects? The merchant nodded with some sort of despair and shuffled forwards, his toes all but coming up against Letter.

The Overlord's eyes flared. 'KILL THEM! NOW!'

Even as the guard started to rush forwards, Sitwell was bouncing low and heaving back up with all he had. The mighty warhammer leapt from him towards its master. Raggar lunged awkwardly, his hands manacled and his ankles shackled. He caught the weapon's handle and brought its anvil straight down on the chain confining his legs. The links parted, and now he pivoted, swinging two-handed and mangling the two guards arriving fastest.

'With the savagery of the Wolf, the venomous strike of Snake and the power of the Bear King,' Elha gasped, tattoos flowing off her and rising up to drive back and harry the rest of the Overlord's elite.

Gardel spread his arms wide, palms up, and met the eye of as many as he could. 'I bear you no ill,' he soothed. 'I do not resist. Garlan heals all, the ailing spirit as much as the tense and overwrought body. Let his care appease you. All is well, truly. I am no threat. Leave off these weapons and bloody thoughts.' His deep tones rolled soporifically through the room. Fully half the guard allowed their spears to loosen in their grips. Men bumped one into another.

Cal somehow still had the leather strap that was his sling – apparently none had realised what it was when they had been taken. And he began to whirl it now with a deadly intent, a stone he'd hidden about him fitted in place. He did not take his eyes from the captain for a second.

The High Instructor was on his feet, speaking arcane words of power. He made grabbing gestures towards Elha's animal spirits, invisible hands catching them up and forcing them together until they merged into one monstrous entity with many limbs and maws. Elha screamed, hands going to her temples and blood trickling from eyes, nose and ears.

'Faithless mab! Did you think He would allow you position and power once you had denied Him? You have damned yourself, and will henceforth be shunned by mortals and spirits alike. All society and association is lost to you forever more,' pronounced the High Instructor.

As Elha wailed and collapsed to the floor, Raggar launched himself at the hulking shadowbeast Sepis had moulded in the centre of the chamber. He hammered into a drooling head as it lowered itself towards the prone witch – as he did so the nightmare visage melted back into the beast and two smaller ones took its place. Raggar bellowed a challenge and battered it high and low, muscles working harder than any normal mortal could sustain for more than a short burst. Yet Raggar had fought on nearly every field of battle the continent had known. He had faced the greatest champions of mortalkind and cast them down. If there was any that could not only stand against such an apparition without being appalled but also hold his own, then it was Raggar of the Pillar Mountains. Had he not recently faced the Keeper himself and survived intact? How then could any mere creature think to succeed?

Beware your self-aggrandisement, fool! the Watchful shouted angrily, as the shadowbeast suddenly changed direction and went for Gardel. It was only by toppling backwards into Cal that the Tender avoided being bitten in two and ravened down by a nightwolf's powerful jaws. As it was, Cal's aim was ruined and his sling released well wide of the captain.

If they were to be taken from you, would you not lose heart? Would you not despair? You do not dare deny it. The Keeper would then hold their shades over you and you would become crazy with grief and self-recrimination. Who knows what would then happen?

We cannot protect them all, the Pitiless responded matter-of-factly. *It is tactically backward to try to do so. We will divide our energies and inevitably fail in all we attempt.*

Even so, Raggar put himself between the beast and Gardel, and laboured against it all the more. His blows sank deeper and deeper into it and, although it seemed to contract slightly into itself, it was suddenly on top of him and he was being drawn into its substance and being pulled back from the others.

Now the scar-faced captain was leaping into the fray, descending the dais in a single bound, going straight for Cal.

And Gardel's priestly magicks were unable to hold back all the royal guard. A dozen had Elha circled and another dozen were closing in on the rest of the group.

'Leave the witch!' the High Instructor directed. 'She is no threat and I will have use of her. Go for the others.'

'The boy is mine,' the captain smiled.

'Lad!' Raggar roared, plunging deeper into the beast to seek its heart, even as it turned to mist and moved back to elude him.

'Great-grandfather!' Cal cried out, whipping his sling round once and releasing at the beast.

The captain's mighty hands encircled the farmboy's neck, nearly breaking it in the first moment. With unnatural strength, the servant of the Empire lifted the youth from the floor and held him on high, waiting for Cal's own body weight to separate his head from his shoulders. He laughed darkly.

'Gkk!' Sepis managed before pitching headfirst down the steps of the dais.

Cal had sacrificed his chance of taking down the captain, instead looking to aid his ancestor. The sling's stone had flown through the dematerialising beast and struck the High Instructor directly between the eyes, creating an ugly and fatal third eye. Sepis was dead.

The shadowbeast became a thin smoke, then entirely dissipated.

Raggar moved with ferocious speed and Letter cracked open the back of the captain's skull. Even then the ogre sought to take his prize with him to the Keeper, looking to jerk Cal and force the end. Raggar let his weapon drop and caught the captain's thumbs, yanking them back till they broke.

Face purple, tongue engorged and eyes bulging, Cal hit the floor. Raggar went straight to his side.

No! the Watchful warned. *We have no time.*

And Gardel was there – careless of his own safety – pushing Raggar away. The priest was praying urgently.

'Save him,' Raggar said distantly, finding Letter back in his hands once more. 'I will end this.'

He barely comprehended his own words, for he had become the unthinking and unfeeling force that was the Berserker. He did not hear the breaking of bones and the desperate pleas, feel the warm blood that sprayed him, taste the acid filling his own mouth, sense that he bit off and spat the end of his own tongue, smell the piss of terrified enemies or see the tragedy of one broken face after another.

'Come down here, little man!' slavered the ancient guardian of the Vale and mortalkind.

The ill-stone glaring like the furious eye of a god. The Overlord swelling until he near reached the ceiling. Crackling magicks scalding him. His grey hair and beard burnt to nothing, but then channelled away by overheating chains. Skin blistering and peeling, but Letter meeting the ill-stone, blackening it, and then closing the disbelieving god's eye forever.

The Overlord was sprawled dead in his throne, something almost childlike about the surprise on his face. The face fell even in death and something like peace became visible there.

Green scintillations danced around the smoking Letter for a few seconds more and then faded. Bizarre images scorched across his mind, Raggar turned to look around the throne chamber. This wasn't his cabin up in the mountains. What place was this? Where had all these dead come from? What infernal field was this? He had found himself fighting on the lowest of the nether planes for a time, hadn't he?

Yet some still lived amid the human debris. A priest – strange and incongruous for there to be such a one. A vaguely familiar youth moving weakly. An unconscious woman – he heard the breath in her lungs. And a sobbing oaf hiding beneath a flag in the corner. Did he know them? Hadn't they been companions of his?

He was tired, he realised. He lowered himself onto the top step of the dais and closed his eyes.

Just for a moment, the Watchful allowed.

Just a moment, the others agreed, spent themselves.

'He will live, but I doubt he will wake for a good while,' Gardel was saying.

'What should we do?' Cal asked. 'We can't just stay holed up here, can we?'

'Perhaps the throne is now ours to claim,' Elha replied. 'I'm not sure what we'd do with it though.'

'I can think of a few things,' Sitwell volunteered. 'We'll be rich, that's for sure.'

'No!' Raggar interrupted them, opening his eyes and struggling to rise. 'The Church still has power here. Given time, the army and the people will organise themselves against us.'

'Never have I known anyone with such powers of recovery,' the Tender murmured.

'It's time to leave. Are all capable of moving?' Raggar pressed. 'Lad, help me up. I'm still a touch woozy.'

'Will we have to fight our way free?' Sitwell worried. 'And I don't know where they took my wagon.'

'Perhaps my animal spirits could guide us to the horses, but I am having trouble calling them.'

'I may have a way,' Gardel nodded, helping Cal raise Raggar, and getting the warrior his warhammer to lean on. 'Come, friends, let us quit this charnel house.'

~

The guards beyond the throne chamber seemed disoriented and at a loss. Gardel gave them instructions in deep reassuring tones, and the men compliantly led them to the palace stables, where Sitwell reclaimed his wagon and animals. The merchant drove them to the palace gates and they were let through without challenge.

Raggar told Sitwell to head for the city's east gate, as any looking to pursue them would likely presume they made for north or south. The people of the city were as listless and apparently directionless as the palace guards had been.

Soon they exited Altimor, passed several mine entrances and reached the edge of the city's environs. They came to a wide crossroads and Sitwell drew them to a halt. He looked at Raggar expectantly.

The ancient warrior breathed deeply. 'Friends, I did not think we would make it this far. Thank you for the aid you have afforded me. Cal, for your unfailing courage, and those surprisingly useful stones of yours. Gardel, for your good faith and the generosity of your healing magicks. Master Sitwell, for your true commitment even in the direst of circumstances, and for this comfortable seat beside you. And Elha, for ultimately standing with us no matter the nature of your own purposes, and for guarding Wormdale against the Empire on behalf of us all. Yet it is now that I leave you, for I must head south to Cha'Ithan, this so-called Enlightened City.'

'But great-grandfather! You have done all that you have sworn. The Vale is safe.'

Raggar shook his head. 'Nay, lad, not till this Empire changes its ambitions is the Vale safe. I must go persuade this Emperor in no uncertain terms.'

'Then I will go with you,' the youth decided.

'I cannot allow it. Your parents will be in need of you. And you should return to mourn properly those you have lost. You have completed all that you set out to do and more. Let it be.'

'Those we killed were but instruments of the ones truly responsible for what happened to Brin and her family. Besides, you stole my revenge from me when you killed the captain. I had him just where I wanted him when you struck,' Cal insisted.

'I too will go with you,' Gardel said. 'For I cannot return to the High Tender till I have secured the Empire's promise.'

'And me,' Elha spoke up. 'For Wormdale will be no safer than the Vale till this is done.'

Even Sitwell barely hesitated. 'And I need to find a new market for my goods, so will accompany you a-ways.'

'Besides, you need us, great-grandfather. Who else will save you from crazed priests when you go rushing in all outnumbered?'

'Yes,' the witch smiled. 'Or when you take all leave of your senses and think to attack the very Keeper himself?'

'And who will heal those injuries you all but never look to avoid?'

'Or throw you your hammer when you have been clumsy enough to let it out of your care?' Sitwell finished with a broad grin.

Raggar threw up his hands. 'Alright, you touched fools, but do not say I didn't warn you. I want no complaining. In fact, I think it's time for a few more rules round here . . .'

They all groaned and began to shout at him at once.

'The gods pity this Empire and that fraud Sharim, that's all I can say!'

Raggar and his companions will return.

From the Diary of St George

A J Dalton

T'S FAIRLY EASY to become a saint. It's far harder to live as a saint. Flawed as we are, we always fail in any attempt to be truly holy. Since our fall from a state of grace, it was ever thus.

I, Georgius Gerontius, know I am flawed. Whatever I do fails to change that. No amount of praying, purging, penance, self-flagellation – Lord, forgive me, I almost enjoy it – or quiet contemplation does aught to correct the error in me.

It makes me wonder if it is even worth trying to be a better man, for it can only end in frustration, anger and further sin. I sometimes wonder if the human Church has got it all wrong. After all, the human Church, in being human, must also be flawed. Of course, it's precisely that sort of attitude that landed me in trouble in the first place.

When a man has both his own nature and the servants of God arrayed against him, what chance can he have? I don't even need Satan's help, it seems, to see myself damned, excommunicate and deprived of my freedom. Truly then, man is his own worst enemy.

Surely the fact that the Church did not choose to end my heretical life – as it did for so many others – is but further proof of that flaw. Oh, there is no doubt that my martial skills inclined them towards a certain leniency and a consideration of how I might best spread their holy word to the heathens beyond Christendom. For truly, where gentle words and reasoned argument can often fail to win over a cold heart or closed mind, a sword can do much to warm the blood and enthuse any number of otherwise reluctant worshippers. It is what they call being a Soldier of God, I suppose. It is how men, flawed though they are, and dark though their deeds may sometimes be, can encourage others towards the Church for their own good. It is how the dark deeds I later committed on behalf of the Church ultimately saw me declared a living saint.

Yet, as I said, becoming a saint is the easy bit, while being a saint every day after is the tricky bit. People simply will not leave you alone, you see. There's no end to their demands once they start believing you have the power to bestow blessings upon them. Belief is therefore one of the most annoying and danger-ous of human pastimes if you ask me. Oh, certainly, it has seen me make plenty of gold from those wishing to win my favour, but I would swap it all in a trice for just a bit of peace.

Ah, peace. I almost forget what it is. The wars and fighting never seem to end. How can they, after all, when man is flawed and therefore always prone to those dark deeds I mentioned? How can a soul know peace in such a world? How can I even sleep peacefully when the bloody faces of the dead are always there begging for an explanation? It's enough to drive a man crazy – and perhaps there would be some escape and relief in such distraction. Try as I might, however – standing in the light of the full moon, saying the Lord's Prayer backwards and so forth – I always remain tiresomely sane.

Others, I've heard, commit dark deeds against themselves to end their lives. But the Church calls that an unforgivable sin, so I daren't attempt it, as I would lose my sainthood, not to mention my soul.

So that only leaves the one choice for the sane and reasoning man, which is not to think about it at all, of course. It makes sense really, since the thoughts of the sane and reasoning man must be flawed in some way, like everything else of man, so it is best to allow the Church and God to your conscience and guide in thought instead. Yes, the servants of God may be flawed in their own way, but they converse with God directly and relay His wishes back to the faithful.

Priests, then, may commit sin, but they are a necessary evil, for they allow you to glimpse the will of God. I have never had a direct relationship with Him myself, despite my best efforts, so have always needed the Church in that respect. I have tried praying to God, entering a trance to commune with him, reading signs and omens in nature, and even casting a spell, but all to no avail.

My creed in life, therefore, is built on just two simple principles. Firstly, avoid sinful thought by not thinking too much. Then do precisely what the Church tells you, even if it asks seemingly dark deeds of you.

That creed has seen me live a long life and seen me become a living saint. I pray it can do the same for you, or God have mercy on your soul, for otherwise you will have caused your own misery and doom.

For all that, it is a difficult enough creed to live by, to be sure. You will only succeed if you make it your life's work, and even if it then becomes the death of others.

Knight of Ages

A J Dalton

'WHAT DO YOU think, Jakh?'

'I think you will have to turn robber-knight, master, or we will both likely starve. Peace between the kingdoms hardly feeds a man of war.'

The knight nodded and eyed the thin stew his retainer stirred over the fire. Although he had eaten little of substance in the last few days, the odours coming from their cook-pot did little to provoke his appetite. 'Are there not even slugs hereabouts, Jakh, with which to make our meal more hearty?'

'I fear the upset stomachs we suffered a few days back were due to the last slugs we ate.'

'They were poisonous, you think?'

'Perhaps. I have not seen slugs of such a colour before. Sorry, master.'

The knight sighed. 'I do not complain. I know you make all efforts you can to see us fed. It is this strange and inhospitable land that is to blame. Never have I seen nature so turned against man.'

Jakh tried to smile. 'But you need your strength, master. Without it, we will not get work. Without work we will not have money, without money we will not be able to afford inn or hospital. We will become destitute and desperate. We will turn to crime and the kingdoms will employ good knights to hunt us down. Without your strength to hold them at bay, we will

125

be captured and hung.' His eyes were wide and staring. 'I see it, master! It is a vision!'

The knight chuckled darkly. 'And all because of some sickly slugs. Who would think they could prove so powerful? Who would think, lowly as they are, slugs could decide the fate of men and the course of whole kingdoms, eh, Jakh? Is this how far man has fallen, then? Are we lower than slugs even?'

Jakh gasped and shook his head. 'No, master, that is not what I meant. It wasn't a vision. That's right. It wasn't a vision, I now realise. It was but my fancy running away with me. It was some toxin in the slugs, I think!'

The knight's voice was deep and changed now, barely human. 'Are you certain, young Jakh? It sounded to me as if you were finally condemning mankind, that you were admitting the golden age had passed and all was turned to mud. It sounded to me that you had at last made your decision that there were none left worth the saving.'

Jakh swallowed hard. He would not meet the knight's eyes, for fear he would be caught by the hypnotic and unnatural shadows that lurked there whenever their conversations took an unnerving and disturbing turn like this. He replied slowly, careful with the words he chose. 'As you said yourself, master, it is this strange and inhospitable land that is to blame. It afflicts my mood and the turn of my thoughts. Indeed, it must also have influenced the people hereabouts and that is why the villages we have passed through have been so unwelcoming. I think they are scared and suspicious of everyone and everything. None has even asked us for news of the neighbouring kingdoms. Far from none being worth saving, then, perhaps all the people of this land need saving instead.'

There was a pause. Jakh held his breath. When the knight spoke again, it was in his normal voice once more, his tone light and matter of fact. 'Yes, you're probably right, Jakh. There are always people who need saving, be it a small farmer who cannot pay the local baron's unfair tax demands, a dispute between villages over hunting, fishing and grazing rights, a maiden who does not welcome the advances of a local ruffian, or a town that is beset by a gang of thieves, a pack of wolves or clutch of forest wites, and so on. So let us not be low of spirit, for we will always find noble service as long as there are people that live.'

Jakh sighed with relief and now glanced up at the knight, whose eyes were the clear blue of a spring day. 'Indeed, master, and if we are not offered anything in the few towns we will pass before reaching the main city of Arla, then we still have some small coin left from your service to the crown of Skarow. Perhaps a glint of gold rather than the show of your sword's steal will be more to the liking of the folk of this place.'

'We still have coin, you say? That is well, for it can inspire the hospitality and good manners of our fellow man even in times of adversity.'

'And, big as he is, Bardas will need proper grain if he is to continue carrying so much weight every day.' Bardas, the knight's haughty steed, chose that moment to snort, as if agreeing. Jakh's mule, also tied up close by, showed its teeth and brayed. 'Yes, and you, Roly! You do your fair share too. If you'll excuse me, master, I will go and set some snares in that small wood, and see if I can find any mushrooms or herbs to add to our stew.'

'Of course, Jakh, of course.'

'You have everything you need for now, master?'

'Yes. I will have a nap, I think, until you return.'

Jakh hesitated. 'You will probably be more comfortable without your breastplate and backplate on, master. Shall I unbuckle them for you?'

The knight grinned broadly at his retainer and shook his head, light from the fire flickering in his eyes as dusk began to fall. 'You know as well as I do that whenever I try and remove this armour something happens to cause me to keep it on. It seems it is the will of the gods. Or I would think this armour was cursed, if it had not saved me so many times. Mark my words, if we were but to start pulling on one of the buckles, a bunch of marauders would come screaming out of those trees and set upon us, or some ogre on heat would come and try to love us death while eating us.' He chortled. 'No, it's best I keep it on. After all, we are in a strange land, so it is better to be safe than sorry, eh, Jakh? Besides, I'm used to always wearing it. I am as comfortable wearing it as not wearing it, I think, so may as well wear it, eh?'

'As you wish, master, as you wish.'

~

The conversation with his master had badly scared Jakh. He sat on a tree root and ran a shaking hand across his brow. There was something wrong with his master, he was sure of it. It was as if something else took control of the knight sometimes, and it was happening with more and more frequency, and for longer periods each time. When Jakh had first become the knight's retainer, the only time he'd noticed any change was in the heat of battle, and then Jakh had simply taken it for some battle rage, fighting spirit or blessing of the god of war. But as the years had passed, the spirit, ghost, demon, or whatever it was, had become increasingly evident beyond battle. Jakh had felt it watching him sometimes – when it thought it had him unawares – measuring him or assessing him. In the words he'd just exchanged with it, he'd got the definite impression it was testing him, trying to trick him or have him make some awful decision. Precisely what it wanted of Jakh and his master, he wasn't sure, but one thing he was clear on was that the main feeling he had from it was one of malevolence.

How it had first made any claim on his master, Jakh didn't know. He suspected it was something to do with the knight's armour, however. Its style was old, it looked like steel yet took on a strange pale yellow burnish, and when the light caught it just so thousands of small runes inscribed into its surface could be discerned. Where it had been made he couldn't even guess, but it had to have been made by a master armourer. And the knight now refused to remove it. No amount of cajoling or reasoning could persuade him, for on the rare occasion that he'd tried, some fight or peril had suddenly descended upon them and people had ended up dead.

Normally, having to wear a chestplate and backplate for a prolonged period would give a knight all manner of skin abrasions and open sores, no matter how well the armour had been padded, but Jakh's master never complained. He never seemed to be in discomfort either. His body should have begun to suffer terribly inside that armour long ago, but far from putrefying and rotting as if inside a metal coffin his body only seemed to get stronger. In a confrontation, none were now able to resist him for more than a few minutes at most, let alone pose any sort of serious threat. Not even time seemed a worthy adversary, for the knight was apparently unaging. Where Jakh had once been a young and bright-eyed squire but was now a middle-aged and weather-faced retainer after a lifetime on the road, the knight himself did not look to have aged a day. Truly, his master was well named the Knight of Ages, but Jakh had started to fear it was a curse rather than a blessing.

It had all been so different in the beginning, when the knight had rescued the young Jakh from the hard monotony of life as a farmhand. Jakh was . . . had been . . . the youngest and smallest of five sons, never likely to inherit their small farm, always given the worst jobs, like mucking out, and ignored by all the girls in the villages roundabout except Simple Sal, and even she seemed interested more often in goats or the shapes clouds made. Jakh had desperately dreamed of making his own way in the world and being in charge of his own destiny. He had prayed to the gods morning and night for some escape, and when the gods had not answered him had given Old Willema a quart of milk, pound of butter and round of blue cheese for a good luck spell. Then the Knight of Ages had ridden through the dale and straight past the gate of their farm, his skin the same colour as the milk, his armour with the same lustre as the butter and his banner with chevrons the same hue as the veins in the cheese. The knight had even looked up into the farm's courtyard and met Jakh's eye before deciding to move on. Jakh had been in no doubt that the world had paused to take a breath for the briefest of moments and that this was his one chance. His one and only choice: to stay working on the safe but humble farm for the rest of his days, or to pull himself up out of the mud and run towards a dangerous sort of freedom. The clang of his pitchfork as it hit the cobbles announced he'd made his decision before he'd even realised it. He blinked. He was vaulting over the gate. Another blink and he was at the knight's side, pledging his life.

'Are you actually free to offer me your service, young man? No man is truly free, you know. Surely you are indentured or indebted to another. You do not look like a farm owner of freeman. If you were such, why would you then willingly give up your farm or freedom for a life of servitude? You would not, unless you were ailing of mind. No, you are either a runaway or a wanted man, which amounts to much the same in the eyes of the law. And if I were to accept you into my service, I might justly be accused of either stealing the property of another or harbouring a criminal.'

'Milord, my father will not even notice I am gone,' Jakh had begged. 'He will be glad of not having another mouth to feed, believe me.'

'Then he will be prepared to sell you into my service for a very small consideration. We will return to your farm to ascertain if that is the case. No, you will not persuade me otherwise! Be warned, it is rarely a happy thing to discover your true value to another. Invariably, they will describe that value as far more miserable or far more excessive than you expected. You will realise that you are worthless or have missed out on magnificent opportunities. You will feel angry, cheated and then sad, and it might never leave you. It might become a blight upon your soul. It may even destroy you. So think carefully, young man, and ask yourself if this is what you truly want. Do you really wish to exchange a warm bed and regular home-cooked meals for an unheroic death upon the blood-soaked battlefield of a foreign kingdom?'

They had returned to the farm and the Knight of Ages had spoken privately with Jakh's father. Then Jakh's father had asked his son with a slight, confused, but perhaps proud smile: 'You want to leave?'

'Yes, father.' Jakh's mother had shed a few tears, told him there would always be a place for him by their fire, given him a kiss on the cheek, placed a tied cloth of food in his hands, and then gently pushed him towards the door.

And for many years his life with the Knight of Ages had been just as he'd dreamed it would be. A glorious adventure, going from kingdom to kingdom, protecting the innocent and punishing evil-doers. They'd brought down tyrants, undone marauders, defended the honour of noble ladies, defeated Wintral the Dark Warlock, and even slain a demi-god who demanded child sacrifice of her enslaved worshippers. When the small kingdom of Nintos had been menaced by the Empire of Greater Asperas – and the knights of Nintos had all suddenly come down with an unspecified illness that meant they were unavailable to face the huge and brutal First Warrior of the Empire in single combat – the Knight of Ages, aided by his fearless squire, had stepped forwards to serve as King's Champion of Nintos. The First Warrior of the Empire had ended up disarmed, with his trousers around his ankles and his bare behind paddled by the flat of the knight's blade. Tears of contrition rolling down his face, the First Warrior had yielded, had promised on behalf of the Empire to mend his ways and peace had existed between Nintos and the Empire for decades after. Songs and poems about the knight had been sung and recited the length and breadth of the known lands. They had been good days, perhaps belonging to a simpler time, when the people were happy to offer thanks for the generosity of their gods, the wisdom of their rulers and the excitement and wonder of great pageants and feast days.

Had it really been a simpler time, or did he just imagine it had been? Was his memory playing tricks on him? Was he confusing the exuberance and enchantment of his youth – when life had seemed so new, different, vivid and colourful – with how things had really been? Had he simply been naive? Whatever it was, something had changed. He wasn't sure exactly how it had happened, but things had gradually become more blurred and ambiguous. Things had become more grey, rather than black and white. Maybe he had just become older, more experienced and slightly more cynical, but he now frequently struggled to separate the good from the bad, and the innocent from the guilty. On behalf of the throne, they had ousted land thieves from the remote regions of Westland, only to discover later that the King of Westland had mining ambitions in the precise same areas. They had hunted a fearsome dragon in the Duchy of Marriswall, a creature that had apparently burned down an entire village and consumed all the livestock, only to find that the large lizard they brought to bay was incapable of breathing fire. Jakh felt sick at the thought they had slaughtered a dumb and innocent beast; and had not had the stomach to ask questions about whether the village had been paying sufficient taxes to the Duke; and why the Duke suddenly had plenty of spare cattle and sheep to sell at a premium to the neighbouring Duchy of Theverell; where disease had recently devastated their own herds and flocks. He didn't want to think about it. They'd caught a murderous gang of thieves who had emptied a merchant's entire warehouse and killed the two warehouse guards. The fat merchant had apparently been left impoverished, unable to provide for his fat family and unable to contribute to the local community that depended so desperately upon him. The Guild of Merchants had paid the Knight of Ages handsomely to see justice done and ensure that their berg and its environs were safe for decent, law-abiding merchants. Jakh told himself they'd done the right thing in tracking down the desperate-looking thieves, but had been unable to watch as the starving men were strung up in the central square of the berg. Was it really the fat merchant who could not provide for his family, or was it these thieves who had hungry mouths to feed and no other recourse? The so-called weapons that the thieves had half-heartedly raised when the knight had found them were actually old and rusty farm tools. The men had been dressed in the rags of peasant-farmers, peasant-farmers who could no longer pay the rent on the mean plots of land that they worked, a rent that had of course been set extortionately high by the land owner, the land owner which was of course the self-same Guild of Merchants. He didn't want to think about it.

He wouldn't think about it. They undertook noble deeds, they were not simple sellswords or amoral mercenaries.

Yet as he'd refused to think of such things, the visions had begun to plague him. They'd only come at first to him when he'd been daydreaming – he'd shudder free of them, but they'd still be lingering there at the edge of his consciousness. He wouldn't remember them clearly until real events began to play out in a familiar way and he realised he'd seen these horrifying things happen before. Just as the rights and wrongs of mankind became more entangled, and the implications of the knight's deeds were more confused, so his visions and reality became comingled. It was just like the increase in the dark influence of the spirit upon his master. Were the things connected? Was Jakh also coming under its thrall? He didn't know how to put things back to how they'd been before. Nothing the knight did seemed to make things any better. The more they tried to help people, the more people took them for granted and became entirely self-interested. People stopped singing the songs lauding the Knight of Ages. The visions and reality of daily life became worse and worse . . . and then nearly the entire continent had been dragged into the inevitable chaos and gyre of all-out war.

They'd been terrible years, like a nightmare that never ends and from which you cannot wake. The Knight of Ages had fought first on one side and then another, continually in a state of battle-rage. So much blood, so many lives. In that war, none were innocent. Yet all were innocent. Acts of villainy would sometimes turn out in the long run to be the greatest kindness, apparent kindnesses tantamount to genocide. Peace only finally came when there were no longer sufficient knights on any side to wage an effective war, and when food shortages had become so bad that the majority had no choice but to put down their swords, pick up pitchforks instead and hitch their warhorses to ploughs. Was it truly peace? Of a sort.

Jakh had found no peace though. The visions now afflicted him during ordinary waking moments. The dark spirit's sway over his master only seemed the stronger. There might be peace, but no one had been saved – quite the opposite. Far from saving others, then, Jakh knew that it was him and his master who needed saving. As much as they searched for those who might need saving, they searched for their own salvation. The knight wasn't aware of it in the same way as Jakh, of course, for whenever Jakh tried to broach the subject with his master, the dark spirit would immediately be there, snarling, forbidding and threatening. His master would later have no recollection of their conversation or anything untoward happening.

Jakh sighed, then hardened his resolve. 'I will find a way. I will help my beloved master, he who freed me and showed me the world, and never asked anything in return . . . except for a stew that did not poison him.'

~

The knight sat with hooded eyes looking into the fire, trying to find sleep, but it would not come. It never did anymore. It wasn't that he felt any particular fatigue, but it would be good to rest properly for once, perhaps to dream of the family he'd had so long ago. He couldn't bring their faces into his waking thoughts anymore, but that didn't mean he loved them any the less. That didn't mean a day ever passed without him thinking of, feeling and praying for them. And there had been so many days, so many battles, so many enemies. He left those for Jakh to remember. The knight's principal thoughts would only ever be of the family he had lost, the family he would find again some day, when his penance was at last done.

Perhaps it wasn't fair on Jakh to have him shoulder the details of their deeds and exploits, but the retainer seemed to have the perfect mind and recall for keeping track of where, who and for whom they had fought, so that they could avoid likely trouble and long-standing grudges held against them. Jakh had a firm grasp of which kingdoms were currently allied to each other, and which were at odds. Jakh knew which noble houses were in the ascendant and well connected by marriage, and which were in decline and probably in need of a good knight's services. Just what he'd do without Jakh, he didn't know. Over the years, he'd become more and more dependent on the boy . . . man, rather. Just how many years had it been? It had to have been a fair few, for Jakh's hair was now thinning considerably. Maybe Jakh's perfect recall combined with all he had seen was a burden greater than any man was meant to bear. The war that had engulfed much of continent had certainly taken its toll on the man. Jakh was far more withdrawn these days. His merry humour and light-hearted observations on life seemed to have deserted him. His words were measured . . . guarded, even. And his eyes – they were haunted.

He worried for Jakh. Jakh was all that kept him connected to the real world. Without Jakh, he would be lost. Without Jakh, he'd never find his family again. Jakh was his family, to all intents and purposes. The knight realised he should be taking far better care of Jakh, lest he become lost like the rest of them. He had to help Jakh rediscover his happy-go-lucky self. He had to ease Jakh's burden, else the retainer's mind might begin to unravel, for the warning signs were there.

Hadn't there been other squires before Jakh, squires who had not lasted very long because they could not bear the strain of forever riding into combat and facing the dark deeds and conjurations of mankind? Yes, Jakh was a rare one. The knight knew he was blessed to have him by his side. 'Jakh, you are a better man than me, I fear. I should be the one calling you master, methinks. Certainly, you have never committed such an ignoble deed as I.'

The knight's eyes were heavy, and for the first time in an age he found blessed sleep.

~

Jakh's snares were empty come the morning, so hunger saw them strike camp early. Bardas bit at Jakh as the retainer loaded the horse with a good portion of the knight's heavy kit.

'Not impressed at being put to work before the sun's fully above the horizon, eh? Grumpy that your beauty sleep's been disturbed? Keep it up, Bardas,' Jakh groused, 'and we'll be having horseflesh for tonight's supper.'

The horse kicked out and Jakh leaped backwards with a curse.

'Jakh, don't take on so. Bardas is just being affectionate. Imagine how he'd be if he really didn't like you.'

A vision came to Jakh – Bardas rearing up, eyes flashing and foam at his mouth, striking out with his heavily shod hooves and dashing Jakh's head from his shoulders. Jakh blinked, his mouth suddenly dry. He quickly moved away from the evil-tempered destrier and went to see to Roly.

They were soon on the road and riding amongst a range of small bluffs and crags. Paths went off in all directions between the strange outcroppings, but the main path through the maze was well worn and easy to follow.

'This must be the Giant's Anvil, master.'

'The what?' the knight asked absently, an eye towards the bruise-coloured sky. 'I would shoot down a bird or two, but it would seem they are all still abed. I heard no dawn chorus, did you? It is not natural. What about finding a river and catching some fish? Maybe the fish are monstrous and ate all the birds.'

'The Giant's Anvil, master. The boy who spoke to us when no other would in Fairhollow – you know, the town in the impossibly muddy valley – mentioned it to us. Local legend has it that a giant was angry with the earth spirit of this place and thus smote the land with his mighty hammer, cracking it open and shattering it like this.'

'The giant was probably ravenous like us. No wonder he was angry with the earth spirit.'

'They say this place is haunted, master, but it is the most direct route to Arla. Going the long way round would take several weeks extra.'

'By which time we would probably have starved to death. What haunts this place, then, Jakh? The giant? The earth spirit? It can't be that dangerous, or trade would never get to Arla. The way looks well travelled to me, although I am surprised we have not met anyone on our journey thus far.'

'The boy did not say, master, although his belief seemed genuine. Maybe there are thieves and robbers about. This place seems perfect for an ambush.'

'I bet they are hungry thieves and robbers, then.' The knight's armour echoed as his stomach rumbled. 'Unless they're cannibals.'

Jakh yelped and frantically looked around.

The knight smiled. 'Fear not, good Jakh. Arla would never allow thieves and robbers to remain at large here. It would be the end of all trade otherwise. Only a fool would set themselves up here.'

'HOW DARE YOU!' boomed a voice from every direction, echoing through all the rocky channels and paths, getting louder and louder.

The knight pulled his battle-hardened mount to a stop. 'Jakh, did you hear something?'

'IT IS YOU WHO ARE FOOLS TO TRESPASS HERE!'

'M-m-master! It is the giant!'

'I WILL GRIND YOUR BONES TO FLOUR AND YOUR FLESH WILL BE THE FILLING FOR A PIE!'

'Sounds like he's a bit of a cook, eh, Jakh?'

'Master, do not antagonise him!' Jakh squeaked.

'THROW DOWN YOUR PROVISIONS AND POSSESSIONS. RIDE ON QUICKLY AND I WILL LET YOU LIVE!'

'We have no provisions!' the knight called back. 'Perhaps you could spare us something?'

'WHAT? NOTHING? NOT EVEN SOME BREAD?'

'No, sorry.'

'AN OLD BIT OF CHEESE?'

'Chance would be a fine thing.'

'ACORNS?'

The knight shook his head.

A thin white-haired man in dark robes loomed atop a nearby bluff. 'An old carrot turning black that you don't really fancy?'

'Not even that.'

The man's brows lowered angrily. 'You must have something! You will give it to me or suffer my displeasure.' He raised his hands above his head dramatically and his wide sleeves fell down around his elbows. 'In my wrath I shall throw lightning down upon you. I will fry you in your armour, sorry knight.'

'See, Jakh? It is no giant, after all.'

'It's just a dirty old hedge-wizard,' Jakh sighed in disgust.

'What outrage do you utter? I am not dirty! I am Lord Hierophant of this land. I tower above you, while you are lowly. Abase yourself before me!'

'What is a hierophant, do you think, Jakh?'

Jakh shrugged. 'Like an elephant, I guess. They certainly smell about the same.'

'I do not smell!' the man shrieked, shaking his bedraggled beard, stamping his foot in frustration and stretching his arms up even higher. 'Take that back or I will cast a spell of a thousand stings upon you!'

'A thousand stings, Jakh. Nasty to be sure, but nothing like a million stings, I imagine. Having said that, after the first few hundred you probably don't notice the rest.'

'Indeed, master, and there are plenty of dock leaves about, to soothe the worst of it.'

'That does it!' the Lord Hierophant frothed, and disappeared from sight . . .

. . . only to reappear right next to Jakh. He reached out and laid a bony hand on Jakh's leg, muttering something unintelligible.

'Gakh!' the knight's retainer managed, going rigid and toppling off Roly. He hit the ground with a thud and lay unmoving.

'Hah! He will remain a living statue forever more!' the Lord Hierophant declared.

'Not if you know what's good for you,' the knight said dangerously. 'None may harm the squire of the Knight of Ages and not end up ruing the day they were born. You will restore him immediately.'

'The Knight of Ages is nothing but a fairy tale,' the wizard replied uncertainly.

'Come feel the edge of my blade and tell me if that is also a fairy tale!' the knight snarled, shadows flickering in his eyes. He unsheathed his weapon while turning Bardas to face their attacker directly.

'Stay back!' the Lord Hierophant warned. 'You have seen nothing of what I can do. Do you think I have lived to such an age with only a few parlour tricks at my command? You will fear me!'

'And you will curse your mother for ever having produced you,' hissed a voice no human should have been able to utter. 'Your father's name will be as a profanity to you. An eternity as a plaything for demons will be a joy compared to what I will do to you.'

The Lord Hierophant gulped as the knight kicked Bardas forwards. 'No! You do not know what you are doing. You are giving me no other choice!' the wizard gabbled. He twisted around and bent over, hitching up his robes in the same motion. Then he let loose a noxious and devastating wind from his backside. 'The gods have mercy on us all!'

The wind grew in force, and Bardas was pushed backwards. The horse would have charged into the gates of hell at the knight's command, but this was too much. It shied away.

'What foulness is this?' the knight laboured, his eyes streaming and becoming unfocussed. He barely kept his seat.

A tempest now hit the knight and he was bodily thrown back into the side of a crag. The impact forced the air from his body and he slid to the ground.

'I cannot stop it!' the old man cried in distress, emptied inside out by whatever magic he had called up. His cheeks became sunken, his body emaciated and his entire strength wasted. The power he had unleashed then propelled him forwards and smashed his head into a standing boulder.

~

Everything was suddenly still. The knight levered himself up and coaxed Bardas back to his feet. Thankfully, the horse did not appear to have any broken limbs, so would not need putting down.

'Lucky for you my horse is alright,' the knight grated as he marched over to the unconscious wizard and picked him up by the scruff of the neck. The man was as light as anything, seemingly little more than a bag of bones. 'Otherwise I would have made you carry me all the way to Arla instead. With so little to you, you would have been finished within a dozen paces.' He shook the wizard, hard. 'You hear me?' Another shake, and finally a pained groan in reply. 'Why must nature wizards insist on being so stupid? How is it any of you live into adulthood, when you are invariably so stupid? Does it never occur to you to draw magic from the world around you, rather than using your own magic? With what you were attempting, I'm surprised you didn't fade from existence entirely. We're no doubt fortunate that you haven't eaten too much recently, else who knows what sort of ruination would have been visited upon us and the entire surrounding region? You might have killed thousands with your poisonous gas and effluence.'

The knight leaned down, yanked some grass from the ground and stuffed it into the old man's mouth. 'Chew. Chew, damn you! Right. Now swallow! Go on. That should give you enough to unfreeze my squire. Get on with it. Any funny business and I'll snap your neck with a flick of my wrist.'

The wizard coughed feebly. 'It will kill me to use my magic again.'

'Would you have me torture you? Believe me, I will see you suffer so badly that death will seem a mercy. Do it! Without delay! I know the spell you have cast will have stopped his heart. If you have not fully restored him in the time it takes me to draw my knife, then I will peel away your skin, carve your flesh and unstring your muscles, all while you still live.' The knight dropped the wizard next to Jakh and reached for the long knife at his waist. 'I will uncover your ribs and splay them apart. I will take your beating heart in my hand, and squeeze it through my fingers.' His knife came free and it glinted wickedly. 'I will insert the tip of this blade between the plates of your skull and pry them apart . . . '

Trembling in horror, the wizard wasted no time laying both his hands on Jakh and hurrying through a cantrip. Jakh spasmed into life and the wizard promptly fell into a dead faint. The squire took great shuddering breaths and was at last able to sit up.

'M-master?' he panted. 'What happened? Ugh. And that stench? Is he-is he dead then?'

'Not yet.' The knight brandished his knife.

'Master! There can be no doubt that he is undeserving of an honourable death, yet can it be entirely noble to kill him when he is defenceless like this?'

'Jakh, he tried to rob us, and near killed you. What happens to him will be of his own making. He will be the victim of his own poor choices and actions, nothing else.'

'And yet he both failed to rob us and kill us, master. I do not think he is a practised rogue.'

The knight frowned. 'Then what would you have me do, Jakh? Bring him round and put a knife in his hand so he can defend himself? Would that suit your strange sense of what is right?'

Jakh shook his head. 'He wouldn't have a fair chance.'

'None do that stand against me. That does not stop me punishing them for their crimes.'

'That is true, master, and you describe the very point – none that stand against you. Master, this wretch is in no condition to stand even, let alone stand against you.'

'What, then, Jakh?' the knight asked in exasperation. 'We should just leave him here like this and move off down the road?'

'He would likely die of exposure were we to do that, master. It would be much the same as drawing a blade across his throat.'

'By all that's holy, Jakh, I do not know what you would have of me!'

'Perhaps we can save him, master.'

141

'What? Do you run mad, Jakh? Save him so that he might then molest other innocent travellers? Truly, his magic has upset the balance of your mind.'

'Master, we have nothing to lose by keeping him alive, and perhaps there may be some gain.'

The knight released his breath slowly. 'Very well, Jakh. I shall be guided by you on this occasion. Let us pray that we do not come to regret it. Gather some grass and put it in the old man's mouth. Stroke his throat to cause his swallowing reflex.'

~

The hierophant sat shaking by the small fire that Jakh had hastily got together to warm him. The old man's face was pinched and his lips blue. 'Th-thank you. I would not have blamed you if you had wanted to kill me.'

'Indeed,' the knight glowered, hand on swordhilt.

'He is being contrite, master.'

The knight harrumphed. 'Contrition always comes after the fact, Jakh. It does not mean he is deserving of mercy.'

'Good sir knight,' the hierophant ventured, 'forgive my previous behaviour if you can find it in your heart to do so. I was desperate and overwrought. Yet, in part, I also wished to ascertain your worth.'

'You presumed to test me,' came the sneered response.

'I meant no offence, sir knight!' the hierophant hastened to reply. 'I did not know who you were at first, no formal introductions having been made . . .'

'I believe you were too busy threatening us as some giant . . .'

'And the tales of the Knight of Ages are so glorious as hardly to be believed. The only way to know you truly was to test you to the utmost.'

Something did not ring true about the hierophant's words, but before the knight could challenge him further, Jakh was asking, 'At risk of your own life though? What would make you do such a thing?'

'I have nothing else left!' the wizard all but wept. 'My brother has stolen the seat of power from me. My own brother! Where once I ruled this kingdom, I am now outcast. Even nature is turned against me. Can there be anything worse for a nature wizard? Other than what I can eat, I must draw from my own substance to use magic. And can there be anything worse for the kingdom?'

'What do you mean?' Jakh urged.

'Nature is not just turned against me; it is also turned against my beloved people. My brother uses the seat of power to draw the life from the kingdom. It gives him and those loyal to him great power. It has even restored his youth and vigour. But the cost to the kingdom is terrible! Where once this land was an abundant garden, now it is drained and desperate. This year's harvest was pitiful. Whole forests have died. Much of the wildlife has fled. Where life remains, it holds on however it may. Taste an apple and it may well poison you so that its seeds can take root in your rotting body. Just to survive, nature now seeks to feed upon the people! The world is turned upside down. And the people are now changed. I have seen neighbour trying to consume neighbour. I have heard of whole villages going to bed at night and none rising in the morning. The people can no longer trust one another or the world around them. I thought the gods had abandoned us, but see! They have sent us the blessed Knight of Ages.'

'Basically, you want us to oust your brother from the throne – seat of power, whatever you call it – and put you in his place,' the knight replied.

'We must save the people!' the wizard declared.

'What do you think, master?' Jakh asked hopefully.

'I think this vagabond is unlikely to have any gold with which to pay us. Beyond that, Jakh, I have already said that I will abide by your decisions when it involves the Lord Hierophant.'

'My Lord Hierophant,' Jakh said politely. 'Do you have anything in the way of, er, well, gold?'

'Gold?' blinked the wizard. 'I never really had much use for it. I tended to leave all that sort of thing to my . . . oh . . . brother.'

The knight shook his head.

'But there's a royal treasury full of the stuff,' the hierophant insisted. 'Restore my kingdom and you can have as much of it as you can carry!'

'Master?'

'It's easy to promise what you don't have. We could just leave him and ride on to the next kingdom.'

'Master! We must save these people.'

'Any people worth their salt would be able to save themselves,' the knight shrugged.

'Good Jakh, the people and Lord Hierophant of ancient Saluria will be forever in your debt. You may call me Altimius, incidentally, for I am the seventh ruler of that name.'

'Then, Altimius, Lord Hierophant of Saluria, my master and I will be honoured to render our service to you and your people.'

The large knight turned and stomped towards Bardas. 'Come on, then. Let's get going, before there's nothing left to save. By the way, Altimius, Lord Hierophant or no, I do not want your unwashed behind anywhere near my horse or the mule. No creature in creation deserves that.'

'You expect me to walk all the way to Arla?'

'You can do that disappearing and reappearing trick of yours to keep up with us.'

'I will be entirely exhausted, good sir knight!'

'Precisely. That is my favourite sort of wizard.'

'I should conserve my strength for the coming confrontation with the usurper!'

'I have seen the unwholesome magic you use in a confrontation, remember. It is an abomination. Now stop talking and start walking, before I think better of having let you live.'

~

The trio came through the Giant's Anvil and soon arrived at a town that boasted a large number of stone buildings organised around a crossroads. It was late afternoon and there should still have been a bustle about the place. Different traders should have been finishing their last jobs of the day before heading home for the evening meal. There should have been a few women gossiping by the well. There should have been children playing, running home from lessons, carrying messages or coming to see the strangers entering town. There should have been dogs barking or sniffing at rubbish. Instead, all was still. The wind whispered at their ears like the last breath of a dying man.

'This is Nearhome,' Altimius said quietly. 'More than a thousand people.'

Jakh shivered. 'Tell me they are all out working in the fields.'

'This town has no fields. It's on the trade route, so has merchants, a blacksmith, a wheelwright, carpenters, an inn . . . a bawdy house . . .'

'The atmosphere of this place makes my flesh crawl. It feels worse than anywhere else we've visited,' Jakh managed, his words slow and heavy, as if they took him effort.

'The effect of the malaise is worse the closer we come to Arla. You must fight against it, good Jakh. Fix your mind and passion on our just cause and it may give you strength. Or offer prayers to sweet Fecundia, nature's goddess, and she may protect you.'

'If my squire begins to fail, you will share your strength with him, wizard,' the knight ordered quietly.

'Of-of course. If he will trust my touch, then I will provide him with more resilience.'

Jakh nodded. 'I would welcome it, Altimius.'

The wizard laid a hand on the squire's thigh. Several moments later, Jakh's gaze had become sharper, there was a slight smile on his lips and he sat taller in his saddle. 'Better?'

'Much. Thank you.'

'Food and wine will also fortify you. Let us find the inn,' the knight said, moving forwards with Bardas and keeping a close watch on the shutters and muddy alleyways to either side of them.

The inn was a squat, thick-walled building. Its main door was shut against them. Having dismounted and tethered the mule, Jakh tried the handle and then knocked. The knight suddenly came past him and shouldered the door, bursting it open.

'Master! What are you doing?'

'No inn should be closed at this hour, especially to tired travellers who are on their way to save the kingdom. Innkeepers are meant to wait on their customers, not the other way round.'

The knight and his companions moved into the darkness of the interior. The scene that confronted them was disturbing indeed. The innkeeper and his family sat at a table, staring vacantly at all sorts of victuals laid before them. There were breads, fruits, meats, cheeses, possits, puddings and what looked to be some sort of congealed stew. Very little of it had been touched, and a fur of mould was on much of it. There were loose folds of skin around the innkeeper's neck, where presumably he'd once had the jowls of a big eater, and his clothes seemed too large for his frame. The youngest child had her head laid on the table. The large fireplace looked to have burnt out a good while ago and there was a slight chill in the air.

'They are starving, but they do not have the will or energy even to raise to their lips that which would keep them alive,' the hierophant croaked.

'Innkeeper! Wine!' the knight shouted.

The innkeeper's gaze drifted to the knight. 'Welcome,' he said without intonation. 'Join . . . us.'

'Wine! Move!'

'Help . . . yourself . . . Some . . . in . . . barrel.'

'Altimius, can't you help them?' Jakh pleaded.

Altimius, who had been eyeing the food on the table, started guiltily. 'Why, yes, I believe so. I will need to replenish myself first, though.'

The old man quickly went to help himself to an apple. He sniffed at it and was about to take a large bite when there was an angry shout from the door. 'Thief! You will put that down at once. Begone, you looters!'

Blocking the exit was a formidable looking woman in her forties. 'She had flat features and wore simple homespun robes, but there was an energy about her that was captivating. She held a crossbow levelled straight at Altimius's chest.

'I have the honour of addressing a priestess of Fecundia, yes?' Altimius judged. 'Mistress, I myself am a nature wizard.'

The woman spat on the wooden floor. 'That would be a second reason to put this bolt through your chest. For too long men like you have simply taken whatever you wanted from the goddess without paying her due. If it is not freely given, then you try to take it by force. Is it any surprise then that she now turns against you? You have done this to us!'

'Madam, I assure you that none of this is my doing!' Altimius bridled, drawing himself up. 'I am the Lord Hierophant!'

'And that is the third reason,' the priestess said with eyes narrowed and hatred plain in her voice. Her finger began to squeeze the trigger of the crossbow.

'Priestess, you will not do this!' came a guttural command from the knight, darkness filling his gaze.

'Wait!' Jakh wailed.

'Demon!' the priestess spat, swinging her weapon towards the knight.

'Master, no!' Jakh cried, throwing himself between the priestess and the Knight of Ages. He squeezed his eyes shut, waiting for the heavy bolt to tear through his chest.

'Jakh!' Altimius called out in despair, dropping the apple.

'He is innocent!' the knight roared.

The crossbow trigger clicked and there was a rushing sound as the weapon released. A loud thud. A scream. The air went out of Jakh. He couldn't breathe. He was weightless. Was he flying through the air or falling? Altimius was suddenly there, catching him.

Silence.

'He fainted, that's all,' said the knight, sounding like himself.

'Thank you for pulling your aim, priestess,' Altimius ventured.

'A devotee of Fecundia would not kill such a one,' said the priestess. 'And my magic will be a more effective weapon than the crossbow against the two of you.'

'Enough,' said the knight. 'There is no purpose to this fight, unless you are intent upon your own death, in which case I will oblige you. Otherwise, you will stand aside and we will be on our way to end this malaise and free the people of this miserable land.'

'I cannot simply let you leave after the damage you have caused here. And how do you propose to free the people, demon, when Fecundia will have no part of you?'

'As Lord Hierophant, I will leave a promissory note to make good on the damages,' Altimius interjected. 'We travel to Arla, madam. We will free the seat of power from my brother's corruption. I will then see to it that Saluria and a proper reverence for Fecundia are restored. You know that a nature wizard would not want to see this land fail, and by that that you can take me at my word.'

'It is true, priestess,' Jakh said blearily from the floor. 'Believe us, as you are a woman of good faith. My master is the Knight of Ages, a warrior of renowned virtue. Surely you have heard of him?'

The priestess gazed at Jakh, weighing him, then at the knight and wizard. Her examination of the knight was particularly hard, but at last she said, 'Very well, but only because innocent Jakh has spoken for you. I will accompany you to Arla.'

'Madam, there is no need . . .'

'Now just you hang on . . .' began the knight.

'I do this for Fecundia!' said the priestess loudly, refusing to hear any argument. 'It is a holy mission to see a proper reverence for her restored. It cannot be entrusted to a fork-tongued demon and a light-fingered wizard only! Besides, there is little more I can do here in Nearhome.'

The knight glared at the priestess. 'Jakh, what say you?'

'Surely a priestess of Fecundia will be useful, master, don't you think?'

'If that is your decision, Jakh. Either way, it is time to be going. I will leave it to the three of you to deal with the innkeeper and his family as you see fit. Be quick, however, for time is against us and Bardas is always impatient to have his head.'

The priestess moved out of the doorway so that the knight would not walk through her. Altimius smiled at her and said, 'Madam, now that we are on better terms, about that apple . . .?'

~

The foursome travelled quickly, only resting for a handful of hours that night, before pressing on with the dawn. Altimius kept up by walking out of view around a tree or rock and then appearing much further down the road, whereas the priestess, who called herself Diahn, would wander off along faint forest tracks that somehow proved quicker than the main route.

They soon came to another town, but there was the smell of death about it, and carrion birds could be seen circling above, so they skirted it. Next they came to a walled village – called Heartsease, or so Altimius thought – yet the gates were closed and they were told to pass on by dull-eyed men with bows.

'It pains my heart to see the people like this,' Diahn said sadly to Jakh. 'The men of Heartsease knew I was a priestess of Fecundia, and I offered them her blessing, but still they were not persuaded to let us in. They would deny the very nature of which they are a part. They would deny their own nature and existence! What hope can there be for such people? It is against all sense.'

'They are scared, priestess. In their fear, they believe we are monsters come to steal from them or kill them. The monsters are in their minds, of course, but those monsters are more real to them than the world and its true nature. In many ways, those monsters are demons that possess and control them.'

'Yes,' Diahn nodded thoughtfully.

'Priestess, can your blessing or magic free people of such demons?'

Diahn looked at him with gentle understanding. 'Only if those people wish to be rid of their demons, Jakh. Only if they can close their ears and minds to the sweet nothings and temptations their demons whisper to them. If they can do that, then they will have the strength to cast out those demons and find the happiness of the goddess's blessing.'

Jakh pondered. 'My master says that some of the gods are just masquerading demons. He refuses to devote himself to just one of them, and never seeks to persuade others of the need to worship a particular god.'

Diahn's jaw tightened and her coal-coloured eyes flared. 'That is a blasphemy, Jakh, and I will not listen to it. You should steer your mind away from such thoughts, lest they corrupt you!'

Jakh sighed as the priestess deliberately stepped away from him. She would not be able to help his master, he now knew.

Altimius drew level with the high-stepping Bardas and called up to the knight: 'We are making good time, no, sir knight?'

The knight gave a perfunctory nod, continuing to watch the road ahead.

'I think we may even arrive there today, sir knight.'

'The sooner, the better.'

'Sir knight, if we are to converse, then perhaps you could share your name with me.'

Now the knight turned his eyes down towards Altimius. 'And why would I do that, pray tell?'

'Why, otherwise you would have me at a disadvantage,' Altimius smiled.

'That is how I prefer to have all wizards.'

'Oh, come now, it is customary for travelling companions to share their names at least.'

'Do you think I would freely give my name to a wizard? Press me again on this and I swear, by all I hold dear, that I will strangle you with your own beard.'

The wizard paled and his smile became crooked. 'Ha! You are right, good sir knight, the sooner we arrive at Arla, the better.'

'And mark me, Altimius, if I find that you go bothering Jakh with questions about me, then they will be the last questions you ever ask. Do you understand, wizard?'

'Good sir knight, I am already sensible of the service you do me and my kingdom. I would be a fool to risk that. Indeed, without such service, I would have nothing, I would be nothing.'

'Indeed, you would be a fool. Men are fools, however.'

'Even you, sir knight?'

'I am beginning to think so, for not letting the priestess skewer you with her crossbow. Not even your subjects want to see you live, it would seem. Now stop talking and start walking.'

~

The sun was past its zenith when they came over a small rise to find Arla towering above them in the distance. Light shimmered off precious glass windows and spires and domes sheathed in metals. Water danced along artificial courses, bright flower gardens caught the eye, and fruit orchards paraded before the city walls. There was a perfume in the air that made Jakh giddy, and he found himself smiling at mere sight of the place. After the drab and muddy towns of Saluria, Arla was a blessed relief to the spirit and senses. He breathed deeply and felt refreshed and strangely at peace.

'See the sky sparkle above the city!' he whispered in awe.

'Golden ravens,' Altimius answered. 'They were a gift from the Grand Magus of Kandala. Magical birds that fly without surcease over the palace. They shit on everything. I had people cleaning the roofs day and night just to stop the smell.'

'Do not let this place deceive you, Jakh,' the knight warned.

'There is so much . . . life here,' the squire wondered. 'Can you feel it?'

'Yes,' Diahn agreed. 'It is glorious!'

'My brother drains the kingdom to feed himself and Arla. He rewards the subjects of Arla well for their loyalty. Yet the beauty and prosperity of this city depends on creating ugliness and suffering elsewhere.'

'Parasites,' the knight murmured.

Jakh had already nudged Roly forwards, drawn towards the city as he was. And the mule seemed to need no second bidding for once. Bardas pulled at his reins, never happy to be in the mule's wake, and soon they were all racing towards the bewitching city.

Rich fields flashed past, and then the orchards. They reached the gates, which were flung wide like open arms, and entered into the city's embrace. The people wore warm colours and seemed relaxed, strolling leisurely among shops and the stalls of beaming traders. Mothers stood smiling and chatting while their children played tag or hide and seek. Friends waved to each other. Many a person sat happily watching the world go by, while others wandered without apparent direction, taking in the scent of the flowers that seemed to grow everywhere. The drone of the bees that bumbled from bloom to bloom mixed with the murmur of myriad conversations. Jakh watched it all as if in a trance. Lovers kissed and made eternal promises to each other. Light laughter lulled him and soothed away his worries. A pretty maid smiled coyly at him, then beckoned him to leave Roly and come walk with her. Her eyes were a deepwood green.

'What are you doing?' the knight's voice intruded.

'Sorry?' Jakh asked dreamily, reaching for the maid's hand. 'We've been travelling a long time. We should . . . rest before meeting . . . meeting . . . you know.' The maid began to lead him away through the crowd.

'We should not let ourselves be separated!' Altimius said sharply. 'Jakh, come back!'

'You rest, then, Jakh!' the knight rumbled. 'I will see you back here when all is done. Let us move on.'

'I think we should make him come with us!' Diahn fretted.

'He does not seem to agree,' the knight observed, 'and I am guided by him while we are in the service of Altimius. Were I to try and force him from that comely maid's side, he would probably seek to fight me – I know I would if I were him. Then all sorts of tragedy might occur. No, he will be safer if I leave him here. Come.'

The knight led the hierophant, the priestess and Roly up through the city. They entered a series of streets that were not as well appointed or maintained as earlier ones. A young woman in a grubby red dress but pristinely white apron sat sobbing on a doorstep.

'What is it, child?' Diahn asked with concern.

'Oh, mistress, the physicker says I can never have children. What am I to do?'

'Have faith, daughter,' the priestess reassured her, murmuring a prayer and making a benediction.

The young woman's hands went to her stomach and she looked up in amazement. 'The goddess be praised!' she cried. 'I am healed.'

Seeing what had happened, passers-by echoed the young woman's thanks. A small crowd assembled around Diahn.

'Priestess, my girl is blind and has never known the joy of looking upon the goddess's fair creation. Have mercy, I beg you!'

Diahn murmured another prayer, the girl gasped in delight and many in the crowd fell to their knees. Others called out to neighbours to spread the word.

'Our prayers are answered!'

'We will make offerings to the goddess.'

The crowd swelled. Two women in similar garb to Diahn pushed their way through to her. 'A true priestess is here! Praise the bountiful mother! We are acolytes of Fecundia's temple here in Arla. Our High Priestess passed on a year ago and we have had no one to lead us in the ways of the goddess since.'

'Lead us!' the people begged, kissing the hem of Diahn's robe. 'Save us! Heal us!'

'Help us find our way back into the goddess's favour!'

'We would have you as our High Priestess, if you will have us,' one of the acolytes said, going to her knees in supplication. 'Think of the good our temple can then perform for the kingdom.'

The other acolyte gently pulled Diahn away. 'Lead us, holy mother.'

'Help me, Altimius,' Diahn said softly, but did not spare him or the knight a backward look.

The priestess became lost from view as the needy closed around her. 'She does not want to go with them!' Altimius shouted.

'Her words say one thing, but her actions another. She does not fight them, wizard, does she?'

'She fears to hurt them.'

'Or she needs them as much as they need her. We should move on, wizard, unless you would have me fight the whole of Arla. I thought you wanted me to save your kingdom, not destroy it.'

'Damn my brother and his wiles!' Altimius railed.

'I told you, wizard. Men are fools. Come.'

They went higher and the palace precinct hove into view. The streets here were wide and neat. Each house stood alone and was at least two storeys high. Metal bars were set across large glass windows, which were internally framed by sumptuous velvet curtains, past which ornate chandeliers could be glimpsed. Street entertainers moved up and down the way, performing for families who watched from balconies and threw down small coins. Street vendors called out their wares, the smell of their hot pies and pastries reaching even the highest balcony, and many slippered servants were dispatched from their respective houses to procure the tidbits.

A juggler caught Altimius's eye with fans and fountains of playing cards. With a flick of the wrist, the juggler sent a card spinning at the wizard. The card caught in the wizard's beard and revealed itself as the King of Hearts.

'Throw it back into the pack . . . if you can!' challenged the juggler, holding a large fan up high.

Altimius took the card, stuck out his tongue in concentration and threw the card. It arced and swooped up in the air and became lost from sight.

'Well done!' shouted the juggler, for the card had somehow appeared in the deck. 'Yet it has landed amidst a host of dark clubs here, you see. The king is surrounded by enemies.' The fan was turned over. 'Come, see if you can pluck him from their midst. See if you can save him.'

Altimius approached, eyes fixed on the card he was sure was the king. He reached for it . . .

'Do not,' warned the knight.

. . . and pulled a club.

'Unlucky!' commiserated the juggler. 'A florin's forfeit is now due.'

'I have no money. I will give you a promissory note for the amount.'

'A promissory note is just another playing card to me, and I already have all I need. Instead, I will let you draw again. Find the king and your debt is cancelled. Fail, and the debt is doubled. Come, the odds are more in your favour now one of the clubs has been removed.'

Altimius stuck out his tongue and hesitantly reached with his hand.

'I will leave you here, then, wizard.'

'Eh? Of course, my good fellow. I will be along presently. I must just settle this debt.'

As the knight rode away, he heard the juggler shout, 'Unlucky! Two florins are now due. It seems that not even a king can defeat his fickle fate.'

'You must let me draw again.'

Approaching the palace precinct, the knight lifted his half-helm – from where it was hooked to Bardas's saddle – and placed it on his head. He unstrapped two throwing axes from his kit and slid them into his armour. He buckled spiked greaves to his forearms and checked his blades were clear in sheath and scabbard.

He came to the palace gates, thick oak set into even thicker stone walls. The way was open, except for six knights standing facing him. They wore curiously intricate armour that looked more woodland thicket than metal. The knight suspected his blade would spring off such material without causing much damage, or would become ensnared by it and rendered all but useless. There were flashes of green to be seen, which the knight took at first to be an enamelled leaf design, but as he got closer he began to think they were real leaves. Was the armour somehow alive? How could it possibly be maintained? Magic? Did the armour grow from the knights themselves? Were these green men, then, knights of legend? The Knight of Ages suddenly became wary – and Bardas sensed it, flaring his nostrils, flashing his teeth and raking the ground in anticipation of the command to charge.

The largest of the green knights – who stood taller than Bardas's shoulder, and dwarfed the Knight of Ages himself – stepped forwards. He had a thick, brown beard, circles round his eyes like the rings of a tree and such flat features that they seemed poorly carved.

'I am Sir Sycamon. You are expected, sir knight. I am to conduct you to the King. Dismount, and your animals will be well looked after. You will also leave your weapons here, for they may not be brought into the King's presence.'

The Knight of Ages remained where he was. 'I will not give up my weapons, good Sir Sycamon. You have my word as a knight that I will not use them unless attacked first.'

The green knight's brows drew down. 'I do not impugn your word as a knight, but it is our King's command that all guests disarm themselves before entering into his company.'

'His commands are not mine to obey.'

Sir Sycamon smiled. 'We will be forced to disarm you then.'

'And I will be forced to defend myself. In your determination to obey your King's command, you will all be killed, for honour will not permit you to yield, will it?'

'Or we will kill you,' the green knight grinned. 'There are six of us.'

'And your King will be angry at how you have treated his guest.'

The green knight hesitated. One of the other knights shifted uncomfortably. Apparently, the prospect of the King's anger was not one to be desired.

'Come, Sir Sycamon. You appear to be worthy knights, one and all. You will surely be able to keep the King safe from me. There are six of you, after all, and I have given you my word.'

'Keep your weapons, then!' the green knight growled. 'This way, sir knight. We should not keep the King waiting.'

~

The Knight of Ages was brought into a large hall by the six knights. Groups of velveted nobles and gowned ladies moved aside so that there was a clear passage to the far end of the hall, where steps led up to a dais and throne. Approving stares and whispers followed them all the way.

'. . . Knight of Ages, they say, as brave as he is lost . . .'

'. . . always looking for something . . .'

'. . . a never-ending quest. Some unrequited love, no doubt. A maiden with looks as gentle as they were cruel . . .'

'. . . I could love such a man . . .'

The knight tried to shut it all out of his mind, but he found himself distracted. Then he was looking up at the King, he of the knowing eyes and features as firm as they were forgiving. He was as youthfully handsome as he was wisely self-composed. He had a mesmerising quality, just as a landscape can enchant the eye, a banquet will make a starving man drool, a child can make the elderly smile, gold can obsess a person regardless of wealth, and a beauty can see people swear themselves to any deed. There was more life to him than any other in the room. Every man and woman seemed little more than a shadow in his presence. He rose from his throne – a glistening red and fleshy plant of some sort – and his court fell to its knees. The Knight of Ages unthinkingly lowered himself to the floor, before remembering himself and straightening back up.

The King smiled magnanimously. The six green knights took up guard position on the stairs before the dais. 'Knight of Ages, welcome to the fair city of Arla and my court. We have heard tales of your heroic deeds in far-off lands, and rejoice that you come to us now, when there is some blight or curse afflicting parts of our kingdom. I pray that you can help us in our time of need, and beg you on behalf of all Saluria to enter into our service.'

His thoughts strangely clouded, the knight shook himself. 'I . . . am already in the service of another – your brother, Altimius, he who was Lord Hierophant.'

The court was silent. The King frowned slightly. 'Brother? I have no brother. I think you are misled, sir knight, but no matter. Whatever it is this person offers you, I will double it. Or you can name your price. Tell me your heart's desire and it will be yours. Tell me!'

The court began to whisper again, praising the King for his generosity and speculating on what the knight might ask for. The knight saw himself in the King's black eyes. Images filled his mind. A place in this court of light, this court of life. No need to fight on and on. No need for all the killing, all the death. He was tired, wasn't he? So tired after all the years. He had earned this rest and reward. No more retribution and punishment. No more penance. The shadows of the past would be expelled by the light of this place. There would be no more dead family. Instead, there would only be a living one. See there! A fine lady who loved him more with every passing day. Strong children who carried his name with pride and went on to marry well. Grandchildren who demanded he pretend to be a horse so that they could play at jousting games. It was all there. It was real, more real than the life he had already lived, no matter how long that life had been. That past life was a shadowy dream, one that had no place here in this waking realm of bright and intoxicating life. That past life was ephemeral at best, a whimsical idea like smoke on the wind. It was gone. Nothing of that life or self was left. Nothing.

The light filled him, pushing out all else. Yet the stronger the light burned, the darker became the shadow cast by that which was fixed in him. So dark that it absorbed the light completely. It pulled in more and more of the light, swallowing it hungrily. Your service to me is not yet done, little knight. You cannot be released so easily, as if your dark deeds were never committed. You know the penance required of you!

In monstrous tones, the Knight of Ages answered the King: 'You cannot buy me with the lives of the people, for they are not yours to offer up. You have stolen the lives of too many already, and you corrupt those that remain. I will not suffer you to sit upon the throne. You have no right.'

'No right?' the King seethed, his court wailing in fear and shouting in outrage. 'The seat of power is mine. Its roots spread beneath the entire kingdom. All that grows is because I allow it.

All that dies is at my say so. The seat of power is the kingdom. That is my right.'

'You are responsible for the malaise that affects the kingdom. You are responsible for the death of entire villages. Those still clinging to life are so desperate that they commit the sort of acts only otherwise seen in hell. And all for what? So that you and your lickspittles can become spoilt with a rude and unnatural health.'

'Those villages that have refused the crown sufficient taxes must pay by other means! They must also be punished as an example to others. It is the King's justice. Those that say otherwise are guilty of treason!' the King raged, his eyes blazing and lightning crackling in the air around him.

The shadow lurking within the knight drew in the King's power, instantly snuffing it out. The King swayed on his feet, seeming to dim for a moment, before falling back into his throne. 'I have seen a child die for want of the strength to feed herself. Would you similarly tax a babe before it has had the chance to suckle at its mother's teat? Would you drain an infant before it had lost the residual heat of its mother's womb? For would that not also be your King's justice? Should I say otherwise? You that call the truth treason can only be dishonest and corrupt of nature. I will not permit you to sit the throne a moment longer!' So saying, the knight drew his sword.

'Sir Sycamon, kill him at once! You two, aid my champion. You three, get the prisoners.'

'It will be my pleasure, my King,' the green knight averred, pulling his sword free without hesitation.

The large green knight leapt down the stairs, his sword arcing downwards powerfully. He moved as quickly as a man without armour, but the Knight of Ages was quicker. The Knight of Ages danced backwards and then, as the green knight's sword struck the floor, came forwards and punched out with his own blade. Yet the green knight caught the Knight of Ages by surprise, following the downwards momentum of his sword and ducking beneath the Knight of Ages's thrust. Sir Sycamore's shoulder caught the Knight of Ages in his midriff and started to lift him from his feet. At the same time, the green knight had taken one hand off his sword hilt and pulled a long knife. It now came up with frightening speed, scoring along the side of the Knight of Ages's torso and causing the armour to scream in protest. It was fortunate the leather straps and buckles keeping the hinged backplate and chestplate together were on his other side, or they would already have been separated and the knife would be finding its way between his ribs and into his heart. As it was, the knife would now be seeking a target lower down.

The Knight of Ages made his decision in the instant and pushed off the floor with the balls of his feet, tipping himself headfirst over the back of the green knight. Sir Sycamon collapsed onto his front and the Knight of Ages clattered to the floor behind him. It was far from the most elegant fighting manoeuvre the Knight of Ages had ever used, but it had probably saved him from grievous injury all the same. He sprawled now as the other two knights moved in on him for the kill.

With no time to get up to defend himself properly, the Knight of Ages sent his sword spinning forwards just above the floor. He caught the knight to the right in the ankle just as weight was brought to bear on the joint. The ankle buckled and the knight went falling into his comrade at the same moment as the latter lunged with his sword for the gap between the Knight of Ages's half-helm and plate armour. The incoming sword was knocked off its line and struck the Knight of Ages's shoulder plate instead of sinking into his neck.

Axes came into the hands of the Knight of Ages and he chopped savagely at ankle and knee joints to left and right. The weapons got snagged in the strange armour of the green knights and he let go of them. The blows he had struck had bought him enough space and time to come to his feet, however. He was about to go forwards for his sword, but instinct told him Sir Sycamon was also getting his feet under him. They were momentarily back to back. The Knight of Ages flung himself backwards, bumping the green knight hard and sending him down onto his front for a second time.

'Kill him, you misbegotten dolts!' the King cried. 'What ails you? You fall about like common tavern drunks. Block his path before he makes for the throne!'

Compelled by their King, the knights to left and right threw themselves in front of the Knight of Ages once more, swinging blindly with their weapons. Yet they had come in too close and their swordarms were easily nudged aside. The long knife of the Knight of Ages sank up to the hilt in the eye socket of one of the throne's defenders, and the spiked greave of the other arm made a ruin of the other defender's face.

'Idiots! Must I do everything myself?' screeched the King.

'No!' yelled a grief-stricken Sir Sycamon. 'For Saluria!'

The green knight was charging him from behind. The Knight of Ages knew he would be cut in two long before he could turn round to face his attacker. Instead, he cast his knife backwards over his shoulder, dropped into onto his hands and pushed himself into a backwards slide along the floor. One of Sir Sycamon's heavy feet came down on the back of the knight's left calf, and then the massive bulk of the King's Champion was crushing the Knight of Ages's head and body into the stone floor.

The Knight of Ages was pinned. He wriggled and wormed backwards, his helm scraping between the floor and Sir Sycamon's armour.

'Now I have you, recalcitrant knight!' grunted Sir Sycamon, sliding his long knife under him and stabbing viciously. The tip of his blade caught against the rim of the Knight of Ages's half-helm. Sir Sycamon stabbed again.

The Knight of Ages thrashed wildly, knowing his death could come at any moment. Then he was dragging himself out from under the giant's legs, even as Sir Sycamon pulled himself round. The two knights rose at all but the same moment, Sir Sycamon keeping close the whole time. Stray bits of the green knight's woven armour hooked into the weaponless Knight of Ages and stopped him from pulling away. The long knife came again, digging at an elbow and then darting up at the Knight of Ages's face.

The Knight of Ages pushed down hard on the green knight's knife arm and leaned his own head back till his neck creaked. The blade sank half an inch into his throat! He tasted blood in his mouth. It choked him, but he dared not swallow, for to do so would be to cut his own throat. He tried to wrench his other arm free, but Sir Sycamon had it clamped against his side.

The Knight of Ages spat blood and it spattered down into Sir Sycamon's eyes. The green knight blinked furiously and shook his large ponderous head. For an instant, the movement shifted his balance ever so slightly to his opposite side. The Knight of Ages exerted his entire being to push down on the arm at that precise moment, drawing the tip of the knife out of his throat and pushing it wide, before releasing it and letting it go past and behind him. The Knight of Ages now had his armpit over the top of Sir Sycamon's arm, so the knife could only rake ineffectually against his backplate.

Sir Sycamon's hot and fetid breath was now on his forehead. The Knight of Ages smashed the rim of his helmet into the green knight's nose, splitting his adversary's face wide. The green knight opened his mouth to cry out in pain and the rim obliterated his teeth and mouth. Sir Sycamon tried to push away, but his magical armour bound him tight to his enemy.

The Knight of Ages crunched the helmet into the green knight's face again and again, until the face was an unrecognisable mush. An eyeball had come loose and burst open.

They were on the floor. The green knight convulsed once and then stopped breathing.

The Knight of Ages disentangled himself from the body, picked himself up and glared up at the King. There were whispers from the court, most of whom had retreated as far down the hall as they could.

'Monster!' the King breathed. 'How could you treat such a noble knight in this way?'

'You left me no choice. From the moment I stepped foot in this kingdom, your self-obsessed possession of the throne meant such an act would be inevitable. Given the chance, you would place every single person in the kingdom in my path, give them no choice but to fight for you, and watch them die without ever shedding a tear for any but yourself. You call me a monster because of the graphic nature of Sir Sycamon's death and how it has been played out before this self-indulged audience. What of the children who have died of starvation and despair without any there to mark their passing? Their deaths are less graphic and far more prosaic, I know. They will never have songs and eulogies sung for them. Are their deaths any less monstrous than Sir Sycamon's?' Shadows stirred in his eyes. 'But enough of this. You have been indulged and allowed to live far too long.' His eyes became voids that devoured the King, aging the monarch until all trace of youth was gone and an ancient and cadaverous creature was revealed, its meanness of face and being promising it would steal life and substance however and from whomever it could. It would eat the living flesh off any person. It would drink their blood. It would suck the marrow from their bones. It would see the entire world become a wasteland, all so that it could live.

The Knight of Ages picked up his sword and took a step up towards the throne.

'Hold, self-righteous knight!' croaked the goblin in the throne. 'Another step and the prisoners die. See them there! Your precious squire. My traitorous brother. The prissy priestess.'

The Knight of Ages turned his head. The three remaining green knights had fetched in Jakh, Altimius and Diahn while the knight had been fighting Sir Sycamon. Jakh's hands were bound, his head was ducked guiltily and he looked at his master with abject apology. Altimius was blindfolded, presumably to prevent his magic of translocation, and his shoulders were slumped in defeat. Diahn was gagged, presumably to prevent her calling on Fecundia, but her head was lifted defiantly and there was a pent up fury in her gaze.

'One more step, Knight of Ages, and all you care about will be lost. At my simple command, your companions, cause and meaning will be gone. See, we are not so different, you and I. You will not give them up, because you need them and want to live. And I will not give up the throne and the people, precisely because I need them and want to live. Is it so unreasonable of me to want to live? Every creature has a right to life, whether you approve of that life or not. By what right do you believe it is for you to choose who lives and dies? Such towering arrogance you have. It is insupportable, unconscionable. I am a king. You are naught but a mercenary and itinerant hedge-knight. You should bow to me for my rank alone. If the people would see me overthrown, it is for them to take such steps. It is not for you. How dare you even think to do this! Stand down, I say. Stand down, over-proud and over-reaching wretch. You would have the throne for yourself, I now fear. My good knights and people will not permit it, do you hear? They will tear you down and throw you into the dust. You will be trodden under and your name henceforth will only be spoken by way of curse. That will be all you ever deserve if you take one more presumptuous step above your station.'

The Knight of Ages gave a hollow laugh. 'What say you, Jakh? Would you have me stand down? Every creature has a right to life, whether I approve of that life or not, he says. Doesn't every creature also have a right to its death? Should the King be saved from the knight, the kingdom from the King, or none saved at all? Are none worth the saving? Come, Jakh, what say you?'

'Master, I only know that I have failed you. I have failed our cause. It is my failure and lack that has made me hostage to the evil of this place. My life is not worth all the lives of the kingdom. You cannot hesitate to dispatch this fiend just because of me. It would be the greatest of wrongs otherwise. Though it costs me my life, you must kill him!'

'No! We should not be too rash!' quailed Altimius.

The being that was the Knight of Ages grinned coldly. 'Ah, Jakh, how can you speak of a lack of worth? Only you would seek to sacrifice yourself for people you do not even know.' The knight rose purposefully onto the second step.

The King pressed himself back into his throne. 'Think about what you do. Their deaths will be on your head!'

The Knight of Ages shrugged. 'I have sworn to be ruled by Jakh in this. He commands me.'

The third step.

'You are not a cold-blooded killer, sir knight! I am defence-less. Regicide is the worst of crimes. Your soul will be damned for all eternity!' the King shrieked.

The knight's voice came from another realm, a realm of smoke and heat. 'Thank you for your concern as to this one's soul, but it is already spoken for.'

The fourth step.

The court began to scream and sob in terror.

The King gathered himself, his face becoming malign. 'So be it, demon knight. If you would deny me life, then all will be denied life!' The red throne pulsed with an eldritch and bloody magic, drawing in life from ground and air alike, feeding it into the King's person.

The court's screams intermingled with groans of agony. A beautiful woman visibly withered, all vitality drained out of her. She collapsed to the floor, little more than brittle skin and hair draped over bone. Nobles clutched at their chests, unable to breathe. They writhed on the ground as their faces turned purple, and then moved no more. The remaining green knights were not spared either – they dropped their weapons, too weak to hold them anymore, and their bones snapped like sticks. Jakh cried tears of blood, Altimius keened for forgiveness, jumbling prayer, spell and despair, and Diahn's hair turned white and began to fall out.

The Knight of Ages staggered, hardly able to keep his feet, suddenly feeling all his years and the burden of all the deaths he had overseen. It weighed him down, and his armour crumpled in places, crushing the man within.

The King was transformed. As all fell before him, he rose a magnificent shining being, almost impossible to look upon. 'I am become the godhead of life! See all prostrate themselves before me. Even you, churlish and jealous knight, will kneel and beg my forgiveness.'

Trembling with effort, the Knight of Ages raised his head to meet the King's eye. The knight sneered. 'I think not . . . vainglorious lyche! Enough of your prattle and self-aggrandisement. Come fight me before your tedious words put me to sleep.'

'I will see you sleep forever!' hissed the King as he sprang forwards. 'I will tear the soul from you and torture it without mercy. It will then watch as I visit my vengeance upon your pitiful companions. Never again will any defy my will!'

Something deep inside the knight tore and he was seared to his core. He threw back his head, his silent scream more deafening than any previously heard in the hall. All that he was was inexorably dragged out of him – all his hopes, dreams, heroism, misdeeds, doubts and horror. As the twisting shadow steadily left him and was absorbed by the King, the Knight of Ages was reduced to a broken and pathetic shell, a frail vessel that looked as if it would be destroyed by the gentlest touch or breeze.

The dark maelstrom of power entering the King warped him and allowed him to grow, until he reached nearly as high as the hall. His booming laugh was madly gleeful. 'It is all mine! All life is here within me. I see the entire span of mortal existence: first crawling, then taking tentative steps; finding ambition and spreading its will by sword, thought and invention throughout the realm. Discovering hidden magicks, the conjuration of fell servants and the ways into other realms. Ah, I see it all now. A greater life! I will take these other realms, just as I take your substance and grow ever more. I will take it all in, becoming the universal god!'

'Yes, you have taken it all in,' came the knight's final laboured breaths, 'including your own death. The other realms are forbidden to those that live, for they are realms of darkness and death. If they were not forbidden to the living, there would be no life at all. He coughed blood down the front of his armour, limning its runes. He smiled. 'And you have just grabbed the substance of a fell servant of another realm for yourself. It will end the life in you. Do you not already feel your blood becoming thick and sluggish? Does your sight not descend into gloom? Your heart stutters and slows.'

The King's eyes widened in panic. 'Take it back from me. Get it out! I did not know!'

'Its black oil slips through your veins and into your mind. Its cold numbs you to the centre.'

'There is no need to do this!' begged the King, as his flesh turned grey and he folded in on himself. 'I repent, truly I do!'

'Its sludge blocks your heart and throat.'

The failing creature belched tar, unable to form any more words. It lost its shape and pooled before the throne. It trickled away through gaps and cracks in the stone floor, until all that remained was a sticky and foul-smelling residue on the flagstones. Only then did the last of the shadow that lingered in the air return to the Knight of Ages, before its thin contact with him could be entirely severed or it could be dissipated by some other force.

The only sound was the desperate chanting of nature magic and the repetition of prayers to Fecundia – Altimius and Diahn had apparently been helped free by Jakh, and then they'd been able to protect their small group. They fell silent now.

The Knight of Ages took the last step upwards and approached the throne. It enveloped him in a heady scent, bitter-sweet but strangely sickly. The stimulant triggered thoughts in his mind of glorious struggles for power and the smell of his enemies' rotting corpses on battlefields. He raised his sword.

'Please! Do not!' pleaded Altimius.

The blade cut clean through the thick stem that supported the throne, toppling the seat of power with a thud and squelch. Disembodied screams filled the hall and everything seemed to writhe. Gradually, the tremors subsided and the fugue in the place lifted.

'What have you done?' Altimius hiccupped, tears in his eyes.

'What you never had the courage to do.'

'It could have made me young again.'

'At what price? See, Jakh, nothing has changed in them, despite all that we have done and all that you were prepared to sacrifice. I think that perhaps they deserved this injurious King who sat upon the seat of power.'

'No,' interrupted Diahn. 'We will become better. It will just take us some time to rebuild and remember who we are, to understand who we should be. We do not need the seat of power. Our faith in Fecundia is all we need.'

'Faith will not make me young again,' Altimius mourned.

'Yet it may make you wise one day, you old fool,' Diahn said in not unkindly fashion.

'Will you rule by my side until that day comes?' the Lord Hierophant asked, with a dawning realization.

Diahn nodded. 'That might be the first sensible thing you've asked of me, Altimius.'

'See, master, there is hope.'

'Perhaps,' replied the knight. 'Saluria may know peace and prosperity for some while, but when these two are gone those with selfish ambition will vie once more and provide fertile ground for a new seat of power to grow up in their midst. Then I will have to return.'

'I pray that day never comes,' Diahn said solemnly.

'Pray that it does not, priestess, pray that it does not.'

Some days later, the knight and Jakh sat around the campfire they had built on top of a knoll. They looked out on the Salurian forest below and the stars above.

'What do you think, Jakh?'

'Perhaps more salt, master, but your cooking is definitely improving.'

'You think? The meat was tough.'

'Arguably.'

'And the vegetables burnt.'

'Well cooked, to bring out their flavour.'

'Leaving an unpleasant aftertaste in the mouth.'

'Added reason to drink more of this skin of rather fine Salurian wine, master.'

'So what makes you say my cooking is improving?'

Jakh smiled. 'Because I was pretty certain I could recognise both the meat and manner of vegetable. I do not even have stomach cramps.'

'No fever or shaking?'

'None, master, so it was certainly better than my Salurian slug stew.'

'There is more in the pot if you would have some.'

'Er . . . I am quite replete, master. Absolutely full, in fact.'

'Really? Yet you had such a small helping.'

'We feasted so well in Arla, master, that I will probably never have much of an appetite again.'

The knight chuckled and looked down into their fire. 'So you have had your fill of Saluria and its people, and Bardas and Roly are laden with more gold and provisions than we know what to do with. You must be ready to move onto the next kingdom, Jakh, or are you finally ready to concede it is a waste of time trying to save people from themselves, and that none are truly innocent or deserving?'

'Master, you have too little faith in humankind!'

'And you have too much.'

'Then we are well suited, master. I am ready to leave for the next kingdom, and will stay with you as long as you should have need of a squire.'

The knight grinned. 'We will see, Jakh, we will see.'

The Non-dragon

A J Dalton

'I HAVE COME TO vanquish thee!' bruited the knight, his horse rearing. The sun shone prettily off the killer's plate armour.

She retreated further into her cave and called out: 'Do you really have to? I'm not that bad once you get to know me, honestly.'

'You are a fearsome dragon and a menace to all.'

'No, no! I'm a giraffe. It's really just a case of mistaken identity. I'm here in the middle of nowhere just minding my own business, not doing anyone any harm.'

'You have been troubling the kingdom's sheep. The King has promised his daughter's hand to the valiant knight who slays you.'

'It wasn't me. I'm a vegetarian. It must have been someone who looks like me. Some of my best friends are sheep.'

'You are a fork-tongued beast!'

'Now you're just being plain rude. If I had a forked tongue, I'd thalk all fhunny like thith, wouldn't thigh?'

'Enough! Leave your bed of stolen gold and face me.'

'Stolen? How dare you. It was already here when I found this place.'

'Very well, then I will come in there and find you, worm.'

Partly from fear, and partly in anger at how unfair it all was, she roared at him, the cave amplifying the sound a thousandfold.

The horse shied and skittered backwards. The knight fought to turn his steed back the right way.

She saw her chance and came barrelling out and past him, before he could get his deadly lance back in place. She took to the skies and was away.

It couldn't carry on like this, she knew. Everywhere she went, no matter how remote, they eventually found her. She had only just managed to survive the last few knights, suffering grievous wounds in the process. She had not dared to face this new one.

There was nowhere left to run. She would have to go confront this King.

~

Under cover of darkness, she winged down into the royal gardens of the palace and secreted herself amongst a stand of trees, only snapping one or two of them. Sighing, she settled into wait, dozing with her eyes open.

'Hello!' said the young girl the next morning. 'My, but you're pretty. Do you want to play with me? I'm a princess, you know.'

She blinked. 'Um . . . hello. I'm waiting to meet the King. Is he your father?'

'Yes. I could order you to play with me, you know?'

And I could eat you up. Yes, that would put an end to the knights looking to slay me in order to win your hand in marriage. 'Do you really think I'm pretty? No one's ever said that before.'

'Ooo, but you are. Your eyes are brighter than my cat's. And you're covered in rainbows. Have you seen my cat at all?'

'No. Cats tend to avoid me. Most people do.' *Except knights, of course.* 'You couldn't fetch your father for me, could you? Perhaps I can play with you after that.'

The princess nodded excitedly and ran off. *If I'd eaten her, there would have been outrage and every knight in the kingdom would have been sent after me. Besides, there didn't look to be much meat on her. Scrawny things, these princesses.*

The princess was soon leading a fat and kindly-looking man towards her. Was this the King? The man stopped in amazement.

'Go find the Chamberlain, Isabelle, at once! Tell him there's a dragon in the royal gardens. Tell him to call out the guard!'

As she watched the princess run off again, she said, 'I'm *not* a dragon, you know? Can't you just stop sending all these knights to slay me?'

The King gave her a look of practised sympathy. 'I am of course a reasonable man but, the thing is, the kingdom needs a dragon. And you're it.' He lowered his voice. 'Between you and me, it's very useful you getting rid of my more aggressively ambitious knights, as otherwise they'd only start trouble elsewhere and destabilise the kingdom. With you around, we've never known such peace and prosperity.'

'But that's just it. I'm not going to be around much longer if you keep sending these knights.'

The King smiled and nodded. 'And that's the beauty of it. Whoever slays you will become the people's hero and the kingdom will rally around them. The hero will be named my successor, they will take the hand of my daughter and the people will be happy. See? It works out both ways.'

'Not for me, it doesn't. I could have eaten your daughter, you know, and put an end to all this.'

'Don't worry, I have lots of others.'

'Come to that, I could eat you right now.'

'I see your point, but I don't think that will really change anything. The Chamberlain will continue to administrate things just as he always does, and every knight in the realm will be out to hunt you down, not to mention every farmer and peasant. I doubt you'd live more than a week. Eating me would be a very dragon-like thing to do, to be sure, but you say you're not a dragon, isn't that right?'

'Then I shall find another kingdom.' She knew it was an empty threat even as she said it, for pretty much every kingdom was the same. Humankind was everywhere now. There were no remote places left. There were no peaks distant or inhospitable enough. No caves deep or dark enough. No forests impenetrable and haunted enough. And that was why so few of her kind now remained.

The King looked almost hurt by her last statement. 'Come now, there's no need for that. Look, no one really minds if you take a few sheep here and there. Would it help if I sent, say, only one knight a month?'

'What would really help is if you didn't send any at all! Can't you just accept I'm not a dragon?'

The King shrugged sadly. 'My hands are tied on that, I'm afraid. There's not a lot I can do. You can't deny your own nature, not with such scales, wings and size.'

'But I don't *want* to be a dragon!' she cried.

'Each of us has their role to play. Yours is to be a dragon. Mine is to be a King who sends out brave knights.'

'But you can stop being King if you want to.'

'If only that were true. If I abdicated and tried to live a normal life, people would still *know*. As soon as the new monarch did something unpopular, people would nag me to compete for the throne again. Or the new monarch, anticipating such problems, would send knights to slay me first. Even if I were somewhere no one knew me, there would still be people hunting me. Sound familiar? It should. There's just no escaping it, you see.'

The princess, a stooping Chamberlain and a host of nervous-looking guards suddenly appeared and advanced purposefully towards them. With a bellow of frustration, she took to the skies once more.

~

She flapped on and on, into the night, through rain and storm. She headed north, desperately looking for some sort of wilderness where none would find her for a while.

Exhausted, she finally descended towards a small and deserted-looking farm. The barn was largely intact, so she manoeuvred her way inside and fell into a deep and dreamless slumber.

'Who are you?' a ragged boy asked her the next morning, upon discovering her.

'Oh, just your invisible friend. I am hiding in here because it's out of the way and seems safe.'

The boy gave a serious nod. 'Yes, that's how the raiders missed me. I should like to have an invisible friend, I think. It's lonely now that my family is gone. Would you like something to eat?'

'Do you really have much to spare? You look very thin.'

'Oh, most of the animals were still out in the fields and woodland when the raiders came. There's still quite a few cattle and such about. I just don't seem very hungry these days, you know?'

She grinned at him, trusting that he would not be alarmed by the sight of her teeth. 'Tell you what, if you bring me a sheep, I'll make us dinner. I can even cook it for you. I can breathe fire.'

The boy's eyes went wide. 'Ooo! Can you really? I'd like to see that.'

'Go on, then.'

~

They spent every day together, the boy and his invisible friend. She told him of far off places, of battles with knights and fights amongst dragons. He would listen all agog and then curl up next to her to sleep at night. On the first few occasions like this, he was restless and fitful, presumably with troubled dreams, but soon he was sleeping better. He began to eat better too, and put on a little weight.

As for her, she had never been happier. She could not remember ever having had a proper friend before, someone who listened so closely and found joy in the stories she told, joy she had not realised was in those stories, and joy that she now shared in and learned to appreciate. As with the boy, her wounds healed and she put on a little weight.

Then the cruel-eyed raiders returned, with wickedly sharp metal and a bloody smell about them. In abject terror, the boy fled to her.

And his invisible friend rose up and killed all those men who would so think to hurt others.

'Thank you,' the trembling boy whispered as he kept warm beside her. 'You're the best invisible friend in the whole world.'

She lowered her head and nuzzled him. 'I am your friend, and perhaps not so invisible. For it would seem, after all, that I am a dragon.'

The Dark Arts

A J Dalton

I NEED YOUR HELP. I know that's a lot to ask when you probably don't know me, but I'm trapped and I've run out of options.

The only way I got this message out was to peel my own skin from my body, wash it, dry it and then write on it with my blood. It is the least of the agonies that I have suffered. Physical torment is all but nothing to me now. But what they have done to my soul . . . no, to speak of it might corrupt my good reader.

If you cannot bring yourself to undertake the task of finding and releasing me, I understand. But perhaps you would consider copying this message out onto something more permanent and distributing it to those who might come to my aid more directly?

How did I get here? It's hard to say where it started, where the path began. I still don't know how art and being an artist could have led me to this. Art has always represented beauty and enlightenment to me. I have poured everything into it, my entire life, and now it is my prison.

My talent has always been in sculpture. Clay beneath my hands almost comes to life. The friends I once had used to tell me that they had never seen art that looked so real. One of them though, sweet Jane, would get strangely upset by my creations. She said they watched her and that she could see them moving out of the corner of her eye. I argued that that was no reason to be upset, but in response she would shiver and murmur that there was no knowing what such creatures got up to when no one was looking.

As any sane man would, I dismissed Jane's fears as irrational. There was nothing even in the theme of my work to cause offence. Take my ballerina for example. She is carved with such delicacy and poise that she balances on the points of her toes. It is only a pity that for draconian health and safety reasons she had to be displayed in a reinforced perspex case so that no freak gust of wind would cause her to fall on an unsuspecting gallery visitor. The authorities simply wouldn't listen . . . but I have drifted away from the point and time is short. Then there was my giant eagle with its outstretched talons catching up a dolphin from the crest of a wave. Yes, some few might criticise the work as violent, but it is only violent within the natural order of things – survival of the fittest. It is no more offensive than God's own creation.

In order to demonstrate the virtue of my work to Jane, I decided to carve a life-sized image of her. I toiled until I was dizzy and the marble was smeared with my blood and sweat. When I tried to wipe the marble clean, I only succeeded in spreading the colours of life further over her body. Her cheeks took on a healthy blush and I fancied she was about to breathe.

As was my occasional habit with studies of the female form, I carved her naked. To my surprise and confusion, I found that I was aroused by my own sculpture. It was proof that I had successfully captured or embodied my fantasy of her anyway. She was utterly bewitching.

Suddenly concerned for her modesty and wanting to spare her from the lascivious gaze of others, I decided to clothe her. For all that, I chose a sheer garment, a semi-translucent dress, so that her beauty would not be entirely hidden from the world, so that it could transport the imagination of viewers and give wings to their spirit.

It was with trepidation but also a secret pleasure that I pre-sented her to Jane. She was my greatest piece of work, something towards which I felt more than the normal, self-deprecating modesty of an artist. I felt . . . I felt an affection of sorts for her, as if she were someone who shared my life.

I watched Jane's face, waiting for a flattered and flattering smile of delight to transform her usual, serious expression. I stood at the edge of the precipice. Her frown deepened. The edge began to crumble. Tears started from her eyes.

'How could you?' she cried, pushing my grasping hands aside and fleeing my studio.

My footing went from under me and I fell screaming into the dark abyss. I do not know how far I plummeted but, mercifully, I felt nothing by the time I reached the bottom.

I awoke in a hospital, a pale-faced Jane sat at my bedside.

'J-Jane?'

'Yes, it's me, my sweet. There was a fire. I'm afraid your studio's gone!'

'My sculptures?' I moaned weakly.

'Gone. But don't worry!' she hurried. 'You don't need a sculpture when you can have the real thing instead.'

'Y-you mean . . . ?'

'Yes, I mean me. I can see now you did it all for me. You just didn't know how else to say it, isn't that right?'

'Yes!' I assured her with a mixture of relief and wonder. 'And-and are you okay? Your skin's so white. Like marble . . .'

'I'm not surprised. I've been worried sick about you. I'll be okay after some sleep.'

And that was it. We moved in together as soon as I left hospital and one of the happiest times of my life began. Before, I'd never even dreamed that Jane and I might share a life together. In fact, it felt exactly like a dream. Even now, my memory of the time has that surreal fogginess that you normally associate with things seen and heard within the sleeping mind.

Where Jane had once seemed so set against my art, she now seemed as obsessed with it as I was. That made me love her all the more. As she helped me to see things in totally different ways, she became like a guide on whom I was entirely dependent.

She helped me see that previously I'd been limiting myself by trying to create sculptures that mimicked real life. I had to break through those limits and rules if I was ever going to be free as an artist and realise my full potential. I had to throw off the shackles of the physical world and start giving form and expression to the non-physical world, the spiritual world if you like. That was the beginning of my spiritual journey, I would say.

It may not surprise you to hear, therefore, that Jane and I were not intimate physically. We did try once but she was stiff and her flesh felt cold beneath my hands. I didn't really mind about that because my work and my spiritual life with Jane were fulfilling enough. In many ways, the very idea of a physical display of our love for each other seemed inappropriate or wrong somehow. It was at odds with what we were trying to achieve between us. It threatened to turn our spiritual pursuit into something quite base or self-indulgent, something backward and bestial.

My world, my physical world anyway, shrank to the size of my new studio. I worked longer and longer hours as I became desperate to free myself as an artist and my work. Always, I felt the goal was just beyond my reach but that if I could just strive that little bit harder, I would finally discover that true and absolute artistic expression of spirit. It began to feel like the breakthrough might almost be some transcendental or semi-religious experience.

I started to work frenziedly, often forgetting to eat. I only stopped when fatigue caused my vision to blur and my chisel to slip from my grasp. There were moments of such utter exhaustion that I would start to cry and be about to collapse, but it was at such times that Jane would be there to steady my hand and help me on for vital minutes more. Once a piece had been started I dared not stop, lest I lose my grip on its direction and inspiration. With Jane's help, I would find I could work through the dizziness and access reserves of energy I'd never known I had. My frequent light-headedness also helped to free my work, as it gave it a surreal aspect and a sense of an altered state.

As you would expect, I lost a large amount of weight, but I hardly noticed it. Indeed, it was somehow fitting that as I diminished physically, my work grew spiritually. It told me I was on the right path and coming ever nearer my destination.

In the traditional sense, the subject of my work became less and less recognisable. But it managed to speak more directly to the spirit than anything I had done before. With each new piece I completed, the closer I felt I was to crossing over into a purely spiritual world. I knew it would be a place where my spirit would soar free, finally unfettered.

And then it happened. The clay I worked with simply quickened. It ran hot like lava and behaved as if it had a life of its own. It continually morphed from one shape into another, responding to my haphazard thoughts. Surely this was the very stuff of creation!

What emerged from it was a giant black skull with molten material flowing from its mouth and nose. I was confused by where such an image had come from but did not question it. Instinct was everything. I moulded a pool to contain the fire-bright liquid and then constructed a path leading up to and away from it. Just carving single pieces of art no longer seemed adequate – I needed to build a whole world from and for my art.

Wiping sweat from my brow, I looked up to see what I had created. Here was a strange, nightmarish world organised around the path I had laid out. I frowned as I realised my studio was gone and there was no obvious way to get back there. The real world was apparently lost to me now and I was trapped in a prison of my own making.

Panicking, I ran along the path, frantically searching for a way out. A giant blade swung backwards and forwards at the end of the path. Where had it come from? I realised that it must represent the shears the fates use to cut the thread of a man's life. It was also a terrifying warning to any unwary traveller who might accidentally happen upon this place.

'Jane!' I screamed into the night, but all that came back was the lonely and forlorn soughing of the wind. Where had she gone? My guide, my mentor, my love, the very essence of my art and life? Had she abandoned me?

I flew back along the cursed path on the dark wings of my spirit, casting left and right to see if she were somewhere here and in trouble. But nothing. I hurtled on as far as I could, only to find myself back at the path's origin again. Had I come in a circle or got turned around in my desperation and anxiety?

Surely not. It was this insane place. The normal rules of nature just didn't apply. It had been designed and developed by my deluded and internally-focussed mind. I sat down on a rock at the side of the path and brooded. Perhaps I'd spent my entire life going in circles and getting nowhere.

Should I just give up? No, I had to hope I might someday find Jane . . . or had she just been another one of the sculptures from my deluded mind? I didn't know anymore. What I did know was that I'd found a way to leave a world before, so surely could do it again. I considered the dark volcanic rock all around me. Perfect. There were pieces of hard obsidian which I was confident I would be able to use to carve the softer surrounding rock. And there were even some pieces of pumice that would serve as a fine abrasive to create smooth surfaces.

I set to work. Time was meaningless in this twilight world and I didn't seem to require any food or drink. And I didn't suffer from fatigue at all. Inevitably, the first thing I sculpted was an image of Jane, but the rock refused to come to life. I gazed upon her for a long while and found myself soothed by the sight of her.

I was calmer and more thoughtful when I started the next piece. I chose an isolated promontory of rock out in the middle of an expanse of water and began to turn the whole thing into a colossus. It was a hundred feet tall, so would be seen from many miles away, not that distance or scale really seemed to mean much in this world except in relation and comparison to my own physical person.

I carved the torsos of a man and a woman fused in an eternal embrace. Where their waists met, I carved them sharing a single pair of legs. Long before I'd finished the enormous statue, I knew it could never become animated, since the defining theme of the work insisted the embrace never end. I contemplated the symbiotic couple and realised it represented Jane and myself. I had created her from myself and in so doing had trapped myself in that eternal embrace. It would not be within my own power, then, to free myself. I would absolutely require someone else to free me. But who would be able to find me here? Only another lost soul.

Then, another – more horrific – realisation came to me. If I was indeed trapped in the embrace of my sculpted art, then I myself might start to become like stone. I looked down at my hands – they did seem to have lost their normal colour, and the skin was somehow harder! Was my movement slowing down too?

In something of a panic, I have now cut a piece of skin from my body, used my blood as ink and a piece of obsidian as a stylus, in order to write this gruesome narrative for you, my dear reader. I pray that someone has found these words and told others of my desperate plight. I only hope that my tale has been coherent enough for you to understand what happened to me but also to give you enough information so that you might devise some way of freeing me. I must confess I do not know myself how you might do it and I fear any attempt might put you in danger.

If you cannot help me then I would but beg two things of you. Tell others of me so that I will not be forgotten by the world, and so that there might be hope for me in the future. And then, if you should ever find or hear of my Jane, please, please tell her that I love her and that I have not chosen to abandon her.

I'm sorry to have asked all this of you but this is my end, I'm afraid. My eyesight is failing, my blood no longer flows as it once did and I can hardly move this makeshift stylus.

A fragmentary document found amongst the personal effects of the spiritualist and medium Dr Anthony Anders, whose whereabouts are still unknown.

Rusalka

Nadine West

S HE KNOWS THAT it is futile to measure the weight of water. Look. You can see her there, in a white gown, in a white tiled room, her palms outstretched, lifting them higher as the ripples wash over them. Her wrists are wet now. If you look very closely, you can see the sheen on her skin. Silvered, colder. Skin drawing itself tighter over her bones to find her body's heat.

And still, she tries. But she cannot measure water. I know. I know because I live in it. I know how to move inside it, and I have learned how to pool, and fall, and break. I sound out the deep places in my own dimensions.

Look again. You can see her, if you shift your gaze a little, towards the polished sheet of metal that serves as a mirror in this place. No glass, not here. Glass might tempt her to draw her hot blood up and outwards, might whisper its silver verses to her poor, faltering mind and make its thin, hungry suggestions there: she will think she sees heat, and colour, and something red opening between the bones of her wrist, hot, longing, like a mouth. But metal is quiet enough. Look through the distortions – you can see, can you not, how the bars on the windows bend inward? How the perpendicular copper pipe of the hot water system begins to undulate, an uneasy reddish serpent swaying through its own reflection? Ah, you do see. I can trace the paths that your eyes take, following the straight lines as they fold in on themselves. But if they come, the hard-handed men and women in white overalls, do not tell them about these things. If you tell them that straight pipes seem bent, that bars dance towards each other, they will not think to look behind you, to the mirror, to see the truth. No, they will tenderly, caringly bind your hands with leather tawses and lie you on a shining metal trolley, and gently roll you down a corridor without windows.

She knows these things to be true. They tell her they want to cure her, to take away the voices. But there are things behind her that they cannot see. And there are voices. They are mine.

~

'Mama?'

'Yes, dear?'

'Do you see a person in the lake?'

'A person? Now? With the frost coming? May the fool freeze, then, and the devil take them.'

'No, not now. But sometimes.'

'When, then? A fisherman? A washerwoman?'

'No. Not them. Somebody . . . else. I don't know.'

Her mother watches, warily. But the child is smiling, bright-eyed. Child? No. Her mother must be truthful. This daughter who sits at her table is perhaps something more than a child. The mother watches, closely. Is there something antic in her movements? Is there a wildness underneath her skin that makes her shift and turn when she ought to be sitting still and shelling peas with her indoor apron on? Her mother is silent. She knows there are many things that can happen to a young girl who wanders, feckless, like her brothers do, in the woods. The fire dances. The girl seems to have forgotten her question, and has taken a fat pea-pod and is holding it up to the fire's light, as if to see through it. The drops of water from the cracked old bowl glisten, and her eyes glisten, and she tilts her head a little, like a hungry bird.

'Maybe,' she says, still gazing at the pod, and her fingers, and the light reflecting from the droplets, 'maybe there is somebody else.'

The mother suppresses a shudder. A sense of an old tale moves through her like a chill in winter.

Is the child witched? Or taken? For in this place, the old tales are not so old, and all the gas lamps in the world cannot quite send every spirit and every creature back into the shadows. But it is a shame upon a family to call on a wise woman to whisper her words, these days, and the priest would frown, and turn them away from the bread and wine with his old head slowly shaking. Well then, is the child ailing? For in these days of telegrams and artificial light, the doctors come with their black bags and their silver tools and their silver tongues, and tell the well folk that they sicken, and take their silver coins for their trouble. She asks herself these questions as she bends to see her own face in the low sink, and washes her hands.

No. She will send for no one.

Not for this child.

Not yet.

⁓

I have been here for a long time. How long? Since your great-grandfather's grandfather walked the fields in his own grey father's boots. Since your great-grandmother's grandmother whispered to her silver-whiskered mother that she had spilled her first blood. I have lived in this place before they mapped it. I have lived in it as they drew down the land and trapped it on paper, cut the ground into pieces with different names and gave the maps to different kings. I was here when they tore up the paper and sent bright young boys to bleed on its black earth so they might change its name and kneel in the dust at the feet of another king. But the dust is always the same dust, and the king is always a king. When the boys fall, by the arrow or the bullet, it is me they feel in the mud against their cheeks, and in their mouths as they gasp in their last air. When the kings sleep, it is me that laughs outside their windows, or watches placidly from their castle moat, their pleasure lake, their gold-plate pitcher by their bedside through the dark hours, the ice that dances a tinkling mazurka inside its shining skin. The king and the soldier both. No one can live, or die, without water.

~

'Papa?'

'Yes, dear girl?'

'When you sleep, do you hear people talking to you, in your mind?'

'Yes, my darling. In my dreams.'

'Papa?'

'Yes, my little dancer?'

'When you walk in the woods, do you hear people talking to you, from the air?'

'Yes, my darling. For the hunters and the farmers and the mushroom pickers range through the woods, and their voices come to me on the soft east wind.'

'Papa?'

'Yes, my gift? My only girl, child of my age?'

There is a silence. She breathes. Somewhere beneath her cheekbones, a shadow stirs itself.

'When you bathe, and drink, and walk beside the lake, and when it rains, do you hear someone talking to you in your ear?'

The father says nothing. He narrows his eyes and wets his lips with vodka and iced water. He folds his hands softly and watches the sun set.

~

In her cell, she puts one arched foot in front of another, and then behind, and then again in front. You can see her through the slit, at eye level, in the green metal door. You might think she dances. The ceilings are high here, the lights lying flush along their flatness so no one will think of securing something from them, their nightgown, perhaps, and winding the white sleeves slowly about their neck like the embrace of a lover, and then, perhaps, for a moment, taking to the air and flying. She does not, for the moment, think of jumping. She dances by herself, and sings a little, her voice hoarse and broken, the soft places of her throat raw: they use a rough-edged tube and a metal clamp because they want to help her, because she will not eat. There is a pitcher of water on a low stool beside her bed. She wets her lips. She makes it last.

~

Vodyanoi. Lorelei. Rusalka. Nix. My names sound like charms. Say them enough and you might summon me, one quiet night when the moon waxes full and pulling, and I cannot help but rise. When the land and the people change their names as trees change their leaves, nothing keeps its one true name for long. Speak me in whichever tongue you please. I will hear you. Question me: I know the answers by rote.

Question: do you come from the water, or do you live inside the water, or are you soul of the water, one and the same?

Answer: yes, most certainly, and other things besides.

Question: do you sing to sailors at sea?

Answer: I sing. I have a voice and I have reasons enough to lift it in song. The sailors will have their own reasons for listening.

Question: do you give chase to water-craft, and dash their wooden ribs against the rocks, and spill the blood inside them?

Answer: a thing that comes when called is never chased. And the rocks do what they must, and if they hunger, it is not of my making.

Question: do you call to men and maidens, the most beautiful of their people, and take them down to sleep in the green, cold chambers that lie beneath?

Answer: what is beautiful? What is deep?

What is a man? What a maid?

How do you know?

How do they?

I like to answer questions. But there is a question you have not asked. I can feel it, smell it, hear it writhe in your lungs and twist behind your teeth. I will tell you a story, then, and you can hear the answer in your own way.

~

Once upon a time, only a moment ago, and now, in this moment, somewhere between dusk and moonrise, a girl turns her strong, young back to her mother's cottage and follows her feet forwards, until she comes to a lake. The banks are shallow; green reeds grow, but the water laps against the low places without breaking, and there is no foam, no spray, no brackish taste of salt hanging in the air. Her slippers are brown leather, sewn with gut, and they dampen, just a little, in the mud. A faint line grows upwards, darkening the hide and swelling like a bruise towards the fine bones of her ankles. She looks out across the lake, her eyes on the horizon. She looks towards the other side, misty now, sliding from view in the waning light, little more than a handful of simple, shining things winking at the darkness: fires, lanterns, gas-lamps, the gold dome of the church catching something else's light and scattering it away. She sees all of this, and smiles, and then, leaning forward and lowering her bright eyes, she looks into the water.

The lake rises a little, and falls, and rises again. Something like a heartbeat. Something like the tightening of the skin on a drum. There is a skin on water. You can mark it, scar it. The feet of the water-insects tickle it into dimples. The girl looks into the water, and her eyes burn, and her face is living, and amused, and her lips part slightly as she reaches forwards.

There is a skin on water. Things can rise through it. I rise. She reaches. Her white hand slides in, and is surrounded. Skin on skin.

In the black pupils in the centre of her black eyes, something blossoms.

~

Here she is, now, by the windows. Beyond the bars, and the sheet of plastic that keeps the glass out of reach, and the glass, and the spaces between them, there is a wide green lawn with a path like a smile running through it. Beyond that, an ornamental pond. Beyond that, an orchard, and a stream. They like the residents to tend the orchard, their slow eyes and clumsy hands, numb with cold and chlorpromazine, kept occupied with the business of apples. They stand beneath the trees, the hard-handed men and women who nurse the lost ones, smoking cigarettes and laughing at the lumbering, fumbling bodies that lurch between the trees. Rotten fruit, they murmur, their quick, un-medicated eyes darting between the figures in grey coats and white gowns. Fallen. Stinking. Worm-eaten.

She is not allowed in the orchard. The first time they took her there, after her arrival, her feet still healing from the wounds that the river-bed rocks had torn in them, she had broken free and run towards the stream, a high, keening noise rising from her and filling the orchard until even the slow-eyed others turned their faces upwards, stopped picking, laid down their fruit and listened to the ghostly sound that tangled with the branches above their heads. The second time, she had lain down in her thin shift, in the dewy grass, and soaked the thin fabric right through, and wept. There was not a third time. They keep her inside, now, and she sits in a high-backed chair by the window, and watches.

It does not matter. There is a slight smile at the edges of her lips. I still tell her stories, at a distance. In the water pipes that wind their way around the walls of this vast place, in the softness of these Autumn afternoons, I croon to her.

~

Watch her. She dives. In the lake before her parents' house, she moves like a silver-tipped weapon through the air. Thinner now, weaker, her hair a cat o'nine tails thrashing behind. But she dives.

Is this love? I move around her, under her, between her fingers and in the corners of her smile. A boy came to court her, and her parents let him in. He laid his hand upon her and she hurt him, she says to me, her lips cracked and sore with defiance. She shattered a glass, used its teeth. He whitened as he bled. He will not use his right hand to catch rats again. Or to catch at girls' bodies as they move past him in the woods, she says. And we spin again, and she comes up for air and lifts herself away from me for a broken, heart-sore moment, and the world stops and somewhere in the skies above us the clouds forget how to rain, because I feel nothing but her absence.

Then she is back, her strong hands and feet pushing her further beneath the surface.

Here, beneath, something happens to the sounds of the world.

Birds quieten, but their songs still seep in, somehow, lissom and coiling like smoke. Voices spill and soften. Leaves fall, flatten themselves against us, but they become patterns on the surface of the water when seen from below. The intricate geometry of light and leaf and red and yellow, turning slowly above us. A map of the world. Continents and oceans, and we are floating somewhere else, and watching it, and our soft laughter fills the spaces around us with shining bubbles that rise, and rise, and never burst.

She opens her eyes. Nothing has changed, but there is a shiver beneath the surface.

One finger on her lips, she lifts herself upwards.

There, on the banks of the lake, set back, are three dark figures. The sky is white with snow that has not happened yet. They rest against the whiteness, blackly, anticipating something.

Her mother. Because these things are a woman's work.

Her priest. Because a witched daughter is still the devil's business, and the business of a fat man with wine on his breath, who stands while others kneel.

And a doctor. Because they have told him that disease of the mind is like disease of the body, and given him a white-walled building and a black leather bag of pills to cure it or kill it. He looks at her, and she can see his hot mouth open wetly, and his white breath spill out and tangle towards her.

She screams, and it slips through the hills and makes the rocks ache.

She screams, and I feel the shaking in her bones.

~

She is good today. Quiet. Peaceful. They used to make her stand with only her skin on, in the middle of a bath made of tin and painted poorly by her lunatic sisters, and sponge her down with hard, sore strokes. They would stare at her skin as they did so, and she would feel bruised afterwards. There is so little softness left. Her whiteness is like the ice that forms at the top of the pitcher: a finger's touch could split it. If she is good, they tell her, they will reward her.

A blanket to warm her.

Sweet things: honey, with her bread. An apple. A pear.

A room alone, to wash herself with her own hands.

~

'Doctor?'

'Yes, my dear?'

'Am I here because of the voice that I hear?'

'Yes, dear girl. And because you harmed yourself, and others, and me.' He extends one white, hairy wrist, thrusts it out of his sleeve, where it has been sleeping. A pink scar like a worm seems to be healing, a crust still on it.

'If the voices stop talking to me, can I leave?'

'Have they stopped talking to you, child?'

She says nothing.

'Don't you want to be well?'

She blinks. Guileless.

~

Look. You can see her there, in a white gown, in a white tiled room, her palms outstretched, lifting them higher as the ripples wash over them. Her wrists are wet now. If you look very closely, you can see the sheen on her skin. Silvered, colder. Skin drawing itself tighter over her bones to find her body's heat.

It is a reward, they have told her. She has eaten. Fattened. Smiled as they combed her hair and seemed to take pleasure from her own prettiness. She has nodded her head to the piano that one kind nurse plays in the late afternoons. She has taken water without weeping, or shuddering, or crying out, and she has picked daisies from the lawn in company and made them into green and white chains. She has shown a suitable interest in new slippers.

They are pleased, the nurses. She has been a good girl. And now she is alone, and she fills her hands and lifts them, and slides lower, until she is covered.

I do not breathe. Nonetheless, the white walls seem to hold their breath.

'My love?'

Yes, my darling.

'Have you missed me?'

Yes, impossibly.

'Will you hold me?'

I will never let you go.

Her kiss, when it comes, feels like something deep inside me breaking. Ice, aching, melting, beginning to rain. And when she breathes me in, twice, three times, we dance again, if only for a moment. And she lies then, so still, so pale, so beautiful.

Silvered. Colder.

Later, when they find her, and their cries fill the silence, and their hard, capable hands lift her up and carry her away, they do not notice the way the water thrashes against the high walls of the tub long after they have broken its stillness, cracked through the surface and maddened the depths. The way it rocks wildly for a time. The way it refuses, stubbornly, to drain. They believe that the lake overflows its banks because the snow melts into it. They hear the high keening within the pipes, and they think, perhaps, that they ought to send a telegram to the engineer and the undertaker both, this afternoon.

The sound persists until, late that evening, they wash and dress the body.

Until I kiss her goodbye.

~

It is an ending, of a sort. Ah. You have one more question. I can feel it scratching against your tongue. Ask it freely, and I will answer.

Question: is it loneliness I feel, after years without number, as another lover becomes still and cold and I surrender them? Is it grief, when I sing, and the one who used to hear my voice has gone across into the shadows?

Listen. Perhaps you hear but do not understand.

Answer: how can I be lonely when you have spent so long listening to my voice? You have stayed with me so calmly, so sweetly, and I have told you my stories. You are still here. You have known my names, and murmured them into the quietness of your room.

Do not be afraid.

Bathe, dive, drink deeply. I will not hurt you.

Vodyanoi. Lorelei. Rusalka. Nix.

I am all around you, and part of you.

After all, no one can live, or die, without water.

The Nine Rules of the Nisse

Matthew White

Hailey Skjervold meets the Nisse

HAILEY SKJERVOLD HAD always wanted to meet a Nisse. But when she finally met one she nearly trod on him. It was not really her fault, because her eyes were gummed shut. She blundered to the sink, and missed squashing her dog – and the little man sitting on her dog.

She splashed her face down and stared at her dripping, crimson reflection in the window.

'Hello!'

Hailey Skjervold turned and looked around. She saw no-one, so she wiped her face dry and tried looking again.

Her dog, Neville, was sitting calmly on the kitchen floor, his paws in one of her crimson footprints. This in itself was unusual: Neville was a Jack Russell, and he was always whimpering, hiding from noises or running from the local birds. He was even scared of his own reflection.

But it wasn't Neville's stillness that surprised Hailey Skjervold. It was the tiny bearded man who sat on Neville's back and gave her a bright, fidgety smile.

'Hello!'

Hailey Skjervold was a 14-year-old day-dreamer; neither, according to Ida Tueboll, was she very intelligent. But she was not rude, despite what Ida Tueboll might tell you.

'Hello,' she replied.

'Why, pray, are you covered with . . .'

The little man jumped off Neville's back and skittered over to Hailey, his bare feet clicking on the floor. He gave her boots a tiny sniff, and then jumped back onto the dog.

'. . . the blood of a pig?'

'Ida Tueboll tipped it on me.'

'Why did she do that?'

'Because she is Ida Tueboll. Are you a Nisse?'

The Nisse smiled even more. He bowed.

'I am the kindly soul who has been washing your laundry, attending to your cattle and bringing you good luck.'

'Well, Mr Nisse, it's good to have you on board. Now if you'll excuse me I need to have a bath.'

'Of course! A clean Human is almost as fine as a clean house. If we both follow the Rules of Nisse then everything will be fine and happy!'

And with that, the Nisse disappeared in what quickly became his usual way: he jumped off Neville the dog and ran out of the kitchen.

Hailey watched him go, before giving Neville an absent-minded pat and heading upstairs – condemning Neville to an hour of torture as he tried to lick the blood from his own head.

Hailey Skjervold takes a bath

Hailey Skjervold ran a second bath. The first had quickly taken on the appearance of blackcurrant soup.

She lay back, rested her head and let her mind drift away into deep thought.

She thought about her Parents. She hadn't seen them for weeks: they were busy being famous, but the occasional phone call would have been nice. It was nearly Christmas after all.

Hailey Skjervold loved Christmas, and she did not want to spend this one with just Neville and Rasmussen. Whilst Neville was the perhaps the greatest dog of all time, Rasmussen was probably the worst housekeeper of all time.

She was sure that Rasmussen had troll blood in her. The way she broke things, and set fire to things . . .

And then there was Ida Tueboll.

Ida Tueboll chose an enemy for each of her major quadrants at school.

In sport she hated Mirjam Ostvedt because Mirjam Ostvedt was best at 100m.

Academically she had picked Runar Sunde because Runar Sunde was the only person better than Ida Tueboll at maths. Runar Sunde was useless at everything else, but maths was his thing.

In artistic pursuits she hated Warren Trusso because Warren Trusso had once done a better Lady Macbeth.

And then, in general life, she hated Hailey Skjervold. Not because Hailey Skjervold was particularly amazing at anything, but precisely because Hailey Skjervold was NOT very good at anything. She had to pick at least one enemy based on reasons other than jealousy.

Ida Tueboll had sat Hailey Skjervold down to tell her this.

'But why pick me? Why not pick Lotte Bjorge? She is intelligent and popular and well dressed.'

'Because Lotte Bjorge is intelligent and popular and well dressed. But you are dumb, lonely and a mess. You don't offend anyone, you just float around reading your picture books and dribbling, and talking about gnomes and Huldra and Nisse . . .'

Nisse.

Hailey Skjervold stopped her daydreaming and stood, the last of the blood running from her hair.

She had just spoken to a Nisse.

Hailey Skjervold was a good person. She did not lie, and she always handed her homework in on time.

But she did spend a lot of time thinking about magical beings, and wishing, quietly so no-one would laugh, that one day she would find out that they were true.

That somewhere, in this dull old world of bullies and useless housekeepers, something magical really existed.

Hailey Skjervold quickly reached for her towel.

Hailey Skjervold makes porridge

That night Hailey Skjervold sat at the dining room table, bowl of porridge steaming away in front of her.

Hailey knew her Nisse, and she knew that they loved their porridge. So she waited until Rasmussen fell into her nightly drunken slumber before preparing piping hot porridge.

It cooled down. So Hailey reheated it.

But the porridge became thick and the stirring noises had made Neville whimper and run out of the room.

So Hailey added more milk, which cooled the porridge down.

So she had to heat it up again,

By the time she decided that the Nisse was not coming she had managed to get through six pints of milk.

That night she lay awake, deep in thought.

Hailey Skjervold was a nice person. But she was NOT tidy.

Rasmussen had 'I will not be expected to clean the girl's room' written into her housekeeping contract, and the last time Hailey had cleaned out her room she had filled half a skip with rubbish.

Every night she navigated the pile of dirty clothes, discarded wrappers, mouldy peel and printing paper.

But tonight, looking out over her room, she did indeed see that stains had gone from the walls. She could see out of her window again. And her clothes were in the drawers.

So she had no doubt that the Nisse was real. But he had not eaten her porridge.

Hailey Skjervold realised that she needed to know more about Nisse.

So the next day, at lunchtime, she snuck off to the school library. She did not need to worry about Ida Tueboll today: it was Friday, and Friday was Ida's day to terrorise Runar Sunde.

So Hailey Skjervold was able to read in relative peace. She knew the book she was after – all she had to do was ask the Librarian for the weird book about folk tales. The Librarian gave Hailey Skjervold her usual look, which meant 'In principle I am glad that you are reading but I was pomading my hair' and fetched the book.

Hailey Skjervold placed the book on the desk and wiped off the pomade fingerprints.

When she read the title page '*The Weird Book About Folk Tales*' she gave a little shiver. Every time.

Hailey Skjervold used to have lots of books – at least thirty in fact. They were all folklore, fantasy or monster books. She loved her book collection, and took great care of them, until the fateful day that Rasmussen had called, in her diary, 'That Day I 'Accidentally' Burnt That Silly Girl's Books.'

Hailey Skjervold did not buy any books after that. She suspected that Rasmussen would 'accidentally' burn them again.

Instead she relied upon the school library, and she had read every book in there that had folklore, fantasy or monsters at least twice. That made twelve books, and at least 24 readings.

The Weird Book About Folk Tales was a favourite, but she did not have a photographic memory, and Nisse were not really her favourite creature (in order of preference, they were the Gnome, the Huldra and the Wolverine, which she knew was not mythical but was still pretty monstrous).

Haile Skjervold did not have a photographic memory, but she knew the book well enough to find her section very quickly: pages 62 to 70: 'The Rules of Nisse'.

She settled down and began to read, mouthing the words to herself, oblivious to the yells as Runar Sunde threw himself around the quadrangle outside, trying to dislodge the angry ferret from his hair.

Hailey Skjervold applies the rules

That night Hailey Skjervold carried the bowl of porridge, steaming and just right, to the table.

She placed it down. . . and watched it hit the floor.

She looked around – the table had moved a couple of feet to the left. She surveyed the cracked bowl, the steaming porridge and just-so-molten butter running into the tiles, and she noticed Neville prancing around the newly relocated table.

As she cleaned the floor she allowed an idle thought to escape: page 62 of The Weird Book About Folk Tales said:

'Rule #1: Nisse are very strong.'

But she pushed that thought away. She did not even pay attention to Neville's prancing, because Neville never pranced. She had often seen him skulk, creep, and scuttle – particularly when the birds were out – but she had never seen him prance.

Hailey Skjervold was focussed on getting the porridge just right – applying what she had read on page 68 of The Weird Book About Folk Tales:

'Rule #7: Nisse adore piping hot porridge – but only when it is served with the best butter.'

So the porridge was piping, and the butter was the best that Hailey Skjervold could buy – smooth, creamy and with that farm fresh taste.

As she watched it, the lovely butter sank into the white slick porridge and spread its beautiful yellow goodness.

And then it dried, congealed and went cold, and Hailey Skjervold fell asleep.

Hailey Skjervold had forgotten rule #2 on page 63:

'Nisse never come when called.'

Hailey Skjervold wakes up

The second time Hailey Skjervold met the Nisse she nearly missed him, because her eyes were gummed shut.

This time, however, there was no pig's blood involved – just porridge.

She wiped her eyes clean and stared.

There was the Nisse, tucking into the cold porridge with congealed butter as if it were the greatest meal he had ever eaten.

His little arms were a blur as he shovelled food into his mouth – which gave the impression of remaining open and accommodating the food like a garage accommodates a car.

The occasional glub of porridge flew off the spoon, incapable of keeping up with the Nisse's lightning fast hands.

Hailey Skjervold blinked – she could barely believe what she was seeing, but not what she was hearing.

That was because the Nisse ate in absolute silence, as Neville sat still below him, and gazed adoringly.

And then, just like that. . . he was finished.

He closed his mouth, turned to Hailey Skjervold and smiled.

'Hello again!'

Hailey Skjervold hesitated.

'Hello.'

'You hesitated. Is there something amiss?'

'Yes, I . . .'

But Hailey Skjervold had to stop what she was saying. The Nisse leapt out of his chair onto the table. He pulled a tiny handkerchief out of his back pocket and, with a couple of barely perceptible flicks, he had wiped up every last trace of porridge – even from inside the bowl.

He sat back down, giving his bare foot the tiniest wipe as he did.

'Please continue.'

Hailey Skjervold stammered, and when she found her voice it was husky.

'The porridge.'

'Yes. The butter was divine.'

'But . . .'

'Ye-es?'

'It was not piping hot.'

For the briefest moment a different emotion flashed across the Nisse's face, but his voice was calm.

'Never?'

'Well. . . it was piping hot – but a long time ago.'

The Nisse laughed. As he did he quickly moved the bowl a couple of inches to the side.

'Are you simple?'

Hailey Skjervold nodded. The Nisse's laughter was so good humoured that she couldn't stop herself from giggling.

'Rule number seven: Nisse adore piping hot porridge – but only when it is served with the best butter.'

'Yes.'

The Nisse moved the bowl back to its original place.

'The rule says piping hot.'

'Yes.'

The Nisse slapped his breeches and guffawed – he struggled to get the words out.

'But it does not say when it has to be piping hot!'

Hailey Skjervold guffawed. She almost slipped off her chair. Neville danced a little jig around the table.

And, just as suddenly as he had finished the porridge, the Nisse stopped laughing. He gave Hailey Skjervold a serious look, and told her, in the kindest way possible,

'Of course, from this moment onwards that rule means: piping hot 'pon the moment of eating.'

And with that he leapt from the table, straight onto Neville's back.

Hailey Skjervold opened her mouth to gasp, but she stopped herself when she saw how relaxed Neville was – and how good the little saddle and stirrups looked on him.

'Well fare well this night my simple dear. Sleep well and keep learning your rules!'

The Nisse raised a hand, and Neville turned and trotted from the room. Hailey Skjervold raised a hand in return and watched them go.

That night she went to sleep with a big goofy grin on her face – after she had spent another twenty minutes memorising the rules.

Hailey Skjervold looks up Ida Tueboll's nose

Hailey Skjervold was glad that she liked trousers. Not philosophically – she just liked them.

No, today she was glad because it meant that no-one could see her underwear. As she swung slowly to and fro, her ankle caught in Ida Tueboll's expertly-rigged noose, she noted with approval the lack of underwear on show.

She also caught sight of a stray thread sticking out of the bottom of the turn-ups. But before she could pay it too much attention Ida Tueboll leaned in close.

'Don't think you can fool me Hailey Skjervold, If That Is Your Real Name.'

Ida Tueboll often told Hailey Skjervold that her real name was Pippy Longstocking or something stupid.

'I haven't been watching you. I'm far too busy for that. But I have noticed you out of the corner of my eye like a person might notice, say, an ugly bug or a squashed cat.'

Ida Tueboll got in close. Hailey Skjervold noticed that she had a ketchup stain on her shirt, and she wondered what the Nisse would think if he saw that.

'And I don't like your behaviour. It stinks. It's wrong.'

'What am I doing wrong Ida Tueboll?'

Ida Tueboll pocked Hailey Skjervold's forehead.

'This. Just this. I don't like it.'

Hailey Skjervold noticed a small crowd of kids gathering, watching her from their upside-down vantage point. She realised that it would not be intelligent to provoke Ida Tueboll – but she also had no idea what she had done that was so bad.

'I am sorry Ida Tueboll, I do not want to provoke you, but I have no idea what I have done that is so bad.'

Ida Tueboll stamped her foot, raising a little cloud of snow-flakes. Every single onlooker flinched.

'You are doing it again! This – thing.'

She poked Hailey Skjervold in the forehead again.

'Floating around, smiling to yourself. You should not be smiling all the time. I know something is going on to make you smile and it has to stop.'

'I am upside down Ida Tueboll. I might be upset, but upside down it looks like a smile perhaps?'

Ida Tueboll balled her fist. Then. . . she stopped. Took a deep breath and smiled down at Hailey Skjervold.

'See, from here, Ida Tueboll, your frown looks like a smile.'

Hailey Skjervold did not intend to make Ida Tueboll angry, but she could not help herself. Ida Tueboll was correct, she was smiling more. But she had a Nisse as a friend – a real Nisse. What teenager wouldn't want a Nisse as a friend?

Only that morning they had spent an hour singing old Christmas songs together whilst folding napkins and placing them in the drawer of the dining room cupboard, which the night before the Nisse had polished to a gleaming shine.

Rasmussen had not heard them singing: she was sleeping off her drinking from the previous night. She had doubled her intake since she had noticed furniture moving overnight.

And then, when the work was over and Hailey Skjervold was about to leave for school, the Nisse had dropped an additional bombshell. He wanted to make Christmas decorations tonight!

For Hailey Skjervold, who had spent most of her life pretending that Nisse were real so that she had an excuse to bring some Christmas cheer into an otherwise cheerless house, this was the best news of all.

So yes, Hailey Skjervold was happy, which was just the wrong thing to be when Ida Tueboll was around.

Ida Tueboll got in close. Very, very close. Hailey Skjervold could see right up her nose.

'Yes, you look happy. Very happy indeed. So do you know what I am going to do?'

'No, Ida Tueboll, I do not.'

'I am going to move you around the quadrant, because I can. So now you are my intelligence victim. Which means that, in three days, I will do something to you that is so fiendishly clever that it shocks you to your very core.'

Hailey Skjervold realised that Ida Tueboll had a hairy nose. Not a fluffy nose, but a nose full of thick, black hair. She thought that Ida Tueboll had stolen the inside of an old sailor's nose.

'In three days' time I will wipe that smile off your face with a stunt so evil and clever that your brain will fall out of your head when you even think about it. You can't beat me girl. And do you know why?'

'Why is that Ida Tueboll?'

'Because Hailey Skjervold is dumb. And Ida Tueboll always wins!!'

And with that, Ida Tueboll leaned back and karate chopped through the rope that held Hailey Skjervold in place.

Hailey Skjervold fell onto her face. As she rubbed the snow out of her eyes and undid the noose around her feet she wondered about three things:

1) How did Ida Tueboll get such hairs up her nose?

2) Exactly what was she going to do in three days?

3) How could she get that spare thread out of her jeans?

Hailey Skjervold thinks about asking for help

That night Hailey Skjervold put Neville's food out, but she did not call him for dinner. She used to – that was part of their nightly routine, which also included lots of hugs (Hailey Skjervold on Neville) and licking of Hailey's face (Neville on Hailey Skjervold).

But, since he had met the Nisse, Neville did not play with Hailey Skjervold anymore. He came for his dinner, but only when he felt like it. It was almost as if Neville thought that Nisse rule #2 applied to him too. He had even been spotted chasing the birds in the garden.

But Hailey Skjervold did not mind. When Neville did decide to show his face he always looked happy, which in Hailey Skjervold's opinion was a good thing. She thought about rule #3:

'Nisse will tidy your house and look after your livestock.'

Neville certainly looked healthy. So she left his food, and ran upstairs to do her homework. She had to be quick: the Nisse wanted to start work on the house as soon as Rasmussen had begun her third drink of the night.

Hailey Skjervold rushed through her maths and English, little worrying about grades or accuracy. She had more important things to think about.

Of course there was the Christmas decorations thing. That was still a source of immense excitement. Then there was Ida Tueboll's threat that day. Hailey Skjervold planned to ask the Nisse about this, and seek his advice about the situation.

The Nisse was already waiting for her. He tapped his little foot on the kitchen table as she ran through the door.

'Sorry! I was late coming home, and . . .'

'What is the rule?'

Hailey Skjervold stopped in her tracks. Every night the Nisse challenged her on the rules. Luckily she knew the rules. She had mouthed them to herself enough times.

'Rule #4, page 67: Nisse need to be treated with respect.'

The Nisse nodded, pleased with her knowledge.

'But I am not late, am I?'

The Nisse hopped down and ran to the lounge door. He peeked through. Then he turned around and nodded.

'She began an hour ago.'

'But I did not know . . .'

'What is the rule?'

Hailey Skjervold had to think about this one. She knew all the rules, but she felt under pressure. Finally she had a stab . . .

'Rule #1: Nisse are very strong?'

The Nisse shook his head slowly.

'Rule #5: Do not choose a Nisse, they choose . . .'

Hailey Skjervold stopped talking. She could see that the Nisse was impatient.

'Rule #8.'

Now the Nisse nodded his head. Hailey Skjervold had to count the words of the rule off on her finger.

'If you break any of these rules the Nisse must leave your house. But if you break the rules you may make him angry, and if he is angry he will beat you to within an inch of your life and kill your livestock.'

The Nisse regarded her for a moment.

'I think that perhaps we need a new rule. Rule #4, sub-rule 1: Respecting a Nisse includes arriving at all appointments on time.'

Hailey frowned.

'And what does on time mean?'

'On time means. . . when the Nisse raps his little hand three times on the door to the kitchen like so.'

The Nisse tapped the door with his tiny fists. The BOOM reverberated through the house. Hailey Skjervold ducked, ready for Rasmussen to come flying into the room.

But Rasmussen did not come flying into the room. Rasmussen was already in a drunken coma.

The Nisse smiled a happy, friendly smile – as if this conversation had not even happened.

'Right! Let's start with the tea towels.'

'But we did those yesterday.'

The Nisse's left hand began to shake a little.

'And I noticed that our work was not perfect. It came close, but perfection was sadly absent, so we can do them again.'

'I thought we were going to make Christmas decorations tonight.'

'Rule #3: Nisse will tidy your house and take care of your livestock.'

'I don't . . .'

'Sub-rule 1: the tea towels are not perfect until the Nisse says that they are perfect.'

Hailey Skjervold was going to claim that this rule was unfair, but when she saw the Nisse's hand flapping more and more violently, and when she heard the hissing noise from his mouth as he tried to calm his temper, she remembered Rule #8 and decided that she would not be making Christmas decorations tonight.

And she would not be asking the Nisse's advice about the Ida Tueboll situation.

Hailey Skjervold is in a rut

Hailey Skjervold could do nothing about the Ida Tueboll situation the next day either. Ida Tueboll was not in school – she was probably planning her attack, and all the other children pointed and whispered at Hailey Skjervold, as though she were a dead girl walking.

And Hailey Skjervold herself was too tired to do much anyway.

That night she had folded the tea towels again and again and again. The Nisse had not helped, other than to point out where the folding was not perfect – which she did at least twenty times. And every time he pointed out an imperfection he came up with a new sub-rule to cover it.

By the end of the night there were eighteen sub-rules; every single rule from 1-8 had been amended. Only rule #9 remained untouched, because it was perfect and not even the Nisse could qualify that.

The Nisse himself had been busy too: he had moved the kitchen table eight times. He would move the table from position A to position B. Then he would look at it from all angles, mumbling to himself, before returning it to position A.

Then he would move it to position C, and leave it there for a while whilst he criticised Hailey Skjervold's work, after which he would move the table to position B, before returning it to position A and beginning all over again.

Hailey Skjervold was troubled by this change. She worked and worked, and she did not even laugh when Neville galloped into the room, dressed as a Spanish matador.

Instead she had kept her head down and focussed on folding those napkins as well as she possibly could. And she hoped that the next day he would be more inclined to make Christmas decorations and talk about bullies.

But it was not to be. Hailey Skjervold staggered home to find that the Nisse was already waiting for her, hammering the kitchen door and making an awful racket.

That night she spent her time scrubbing the paving stones on the patio whilst the Nisse concentrated on moving the rose bushes from one side of the garden to the next – pausing, of course, to criticise Hailey Skjervold's work from time to time and to make her do it again.

All the while Neville jumped around the garden, dressed like an astronaut.

Hailey Skjervold almost angers a Nisse

The next day things got much, much worse.

School had passed in a blur. Hailey Skjervold was too tired to even notice that her maths and English homework had got her lowest marks ever. She actually fell asleep as her maths teacher yelled at her.

And when Runar Sunde quietly suggested that, you know, Hailey Skjervold might consider moving to another country, Hailey did not answer – she was dreaming about re-arranging Ida Tueboll's nasal hair into a more regular pattern to soothe the Nisse's ever more flappy hands.

So that night, when she got home, Hailey Skjervold dropped her bag onto the floor, stumbled up the stairs and fell asleep before she even made it to her room.

She slept, dreaming ever more crazy dreams about Ida Tueboll and the Nisse.

She did not notice when Neville came up to her and circled her a couple of times, before tossing his headdress and prancing off.

She did not notice when Rasmussen tripped over her, banged her head and fell into an early stupor.

Hailey Skjervold did, however, wake up when the Nisse hissed into her ear. It was a special Nisse hiss: quiet but painful at the same time, reaching into the depths of Hailey Skjervold's dream and waking her up with a jolt.

She focussed on the Nisse, who was so agitated that he was levitating a foot above the ground. As her eyes began to work she noticed how red his face was. And how much his hands were flapping.

He beckoned to her, and Hailey Skjervold pushed herself up, making her slow, unsteady way down the stairs. The Nisse floated in front of her, continually beckoning.

She glanced back at Rasmussen, and whispered . . .

'Do you think that she is . . .'

The Nisse placed a hand on her wrist. And Hailey Skjervold looked into his eyes, and realised that she should not say any more.

She followed him silently down to the kitchen. The Nisse beckoned her inside, closed the door carefully, and floated to within an inch of her face.

'WE HAVE RULES!'

The yell came from nowhere – but it sounded like it came from everywhere. Hailey Skjervold clapped her hands over her ears and cried for a moment.

The Nisse was floating in front of her, his arms folded.

He waited until she finished crying, not saying a word, until . . .

'What are the rules, simple child?'

Hailey Skjervold was shocked by him – now he was quiet, calm.

'Do. . . you want to hear the sub-rules first?'

'Leave the sub-rules! For the moment.'

Hailey Skjervold stopped her tears. She was scared and bewildered, but she knew the rules. She had learned them off by heart.

'1, Nisse are very strong. 2, Nisse do not come when called. 3, Nisse will tidy your house and look after your livestock. 4, Nisse need to be treated with respect. 5, Do not choose Nisse, they choose you. 6, Nisse do not play pranks – gnomes play pranks. 7, Nisse adore piping hot porridge – but only when served with the best butter. 8, If you break . . .'

Hailey Skjervold hesitated. The Nisse gestured impatiently.

'If you break any of these rules the Nisse must leave your house. But if you break the rules you may make him angry, and if he is angry he will beat you to within an inch of your life and kill your livestock.'

'And what is rule #9?'

Hailey Skjervold took a deep breath.

'If you do make a . . .'

The door burst open, shocking both Hailey Skjervold and the Nisse. They turned to see Rasmussen, unsteady but defiant, at the door.

'I knew it!'

She stepped into the room and grabbed a frying pan from the wall. The Nisse did not move as Rasmussen marched up to him. Rasmussen's swing was ungainly, and the Nisse dodged it easily.

So Rasmussen kicked him as hard as she could, and he flew through the window into the garden.

Hailey Skjervold put her hands to her face. Rasmussen turned to her and, without a word, shoved her out of the room.

'No! I need to help, he'll come back!'

Rasmussen pulled Hailey Skjervold close, her foul whiskey breath making Hailey's nose wrinkle.

'Have you deliberately annoyed him?'

'What kind of question is that?'

'Listen to me child! Have you made him angry?'

'Yes, but . . .'

'Did you mean to? Did you?'

Hailey Skjervold was shaken, she could not think of an answer. So Rasmussen shook her and whispered in her face.

'Remember rule nine.'

'If you do . . .'

Rasmussen looked up. The Nisse was floating at the other end of the corridor. She looked down at Haile Skjervold one last time.

'Rule nine.'

Rasmussen pushed Hailey Skjervold to one side, before jumping back into the kitchen.

The Nisse moved. . . he dropped to the floor, ran to the kitchen, and kicked the door off its hinges.

Hailey Skjervold screamed . . . as the kitchen door fell onto her head.

And she did not remember any more.

Ida Tueboll chooses a new victim

Ida Tueboll gave the piano wire a tug. It held, which was a good thing, as it was holding two hundred litres of animal slurry above the ground.

The wire had not given out for the last two hours, but she kept on testing it.

She glanced up at her contraption.

It was, she was pleased to note, an act of genius: the most evil combination of humiliation, physical threat and stink – without actually putting its victim at risk.

The entire gym was a trap for one person.

And that person was not there.

Never, in all of her life, had Ida Tueboll failed to deliver one of her humiliations. She could adapt to every situation.

Except this. She could not take this contraption to Hailey Skjervold's house – it needed a gym.

And she could not drag Hailey Skjervold to the gym. That would be humiliating.

But Ida Tueboll was not bound by convention.

In her mind she returned Hailey Skjervold to the general hatred quadrant and pointed at the smallest kid in the crowd.

'Come here Runar Sunde. I've got a treat for you.'

Hailey Skjervold works hard

A few weeks passed. Now there was a new routine in Hailey Skjervold's house.

She did not go to school – she had no time. She would wake up at six for a debrief with the Nisse. He would run through all of the new amendments to the rules that he had made up during the night.

He had amended every single rule at least a hundred times.

But he still could not change rule #9. It was almost as if something horrible climbed into his mouth when he even said it. It was too perfect for him.

After the debrief Hailey Skjervold would work all day, feed the Nisse his porridge, do more work and then go to bed.

Rasmussen was nowhere to be seen. Hailey Skjervold had no idea about what had happened to Rasmussen, but she feared the worst.

So now it was Hailey Skjervold and the Nisse. The Nisse had phoned her school, imitated her parents and told them that they were taking Hailey Skjervold to Sweden. And the school had let them.

But the Nisse was not in this for his own gain. If anything he worked even harder than Hailey Skjervold. Whilst she spent all day cleaning, dusting, washing and wiping, he spent all day rearranging furniture and decorating.

He had rearranged the inside of every room at least three times, moving every single piece of furniture from position A to position B then position C then back again.

He had then decided that the rooms themselves were in the wrong place, so he had swapped room A with room B, and involved room C in the process.

And every time he filled a new room he would rearrange the furniture in that room.

Whilst he worked he talked to himself, and he sang, and his little hands would not stop flapping and moving.

Sometimes he would criticise Hailey Skjervold. And every night he would compliment her on the excellence of her porridge – which now, according to the rules, had to be served in a particular bowl, with the individual design elements pointing in a particular direction. The ratio of porridge to milk had to be just so. The temperature had to be just so. The butter had to come from a cow of a certain age . . .

But other than the compliment, and the daily rules update, he barely spoke to her, not now that she could be relied upon to do an exceptional job.

Every day she worked her fingers to the bone. Her tasks included:

- Collect all laundry
- Wash laundry
- Hang laundry up to dry
- Iron any dry laundry

- Take dog for walk
- Feed dog
- Clean up after dog in case of accidents
- Polish all door knockers

Plus everything else that had ever needed doing in a house.

All this time Neville lived the life of a king. He was walked every day until he was almost asleep on his feet.

He was fed the finest foods known to man (or dogs) – the Nisse would always have a fresh supply of fresh meat.

He would bring a different bird into the house every day, and take great pleasure in tormenting it before biting its head off.

And best of all: he was allowed to make his mess anywhere in the house, and Hailey Skjervold would have to clean up after him in a matter of seconds. What constituted an acceptable number of seconds changed from day to day – with a related rule change.

There were two reasons why Hailey Skjervold did not just run away. Firstly, she wanted to take care of Neville. And secondly, because she knew what the Nisse would do to her if she broke the rules.

She knew that something terrible had happened to Rasmussen. And, the Nisse would, occasionally, drop a hint about what might happen to her, including:

- Smashing her Father's spare car with his bare hands
- Levitating
- And making strange crying noises all night.

So Hailey Skjervold continued to do what she was told: she continued to work and work and work.

Until the day that everything changed – until the day that the Nisse went too far.

That was the day that he hit Neville.

Hailey Skjervold gets angry

Hailey Skjervold rested her head on the workbench as the Nisse cracked his fingers and looked down at his porridge.

'I would say we have earned our porridge today, have we not?'

He had been busy. He had decided that the reason why he could rearrange the house was because the house itself was the problem. So he had spent the day swapping the house's furniture with items from the shed.

Neville, meanwhile, strutted confidently around the room, dressed in his new Roman centurion outfit.

Hailey Skjervold barely heard either of them. She could not remember when she had been awake enough to pay attention to anything that anyone said. Instead she worked, ate, slept – and prepared porridge every night.

'That was one fine heck of a day. That was . . .'

Hailey Skjervold did not notice the silence straight away. She was THAT tired.

But eventually Neville's stillness, the silence where there had been clicking claws, made her look up.

The Nisse was staring at her. He had THAT look again. The look that said she had failed somehow. And this time it was serious.

He moved his hand and picked up the bowl. She looked in it – and saw the porridge.

The picture on the side of the bowl was out by 12 degrees. Neville whined.

The Nisse stood. Hailey Skjervold began to shake.

The Nisse spoke slowly and quietly. He too began to shake. . . with suppressed anger.

'There is a right place for the bowl. I need. . . the. . . bowl. . . in. . . the. . . right. . . place.'

With every word the Nisse got a little louder. Then he changed tack. . . he began to move, making Neville whine louder.

'Which rule is it? Hmm? Which rule is it, you stupid little girl?'

He stopped in front of Hailey Skjervold. His tiny lower jaw jutted out, less than an inch from her face.

'Hmmm? Which rule is it? Hmmm? Stupid? Which. . . rule. . . is it?'

Hailey Skjervold was no longer tired. Now the only thing she felt was the prickling of her skin, the tiny hairs on her face rising as the Nisse's power radiated off him.

She was too scared for fear. She was prickling – that was all she knew.

Neville had stopped whining. Now he was growling, a low, threatening little growl in the throat.

'I didn't mean to . . .'

'TELL ME THE RULE! STUPID GIRL, TELL ME THE RULE!'

Neville charged. A blur of movement and he was scrabbling his way onto the table, his teeth bared, his eyes fixed on the Nisse.

Hailey Skjervold opened her mouth to scream. . . but the Nisse was quicker. He flicked out a hand, barely visible, and Neville flew backwards across the kitchen.

Hailey Skjervold's hands went to her face. Neville bounced off a cupboard and landed on the floor. He was down for barely a moment before he got up and ran from the kitchen, howling, the remains of his Roman Emperor outfit trailing behind him.

Hailey Skjervold's hands went down from her face. The Nisse was still staring at her. Without saying a word she took the bowl of porridge and added the right amount of butter, before placing it back by the Nisse's feet.

And not for a moment did her eyes leave his. Now she no longer felt the prickles of fear on her skin. Now Hailey Skjervold felt a cold, deep certainty inside.

And, looking at her, the Nisse knew.

You could pour pig's blood on her.

You could kill her housekeeper.

You could call her stupid again and again and again.

But you never, EVER, touched her dog.

Ida Tueboll gets an invitation

The call was unexpected, to say the least.

Ida Tueboll had forgotten all about Hailey Skjervold. It had been a couple of months since the girl had been taken away from school, and since then Ida Tueboll had picked Lotte Bjorge as her fourth quadrant victim.

And since then things had gone swimmingly. Lotte Bjorge took her punishment the right way: she yelled and moaned and cried.

And when the others breathed a sigh of relief that they were not the victims, Ida Tueboll would change the quadrant around the ruin their lives again.

In fact, that very day, Ida Tueboll was planning to almost drown Mirham Ostvedt in an epic re-enactment of the sinking of the Titanic.

So when her phone rang she was rather busy trying to secure a large watertight tank to the back of her Father's pick-up truck.

'Hello?'

'Ida Tueboll!'

Ida Tueboll frowned. Did she recognise that voice?

'It's Hailey Skjervold! You poured pig's blood on me.'

'I've poured pig's blood on lots of people.'

There was a silence at the other end of the phone. Ida Tueboll was ready to put the phone down when . . .

'That does not matter. You will remember me when you come to my party next week.'

Ida Tueboll let out a little whistle. No-one told Ida Tueboll when she was going to a party.

'And what makes you think . . .'

'You'll come. If you want to meet my pet Nisse.'

And with that Hailey Skjervold disconnected.

And then Ida Tueboll remembered Hailey Skjervold. Now it was Ida Tueboll's turn to feel the prickly feeling under the skin. Hailey Skjervold, the boring little girl with the Nisse obsession. The little baby who summed up everything Ida Tueboll hated.

The little baby who had disappeared before Ida Tueboll could fully ruin her life.

Of course Ida Tueboll was going.

Ida Tueboll goes to a party

Ida Tueboll was pleased. It was the day of Hailey Skjervold's party and everything was complete.

She had spent a week planning the most outrageous humiliation for Hailey Skjervold. Things were going to get spectacular, and she had even made enquiries about deliveries of two tonnes of horse carcasses.

But then. . . Ida Tueboll was the smartest kid in the school. She knew that.

And she also knew Hailey Skjervold, the dumb insect who lived with her head in the clouds, and who loved Gnomes and Huldra and Wolverines.

Now Ida Tueboll did not know Nisse. But she did know how to hurt people.

And she knew exactly how to hurt Hailey Skjervold.

So she had been to the library, and she had found a strange old book called The Weird Book About Folk Tales. It had taken a while for her to get her hands on it: the Librarian was very protective. She kept dropping hints about dark forces trying to steal it.

But all Ida Tueboll had to do was threaten the Librarian with her Father's money and lawyers and the stupid old woman had caved in. And as soon as she had rubbed the pomade off the cover, Ida Tueboll had her information.

So now Ida Tueboll knew all about the Nisse. And now, as her Father pulled up at Hailey Skjervold's house, Ida Tueboll had a special surprise for her host.

'Is this it?'

'No, Dad. This is the island from Jurassic Park.'

'I've never seen a house gleam like that.'

'Whatever, Dad. Come back in four hours.'

Hailey Skjervold was very, very thin, with bags under her eyes.

But she couldn't stop giggling and smiling. Ida Tueboll thought that perhaps she had gone a little bit mad.

Hailey Skjervold sat her in the lounge and went off to fetch orange squash, and Ida Tueboll took a sneaky peek around the house.

It certainly did gleam. It was the brightest, most spotless house she had ever seen in her life.

'Here's your orange squash.'

'Your doorknobs look amazing.'

'Thanks, Ida Tueboll. I do my best.'

'Did you nail that furniture to the ceiling yourself?'

'My Nisse did. Right now he considers that it will look nicer up there.'

Hailey Skjervold sat down, invited Ida Tueboll to sit next to her. Ida Tueboll considered pouring the squash on Hailey Skjervold's head, but she had to be patient. Her moment would come.

A stupid looking mutt skulked in. Ida Tueboll thought he looked a little like Hailey Skjervold: all sticking out ribs and sunken eyes.

'Is this the party?'

Hailey Skjervold's smile got bigger.

'They will come.'

Ida Tueboll noticed that Hailey Skjervold's hands were fluttering on her lap. Because she was focussing on Hailey Skjervold's lap Ida Tueboll did not notice that Hailey Skjervold was leaning over, and was right in her face.

That manic smile was too close.

'Do you want to see him?'

Ida Tueboll had her answer ready. She had been working on it all morning. The first time she had practised saying it she had retched, but now she was confident she could make it sound genuine.

'Yes. Yes I do want to see him Hailey Skjervold.'

Hailey Skjervold gave her an excited little look, and she called out.

'Oh, Mr Nisse! Mr Nisse come and see your latest admirer!'

Ida Tueboll did not like all the pleasantry – being nice made her skin crawl.

And as the house greeted Hailey Skjervold's words with silence Ida Tueboll was close to pushing herself up, pouring her orange squash over Hailey Skjervold, pouring Hailey Skjervold's squash over the dog, and going home to arrange the delivery of that manure.

But she did not do any of these things. Because that was when the Nisse appeared.

Ida Tueboll Meets the Nisse

'I was here anyway.'

Ida Tueboll turned around. There, standing on the back of the sofa, looking down at her, was the smallest little man she had ever seen.

He was dressed in the strangest, most old-fashioned clothes she had ever seen too. These clothes were even less fashionable than her Father's, and that was saying something.

Just like Hailey Skjervold, he smelt of nothing. But unlike Hailey Skjervold he did not appear to be pleased that she was there.

'Hello, Mr Nisse. This is my friend Ida Tueboll. I invited her to come and see you.'

The Nisse barely glanced at Ida Tueboll, before staring at Hailey Skjervold. It was not a friendly stare, or a happy stare. Instead it was the kind of stare that made Ida Tueboll feel, just for once, the slightest ounce of sympathy for Hailey Skjervold.

She quickly squashed that feeling with a little shudder of disgust.

'I was here anyway. I did not come when you called. The Nisse does not come when called.'

'Oh no, Mr Nisse, that's rule . . .'

'I was already here! I did NOT come when called!'

Ida Tueboll had had enough.

'Hello, Mr Nisse. Hailey Skjervold has told me all about you. I am so excited to meet you.'

The Nisse raised an eyebrow. He was clearly unhappy.

'I would not pay too much attention to the words of Hailey Skjervold. She is an untrustworthy worm, who has taken to sneaking out of our home in the middle of the night when all of the work needs doing.'

Ida Tueboll wondered for a moment where this was leading. She had to steer the conversation back in the right direction.

She had to win his trust. The Nisse continued . . .

'In fact, I have two new sub-rules for you Hailey Skjervold. Rule eight sub-rule six hundred and twelve: no sneaking out under any circumstances, even if the Nisse is asleep. And rule . . .'

'I've heard so much about you, Mr Nisse. About the lovely things that you have done to this house, and the way that you have turned Hailey Skjervold's life around. Before you came along Hailey Skjervold was a horrible, horrible person. But since you came along she has turned into quite the nicest person on the planet.'

Ida Tueboll knew her stuff. She had read the Eight Rules of Nisse. And judging by the Nisse's reaction, Ida Tueboll's awareness of the rules was working. His expression did not change, but he puffed his chest out a little and stood a little straighter.

Hailey Skjervold gasped. The Nisse showed his irritation.

'Please forgive her, she does not know the rules . . .'

The Nisse shook his head.

'We all have nine rules, Hailey Skjervold. You have more because you are bad.'

Hailey Skjervold sunk into her chair. Ida Tueboll took this opportunity.

'Mr Nisse, we know all about you and your kind. We know how wonderful you are, and everyone knows how to give a Nisse the respect that they deserve.'

She saw a flicker of fear in Hailey Skjervold's eyes. Good. Let her suffer.

'And I would like to see how that is done. Hailey Skjervold, would you show me how to make porridge?'

Ida Tueboll makes porridge

Hailey Skjervold's hands were flapping even more, almost as if her lap was on fire and she was trying to put it out.

But the Nisse was nodding. He was clearly falling for this act.

Before anybody could spoil the moment Ida Tueboll was on her feet.

'Great, well come on then!'

The kitchen was a tense, tense place. But Ida Tueboll did not care. She could see how much attention Hailey Skjervold had to pay to every single element of the cooking process.

She could see how hard Hailey Skjervold had to work to get the measurement of milk and oats just so, and to get it to the right temperature.

Ida Tueboll did not ask questions, she just watched. She wanted Hailey Skjervold to be completely focussed on the task.

Which made the next stage a little easier.

Just as the porridge was approaching the optimum temperature, Ida Tueboll opened the butter dish. It was not hard to find. . . perhaps there was an upside to having a Nisse in the house. She could not imagine the little twerp Hailey Skjervold having a house this well ordered before the Nisse came along, even if there was a kitchen table stuck on the wall and a workbench in its place.

Ida Tueboll was working only by feel: her eyes were always on Hailey Skjervold. She carefully scraped the butter out of the dish with her fingers and deposited it in a pocket.

Then she pulled a cube of greaseproof paper out of another pocket.

She fumbled with the paper, and the stuff inside was pretty molten, but when she scraped it into the dish it looked passably like butter.

When the porridge was ready Hailey Skjervold reached for the butter dish. Ida Tueboll quickly manoeuvred it into position, and sure enough Hailey Skjervold scooped a single, flat teaspoon of butter in.

She poured the porridge into a bowl, took a deep breath. Then . . .

'It's ready!'

Hailey Skjervold serves porridge

The kitchen door did not open.

'Ooooh, I'm hungry!'

Ida Tueboll spun, and had to stop herself screaming a little.

The Nisse was already at the workbench. He had his spoon ready to go.

Ida Tueboll picked up the porridge bowl and handed it to Hailey Skjervold.

'Here you go, Hailey Skjervold, I think that you should serve him.'

The Nisse rapped his spoon on the table.

'I said I am hungry! And I was here anyway.'

Hailey Skjervold swallowed. She took the bowl from Ida Tueboll, who gave her a malicious glance.

Hailey Skjervold's face was blank as she placed the bowl on the workbench, carefully arranging it. But before the Nisse could eat she blurted something out:

'I do not think that you should eat that porridge!'

The Nisse gave Hailey Skjervold a look. A look that only thousands of years of hating things could produce.

The Nisse turned away from Hailey Skjervold and took a mouthful of porridge . . .

He chomped, and chewed.

And he chomped again. His face furrowed – he was concentrating.

Then. . . he spat the mouthful back into the bowl. Hailey Skjervold took a step backwards. Hailey Skjervold did not intend to – but when the Nisse glared at her she could not help herself.

'What is rule #7? What is rule #7?'

Hailey Skjervold looked devastated.

'What do you mean? It looks perfect. Please don't . . .'

'The butter! The butter!'

He was pointing at the butter dish. The dog whimpered and ran from the room.

'The butter!'

The Nisse hacked up a glob of phleghm.

'That will require cleaning too!'

Hailey Skjervold crept up to the butter dish. She smelt it . . .

'This is not real butter.'

225

'I can't believe it! It's not real butter!'

The Nisse bawled his little hands into fists.

'You knew. You knew. You silly, stupid little child . . .'

The Nisse pulled his sleeves up.

Hailey Skjervold gets her just desserts

Ida Tueboll let out a little cackle. Things were going perfectly. Rule #7 had been broken. And the words of rule #8 came back to her in a rush of excitement:

'If you break any of these rules the Nisse must leave your house. But if you break the rules you may make him angry, and if he is angry he will beat you to within an inch of your life and kill your livestock.'

Ida Tueboll watched as Hailey Skjervold closed her eyes . . .

The Nisse leapt at her. . . swung his fist . . .

And then he was on his back on the other side of the room. Ida Tueboll let out a little screech. The Nisse pulled himself up onto his feet. He shook his head, balled his fists and leapt again.

And again he ended up on his back. Ida Tueboll had watched carefully this time – and the Nisse seemed to bounce off Hailey Skjervold, who had not moved a single muscle.

The Nisse looked dumbstruck. Ida Tueboll WAS dumbstruck.

'What's happening? Beat her up! Kill the dog!'

Hailey Skjervold opened her eyes, and gave Ida Tueboll a proper smile.

'But he cannot, can he, Ida Tueboll?'

'He ate fake butter!'

'I ate fake butter!'

Hailey Skjervold shook her head.

'Oh, Ida Tueboll, and I expected so much from you!'

She reached into her own inside pocket and pulled out a piece of paper. As she unfurled it Ida Tueboll recognised it – it matched the pages she had been reading in the weird book.

'I read that book! It's in there! You served him bad porridge.'

She gestured to the Nisse.

'You have to beat her up!'

But the Nisse folded his arms. Something had disgusted him.

'Ida Tueboll, I think that you should read this.'

'I know all the rules!'

'All. . . nine rules?'

Ida Tueboll blinked.

'No. Not nine.'

Hailey Skjervold gave Ida Tueboll a pitying smile and handed her the piece of paper. Ida Tueboll looked down.

'The Rules of Nisse.'

She read the rules. She got to rule #8:

'If you break any of these rules the Nisse must leave your house. But if you break the rules you may make him angry, and if he is angry he will beat you to within an inch of your life and kill your livestock.'

But that was not the last rule.

There was a rule #9. She looked up at Hailey Skjervold.

'What is this?'

'Read the rule Ida Tueboll.'

'There were only eight!'

'There were only eight by the time I had finished altering the book. Pomade is perfect for rubbing out old ink.'

Ida Tueboll read the rule:

'Rule # 9: If you do make a Nisse angry: try not to make a Nisse angry.'

Ida Tueboll looked up.

'But. . . you made him angry.'

Hailey Skjervold nodded her head wildly.

'I tried not to make him angry, remember?'

'But you gave him fake butter! Horrible fake butter – I put it there!'

Hailey Skjervold giggled.

'Yes. You made him angry. And you tried to make him angry.'

Ida Tueboll twisted her face . . .

'Stupid, dumb Hailey Skjervold!'

Ida Tueboll threw a wild punch at Hailey Skjervold.

But before it landed she was grabbed by the Nisse, who beat her. Not to within an inch of her life, but enough to teach her a lesson, because she had made him angry – and she had tried to make him angry.

Luckily Ida Tueboll had no pets, so there was no livestock for the Nisse to kill.

But because Hailey Skjervold had broken the rules, the Nisse had to leave her house.

And as he sloped off into the cold, and Ida Tueboll limped away behind him, both of them took a rueful moment to peer back at the simple 14-year-old, cradling her beloved dog and smirking at them both.

And they both realised that they had learned Hailey Skjervold's rule #1:

'If you are thinking of messing with Hailey Skjervold. . . try not to mess with Hailey Skjervold.'

About the Authors

A J Dalton

A J Dalton (the 'A' is for Adam) has been an English language teacher as far afield as Egypt, the Czech Republic, Thailand, Slovakia, Poland and Manchester University. He has lived in Manchester since 2003, but has a conspicuous Cockney accent, as he was born in Croydon on a dark night, when strange stars were seen in the sky.

He is author of the best-selling fantasy novels *Empire of the Saviours* (2012), *Gateway of the Saviours* (2013) and *Tithe of the Saviours* (2014). He maintains the Metaphysical Fantasy website www.ajdalton.eu, where there is plenty to interest fantasy fans and there is advice for aspiring authors.

Nadine West

Nadine West is a poet, short story writer and spoken word performer from Manchester. She has been a guest artist at a range of venues, and has won acclaim for her work, which combines a lyrical style with a feminist sensibility. This year she has seen one story shortlisted for the Bridport Prize; a second story received a Highly Commended prize in the same competition, and was published in the 2014 Bridport Anthology. Her first novel, set in Australia in the 19th century, will be completed in 2015. For news and updates on new work and performance dates, follow Nadine on Twitter @andiekarenina

Matthew White

Matt White's first novel, *North by North Ryde*, sold four copies in Australia a long time ago. So he tried writing scripts and got an MA in TV and Radio Scriptwriting from Salford University. He also wrote a number of shorts which won awards and were shown at festivals around the world, including the LA Film Festival – LA in this case standing for 'Lewiston-Auburn'. His co-written feature film, The Final Haunting, is being shown – as he writes this – at the Mumbai Women's International Film Festival. But Matt has always loved his books, and he saw working with Adam as an opportunity to dip his toe back into that magical pond. His toe enjoyed it, so now he is writing a YA ghost story.

Matt lives in The Quietest Place Under The Sun (look it up) with his wife, family and fur-shedding dog. You can follow him on Twitter via @treeandtroll, or find out more via his website (mattwhitescripts.wordpress.com).

Acknowledgements

A whole slew of people have helped put together the The Book of Orm. I'd like to thank . . .

- Sammy HK Smith of Kristell Ink, whose enduring faith and good humour are equally rare amongst publishers

- Oliver Flude, my long-suffering cover artist (www.oliverflude.com), who constantly has to balance the commercially attractive with the genuinely artistic

- Nadine West and Matthew White, my inspiring co-authors, who have contributed their work, hearts and minds in return for little more than a few pints of (very thin) ale

- Mum and Dad, who corrected a disgraceful number of typos in early drafts of the manuscript, and have supported the literary ambitions of their son against all good reason and common sense

- Pete Sutton, a valued supporter of Grimbold Books and its imprints

- and all those fantasy fans who keep insisting it's all worth it!

I humbly salute you all!

Adam Dalton

A Selection of Other Titles from Kristell Ink

In Search of Gods and Heroes by Sammy H.K Smith

Buried in the scriptures of Ibea lies a story of rivalry, betrayal, stolen love, and the bitter division of the gods into two factions. This rift forced the lesser deities to pledge their divine loyalty either to the shining Eternal Kingdom or the darkness of the Underworld.

When a demon sneaks into the mortal world and murders an innocent girl to get to her sister Chaeli, all pretence of peace between the gods is shattered. For Chaeli is no ordinary mortal, she is a demi-goddess, in hiding for centuries, even from herself. But there are two divine brothers who may have fathered her, and the fate of Ibea rests on the source of her blood.

Chaeli embarks on a journey that tests her heart, her courage, and her humanity. Her only guides are a man who died a thousand years ago in the Dragon Wars, a former assassin for the Underworld, and a changeling who prefers the form of a cat.

The lives of many others – the hideously scarred Anya and her gaoler; the enigmatic and cruel Captain Kerne; the dissolute Prince Dal; and gentle seer Hana – all become entwined. The gods will once more walk the mortal plane spreading love, luck, disease, and despair as they prepare for the final, inevitable battle.

In Search of Gods and Heroes, Book One of Children of Nalowyn, is a true epic of sweeping proportions which becomes progressively darker as the baser side of human nature is explored, the failings and ambitions of the gods is revealed, and lines between sensuality and sadism, love and lust are blurred.

June 2014

The Sea-Stone Sword by Joel Cornah

"Heroes are more than just stories, they're people. And people are complicated, people are strange. Nobody is a hero through and through, there's always something in them that'll turn sour. You'll learn it one day. There are no heroes, only villains who win."

Rob Sardan is going to be a legend, but the road to heroism is paved with temptation and deceit. Exiled to a distant and violent country, Rob is forced to fight his closest friends for survival, only to discover his mother's nemesis is still alive, and is determined to wipe out her family and all her allies. The only way the Pirate Lord, Mothar, can be stopped is with the Sea-Stone Sword – yet even the sword itself seems fickle, twisting Rob's quest in poisonous directions, blurring the line between hero and villain. Nobody is who they seem, and Rob can no longer trust even his own instincts.

Driven by dreams of glory, Rob sees only his future as a hero, not the dark path upon which he draws ever closer to infamy.

June 2014

Cruelty by Ellen Croshâin

Once a year, in the caves deep below the house, the Family gathers to perform a ritual to appease their god. But Faroust only accepts payment in blood.

Eliza MacTir, youngest daughter of a powerful Irish family, was born into fae gentry without the magical gifts that have coursed through the Family's veins for millennia; she was an outcast from her first breath. Desperate for freedom, Eliza's flight from rural Ireland is thwarted by the Family's head of security. The only weapon she has to fight her captor is her own awakening sexuality.

Drawn into the world of magic and gods, Eliza must find a way to break free, even if it means breaking the hearts of those she loves, and letting her own turn to stone.

Cruelty, it runs in the Family.

www.kristell-ink.com

Made in the USA
Charleston, SC
08 April 2015